Princess of Galilee

PRINCESS
of GALILEE

Charles Redden Butler Neto

iUniverse, Inc.
New York   Bloomington

Princess of Galilee

iUniverse books may be ordered through booksellers or by contacting:

iUniverse
1663 Liberty Drive
Bloomington, IN 47403
www.iuniverse.com
1-800-Authors (1-800-288-4677)

ISBN: 978-1-4401-7405-6 (sc)
ISBN: 978-1-4401-7941-9 (ebk)

Printed in the United States of America

iUniverse rev. date: 04/02/2012

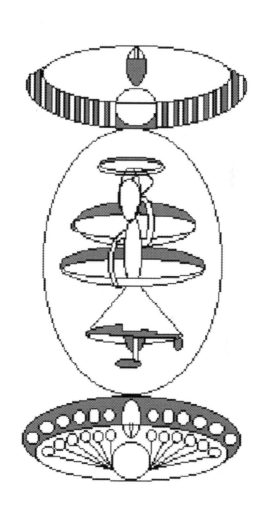

Table of Contents

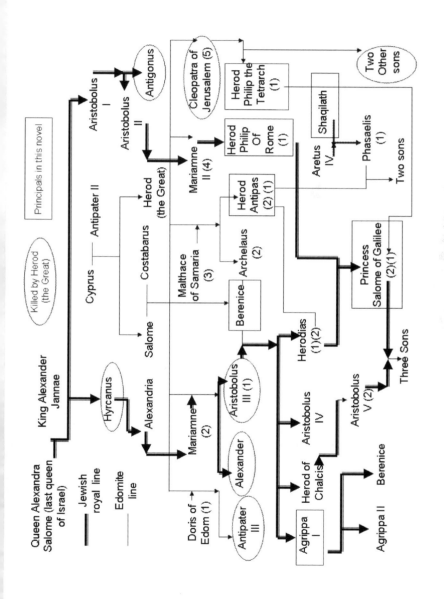

INTRODUCTION

THE HOUSE OF HEROD

Herod the Great was put on his throne by Marc Anthony of Rome. Though Herod was not Jewish, he married into the family of the High Priest Hyrcanus, one of the last contenders to the throne of the Maccabees, the last descendants of the rulers of Judaea.

Salomé Alexandra, the last ruling queen of the Maccabees, was known as a woman of peace. She died leaving two sons to contend for the throne. Herod married one of her granddaughters, Mariamne and claimed the throne, though he was not Jewish. His reign, in contrast, was one of terror and he married more than 9 times. He had two of his wives strangled, and had his favorite son, Antipater II, murdered upon a rumor. Upon Herod the Great's death, the Kingdom of Judaea was divided into multiple territories among the children of his five wives. Herod Antipas was named Tetrarch (ruler of the land) and received Galilee, Samaria, and the Decapolis.

He maintained palaces in all three territories, as well as one in Jerusalem. Archelaus was made ethnarch (ruler of the people) and lived in Samaria. Herod Philip of Rome received an estate in northern Syria, Herod Philip the Tetrarch ruled western Syria (now the Golan Heights). Aretus IV, King of the Nabateans, Herod's distant cousin, ruled Damascus and Petra. Herodias first married Philip of Rome by whom she had Salomé. She then divorced him and married Antipas, who divorced his wife, Phasaelis, daughter of Aretus, by whom he already had children. This caused a war which is in progress at the opening of this book.

DEDICATION

This book is dedicated to Salomé of Galilee and is a work of fiction. Though due diligence has been observed in historical precedence and background, exact timelines cannot be preserved. The Interpreter's Bible, the works of Josephus, archeological records, legends of Greek, Roman, and Phoenician sources, and dramatic opera all are acknowledged as source materials.

Many thanks to my partner Frank, for endless hours of listening to drafts; to my sister Georgia who encouraged my bardic study; to Bambi for the original inspiration, to Kallina for not giving up, and for all my devoted readers.

SPARROW OF JERUSALEM

Synopsis

Salomé, the notorious daughter of Herodias, thinks back upon her life from the age of 75. She begins with learning her famous dance for the head of John the Baptist from a Babylonian dancer, learns of the war that has been fought over her mother, and finds herself confronted in a theatre in the Decapolis by Shaqilath, the Queen of Petra, her stepfather's enemy.

CHAPTER 1

Reminiscence

I am old and the breeze of the sea creeps into my bones. Three-quarters of a century separates me from my childhood. An Arabian horse tosses its head with a jangle of bells and I think back to a time when my hands were covered with jewels and my hips swaggered when I walked. I burst into tears, and my husband's hands are no longer here to comfort me.

That first lifetime, I was the toast of the court, the envy of my mother as my stepfather vied for my affections. But now I am a matron of many years, far older than any ever expected me to survive. All of my companions are now dead, and I sit in my villa and count the stones in the mosaic floors to pass the time.

The breeze of the sea gathers the scent of the quinces in bloom. These trees were planted as a wedding gift from the Emperor Gaius, and now after more than 45 years they are as gnarled as I. My servants gather the fruit every year for wine, and I sip it even now as the sun sets red behind the mists. It has been a day with time for melancholy without bitterness, and the wine clouds the current thoughts and brings my childhood to me, and the savor of court.

Herodias dropped a cabochon back into the brass bowl on her alabaster dressing table. This color of red would just not do today; it would show her swollen eyes too much, which she carefully hid with kohl so as to not appear cross in court. Perhaps the blue instead—to highlight the shadow in her cheeks and make her appear like some Grecian urn. This was, after all, the court of the Herods, even if she now felt like an outsider.

Adultery was nothing knew to her, her husband Herod Philip had been weak, and such a pompous ass, resigned to a quiet life in an isolated estate near Rome. She had hoped that siding with his half-brother Herod Antipas would win her the excitement that a young woman of station was promised— one of the few ways to escape from the boredom of Judaea. Her husband's life had originally been the bargain for her adultery, so there was a reason for it after all, but now her daughter Salomé was nubile, no matter how she tried to hide it, and the suppleness of her limbs was a mockery to her mother.

•   •   •

Yet I, that daughter, was unusually loyal—I told my mother everything, including about the midnight calls from my stepfather. Better that she know first hand than be the brunt of court gossip without knowledge. Herodias chose to be gracious in court, and hide the redness of fury with kohl, but it was becoming tedious.

I had merely tempted my stepfather, that fatal step had not been made to a very twisted triangle, but the calls were becoming more and more frequent, and I was having a hard time keeping enough poise to be tempting, yet somehow managing not to consummate the affair.

"Good uncle," I whispered, slipping carefully out of his reach. "I know you find me lovely, but I am your daughter."

"But you speak to me, even when you are angry," complained Antipas, "and I find you most affectionate."

"Good uncle," I repeated, "even I have my limits. You are drunk, and are light-headed," squirming out of his hold.

"No matter, I only want a comfort, and a sigh, and I will let you go."

Some variation on this theme had been going on every other night for almost a month—and wearying—I was beginning to feel my control slip more at every call. But what could I do, there was no place in court he could not find me, and it would not do to refuse him in public.

Scandal was already in place with my mother's affair and my adoption. Let's not give them more to talk about—as if they had not already. And so I slipped out of his bedroom for the twentieth time, and managed to join my mother without mishap.

•   •   •

There were always agitators on the palace grounds, crying after one cause or another, but one stood out above the rest. Rather than come to the palace at Jerusalem or in Caesarea, he wandered in the desert, gathering followers by his outspokenness. His name was John, and he had taken the old Jewish custom of mikvah, ritual washing, and turned it into a sign of religious "renewal,"—as he called it— calling for people to immerse themselves in the river Jordan.

But it wasn't enough to just bathe and go on your way, he pushed people to their limits. He did not respect rich people or any of the political leaders. He spoke out against injustice and the Zealots and desperate people listened to him.

•   •   •

"And John the Baptizer, who had spoken against Herodias, was shut up in prison, but his disciples came to him daily..."

•   •   •

"Will that wild man never shut up!" screamed Herodias. "So I break his people's law, does he have to be so pointed? All the people think the Baptist a prophet, and I thought divorcing my husband would shut him up!"

"Mother, he will never shut up as long as he is alive," I screamed back, just as furiously. "Antipas has taken him under his wing, for God knows what reason."

"I know, and when Antipas makes up his mind, heaven and earth may pass away before he can be bent," sighed Herodias.

"Mother, you have just said the very words which may break his will," I spoke, feeling my eyes suddenly grow wide. "You may not shut the Baptizer up for now, but I have a plan which may get rid of him for good, and leave even Herod speechless!"

My voice dropped to a whisper, "Remember when I was only six years old, when we were in Rome, and you fell in love with Antipas from afar? You may have thought me sleeping, but I heard you whispering to that old woman who had been a Persian dancer."

"What do you mean? What dancer?" spoke Herodias, suddenly falling silent.

"The old one, who came heavily veiled. You spent many nights with her, learning every move, for though her beauty had faded like the winter sun, her suppleness remained."

". . . that dance, I shall never forget that dance, and Antipas was like a young Apollo, or a young bull in rut," breathed Herodias.

"It was but eight years ago, Mother, and your beauty has not faded beyond recall. My stepfather seems to have eyes only for me, but perhaps we can make this turn to our liking."

•   •   •

The nights continued. On the seventh night following, the conversation turned. "Good uncle, you find me beautiful?"

"More than you can know," my uncle gasped. "How could you not know this by now. I have quoted more poets than I can think to describe your beauty. Persia, Pamphilia, Saba, do not compare," he continued drunkenly.

"I would show you more, you have never seen me dance!" I murmured, preening.

"Ah, Salomé, but I have, on the terrace at night," he leered.

"But that is but a small dance, I would learn more to please you. Would you like that?"

"Yes, the best dance instructor in the land will be bought, if necessary," he expounded. "What can I do?"

"Allow me two months of solitude," I declared. "Away from the palace and its distractions I can concentrate on a dance which will please you and all of your friends," I spoke, enticingly.

"How will I survive without your presence, you are like the moon each night, waxing more beautiful." He clutched at my ankle from the couch.

"I would prepare you something special. The Festival of Lights will come in three months, allow me to adorn myself and study," shaking him off.

"Always, beloved, always," he moaned.

I spoke almost as an aside, "May I take my mother with me? She has wearied of the palace and needs a respite."

"I have plenty of charming courtesans to keep me company, tell Herodias she has no need to worry on my behalf. Take her, take anything else you need. Massada is well prepared for this season. The Days of Awe have just finished, so even my religious counselors will not be surprised if you disappear for a while."

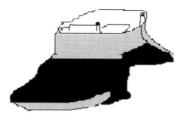

CHAPTER 2

Massada

I had been to Massada in the springtime, but this was the first time I had visited the stronghold in the fall. The air was dry and sweltering, so I looked forward to its deep wells. The great retreat had been carved out of solid rock under my grandfather's orders to be both an escape from Jerusalem in the desert, and a fortress against the Persians and the Nabateans, but I had not realized until this ride through the heat what a monumental task it must have been.

The dusk was falling as we rode up the last mile to the guard's house. The dance instructor had kept silent the entire journey, though my mother tried to entice her to speak. I could get no word from her as we were taken to apartments. With a sign she indicated she would wake me at first light, and she turned to her own quarters.

At dawn, I awoke to the sound of a small bell. At the door was the old woman, with her garments tied back so that she could move freely. Without preface she spoke, "You prepare for the Feast of Lights. It will take you many days to prepare, for each dance must be done in sequence. Nothing must be left to chance."

"We weave the dance of seven veils to the words Chanukah Asher," she spoke, "a night for every letter of the words, for Antipas is Tetrarch, and must preside over this Feast of Dedication."

"You will spend seven nights and days learning each veil, and seven more days at the end to bring it to completion, eight weeks in all, and then the Feast will be nigh upon us."

"Come with me to the garden," spoke the old woman, leading the way to the tiny expanse at the edge of the cliffs, "What do you see, Salomé?"

"I see small birds, tumbling from the heights."

"Those are sparrows. Were it not for us they would starve in this wasteland." Even as she spoke a brown bird hopped from a bush and fluttered, barely flying.

"It is but a baby," I exclaimed. "Let me help it back."

"No, no! It is not tame, and if you take it from its mother, she will never reclaim it," spoke the old woman, silencing me with a gesture. She held out her cane and the young bird hopped on it. She then put it back in its nest above the porch, saying "Do not touch it with your hand, mother birds do not forget."

** ה **

"The first lamp will be for Chai 'life', the palest of pinks, this is your first veil, to capture his imagination," spoke the old crone. "You wish to appear innocent as you begin your dance. "Imitate the movement of a bird just learning to fly."

I tried to lower myself slowly, following her guiding. I got down to a squat but when I tried to rise, she held my shoulder. "Slowly, slowly, you are just learning to use your legs." I tried, but I spasmed, and fell.

"Think of the bird, a trembling thought at the merest touch of trouble. Remember, you are showing both trust and fright, something Antipas cannot see in himself right now. Your dance is to teach as well as terrify. It is something to learn, and each step builds on the one before."

I squirmed under her touch, the pain of my thighs was unbearable, but she was stern and I tried again, to slowly get up, and try to be graceful. Oh, such agony.

"Again, Salomé," her voice was like iron and felt together. How did she do it?

And so it began. Day after day, I struggled those long weeks, not knowing how I was to learn. Patience was not a virtue I had ever cultivated, but this dance was not about to be taught to me overnight.

**] * *

Seven days, and again we found ourselves on the battlements, this time toward dusk. "The second lamp, for the letter Nun, will be for "Noah," happiness, purples of sunset, mauves of a whisper of shadows."

"The birds are not now so tame, look down from the battlements, Salomé."

I looked below to where the scraps of a meal had been thrown. Ravens were beginning to wheel down, arguing with each other over a scrap of meat.

"It is a parable, Salomé. The royal purple is not easy to wear, and you will always be pawed over, and fawned over."

The dance this time was a stalking dance, first a feint, then a quick touch to the center of attention, then walking away as if having stolen a prize, a look back. Over and over again.

It was dizzying at first, like being suspended over a gibbet. I felt as if I was losing my bearings altogether.

"You are Noah's raven," spoke the old woman as she beat the tambor for a rhythm. "You bring sunset and good news, and even food to the wilderness, but you are not tame. You must not forget this. He may think you a tamed purple finch, but remember your raven heart."

I thought of how Antipas had had me bring him sweetmeats at midnight, and trembled. Purple finch indeed!

* * ˥ * *

The lessons continued, and the weeks passed. I was used to rising with the dawn by now, and yet this morning the old woman was delayed. "Come with me to the well," the old woman spoke. "It is high noon, and a clear day. Come, look deep into the well."

"There is a star there!" I cried.

"Yes, it is the Day Star. When the light is just right and the well cuts out the reflection of the sun, you can see the Day Star in any well. This is not magic, just knowledge of the sky, and that is what this next dance is about.

"The third veil is Kappa, Kadosh, holiness, a blue veil to set you apart, my Young One. Though this dance may seem strange to you in this context, it is a lesson to Herod."

"How do I capture knowledge in a dance, Old One?"

"By singing, as you dance, a wordless song of beauty, recalling the heavens and the earth, and the waters under the earth. This is your song of rain, and the veil of tears which your mother cries and Antipas does not hear."

"Remember, Salomé, you are set apart, something Antipas has heard many times, and does not believe. You are yet a virgin, and that is what he most desires, and fears. And remember, you will be learning this dance for seven nights, so every lesson is important, nothing must be left to chance."

I sighed, and began the slow learning process of a song without words, a song which called rain to my eyes, and sorrow to my breast. This song would set me apart from the world, and from all my memories.

Ah, beloved husband, it has been years since that time, and I sit and think of Galilee's deep waters again. The tears I have now bring up even that dance to my mind, one is forgiven, but one can never forget something forged so deep.

* * ה * *

I woke in the darkness to the insistent shaking of my teacher. "Come at once," she whispered.

"Here in the darkness you learn the heartbeat of Creation, the night which turns to dawning. Your veil here will be the green of dawn, which you can only know if you have waited the night for it."

"Listen for the crickets, and the night creatures," she murmured. "I have woken you so you may hear their rustle at the last watch, the two hours before dawn."

I sat in silence, as even my breathing had become hushed. She had led me with only a single tallow candle to our watching post, looking east, across the desert to her homeland. An owl arose with something in its talons, visible against that faint light which I had learned this night rises just before dawn, a faint crescent arch that followed the circle of stars the Babylonians watched to predict the future. I thought of myself as that poor mouse, caught away in something far beyond me.

"Hush my Young One, you must be brave, a living mouse can survive when a lion would be killed for its growling in the night."

"Now watch the dawn with me. You must watch carefully for that first light. See that pillar far off in the desert? That is marked for this season; the sun will rise behind it."

I watched where her old finger pointed, and suddenly there was a flash of green, then the light of the sun, too bright to look at.

"Yes, my young mouse. That is the green sun, a flash that is only seen in the desert and on crystal days at sea. It is a mystery which you can hold within. This is now your veil of He, for Hevah, Mother of Life."

"Within each of us is a hidden mystery, something which only we can hold and which holds us together. It is a green something at the heart of us that few can see for they are impatient and are not willing to wait for the moment of intimacy. It separates us from brutish souls, who if they watched the animals would learn that center again."

"You are called, even in your pain, to be Hevah, Eve, a green canopy, whirling out of darkness, speeding on its way. This is the fourth veil, something I did not teach your mother, as she wished for passion, which comes in a different time and place." You are here to bring justice as well as pain, so remember even in your weaving of this dance that brings death to a prophet, that you cannot forget life."

* * *

Herod kept a tower at each of his fortresses for messages. Through a series of mirrors and watchfires, he could keep track of all that was happening in his scattered holdings, from Jerusalem, to the Herodium, to Macherus, to Massada, even up to Galilee and out to the Decapolis. By day and night the signals danced over the desert and brought news.

It had now been four weeks since we left Galilee. We learned from the guards at the signal tower that a supply of goods would be delivered this afternoon. Though we had only a skeleton staff at Massada at this season, still four weeks would devour staples. Nothing grew well on this height, except for the plane trees that seemed to grow in any crevice they could find.

I watched the road to Galilee with my teacher. Many miles away we could see caravans coming up the desert road, but nothing turned in this direction for hours. Finally, something began to crawl its way toward us. They edged closer and closer along the winding wadis until I could recognize the slow moving figure in front.

"Why it is Tobias and his oxcart," I shouted. "Let me down, let me down. Quickly! Quickly!"—I was still impatient.

Massada's stronghold ended with a high cliff from which soldiers would let down baskets the last 20 feet to the road. This prevented anyone from assaulting the heights, but it acted as a strain to anyone who did not know the way. The soldiers operated baskets for the suppliers to leave goods, but this time I could not resist.

"What, my sparrow? You are here? I had no idea. I was just asked to bring letters and some dried fish to supply the garrison," he spoke. "I can stay but one hour, and I am forbidden up on the hilltop this time, my songbird, but let me look at you. You seem in good health. Without all that makeup from court you actually look like the young girl I remembered."

"Ah, Tobias, that is one thing that only you may remember of me now," I chattered.

"Well, try to remember for me, if for no one else, that innocence is not such a bad thing." Tobias finished unloading his oxcart and turned back toward Judaea. "Be well, my daughter." His voice floated back through the desert air.

* * א * *

"Patience, my youngling, patience!" The old woman was exasperated with me. "Once again, take the step slow and even. You must ignore the music here and plod unthinking."

"But the music is violent, and quick, and bright, and lively," I complained.

"Even so, for this is the dance of the ox, Aleph, who turns the wheel which makes the grain to grow, the yellow of wheat, and harvest, and the sun. Everything else is bright, as the chaff is whirled away, but the ox plods on at the mill, looking inward, seeing nothing of the outward changes, concentrating only on the end result of its labors."

"This is the yellow veil, Salomé, the veil of the sun's heat, steady, eternal, something that comes from your bowels, that deep source of feeling, something Herod has put aside, but must remember when all is done."

I plodded like the ox, trying to deafen myself to the music. This was trust in its most basic form, that my dance would be meaningful and strike the heart, even when I could see nothing and feel as if it had no purpose in it.

* * שׁ * *

"Now the last two veils, my daughter, are the hardest of all," spoke the old woman, "for they strike at the heart of Antipas' faithlessness, the womb and the passions. He could have learned much from his advisors, but he chose to surround himself with sycophants instead."

"The orange veil, the letter Shin is the veil of Sheba, the forbidden woman, and the Queen of the Desert. You are to become that queen, Salomé, and this is your dance of possessing your birthright."

"Solomon was fascinated by her, and she came seeking him, but this time you come as Sheba in her anger, Sheba spurned, Sheba ennobled. You are lioness, and panther, and desert wolf. You are Salomé, the female Solomon, bringing Herod to task for your mother."

I did not know what had caught me up in this woman's passions, what drove me to respond to her words. All I knew was that I was caught up for seven days in a dance of wild things, of desert heat, and rage, barely controlled, forging a chain of golden wrath for myself to contain this dance until the Feast of Dedication.

The dawn of the last day I woke slowly, like a cat, stretching every muscle, and knew that I had learned this lesson deeply. Antipas would not like this dance, but he would be ensnared by it.

* * ⅂* *

The last day, the day of Resh, you play the fool, Rachah, to dance for the head of the Baptist, Rosh. This is the veil of red, the one so tightly wound it clings to your body like a second skin. There is nothing hidden here, all is unveiled in this dance, but you show nothing you do not choose to show."

Today my teacher had a whip in her hand. "You must use your skills to wrap this veil tightly, for you will be tempted to drop all of your defenses. I will never strike you Salomé, but this whip will strike around you to remind you of how close you are to danger at every turn. This is the dance you feel compelled to do—and you bring a king to ruin in it."

"Strike, strike, strike" I called, as the dance grew closer and closer, the rhythms more hypnotic. The drummers took the heartbeat of the dance and it grew to a great swell and then a close.

"Rachah, I am a fool to do this!" I gasped exhausted.

"Get up, you must continue," spoke my teacher. The whip moved again. "Remember, this is the dance for which you have spent 50 days of your life." "It will not be done until that last gesture," she breathed. I dared not bring a man into this chamber, other than the eunuchs who have been your drummers, for they would have gone furious with desire. But it is not yet over." She spoke tautly as if holding herself in check.

"Not yet done!? Where do you get your stamina? I am the one dancing!" I sputtered.

"I have breathed with you with every lash of the whip, that is why I know your limits. I know every hurting muscle and every tear of your heart. I pour myself into it with you, for this is a strike for my own justice, as well as yours."

"Your own justice?" I spoke, now frightened.

"Yes, Salomé. I am not just any dancer, but I cannot speak of what I know until the deed is done. Just remember, you are not alone. Your mother and I dance with you!"

I thought deeply of the dance I was weaving. A dance of vengeance, and justice, and death, woven to be presented almost as a sacrifice at the Feast of Dedication. What hand was guiding me? Who was my teacher, and why did she care so much for my welfare?

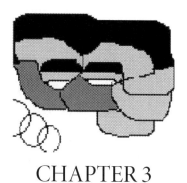

CHAPTER 3

The Baptist

Jerusalem was a cosmopolitan city in those days. With Romans and Greeks rubbing elbows with the Sanhedrin, the city's ruling class, though they would not eat with them, the mixture of customs became rather strange.

My stepfather Herod Antipas was often considered both outcast and insider. His father, Herod the Great, had been mad, murdering three of his wives and four of his sons before toppling from his throne, exploding across the pavement, putrefied by his own hatred from within. Herod Antipas, one of several surviving sons, had himself barely managed to survive all of the attempts at coups until direct support from Tiberius, the current Emperor, had enabled him to be established as Tetrarch of Galilee instead of his brother Archelaus, though he more often stayed in Jerusalem or the nearby fortress of Herodiam, the family compound.

Even so, Antipas tended to posture on both sides of the political fence. My mother sat in the background at every court, watching everything, and I was often forced to sit next to Antipas as his current favorite lust object, though not yet his bedmate. I can only appreciate now, after years in endless court functions with my husband, what patience it took for her to ignore the subtle insults his attentions on me heaped upon her unhappy life.

Now that the winter court was near, we were constantly on display, and with Antipas knowing that we had been especially preparing for him, he was anxious to ensure that I was seen with him.

Unbelievably, my eunuchs had been loyal, and we had disguised our intentions from the garrison that we often knew had spied on us at Massada, but my teacher, my mother, and I were all anxious for the court to be concluded after many days, culminating in the Feast of Dedication.

As we prepared ourselves, we learned that the mirrors had been flashing for weeks from Massada and from Galilee to Herodiam. In response, Antipas chose to move his court to Macherus, the fortress opposite Massada on the near side of the Dead Sea, as he was still at war, even after seven years, with Nabatea and wished to find friends in Arabia. We were still unpacking at midnight in our new quarters when my stepfather came with guards, and requested I accompany him to the prison below the fortress.

•   •   •

"Salomé, my beloved, I know you do not understand him, but I wish you to listen to the prophet tonight," spoke Antipas quietly as court began to close. I blanched. "What does he know?" I spoke to myself. "But he is so dirty and you know Mother hates him." I spoke aloud.

"Even so, accompany me this once. You see all sides of court, perhaps you can see what your mother does not."

I shuddered inside—I had heard screams many times from the towers, I never thought to have to visit them. "Let me at least cover myself. Who knows, he might desire me," I tittered nervously.

"He is not moved by women, but by visions, Salomé," he spoke, unexpectedly sober.

I walked three steps behind Antipas, staying always in his shadow, even though surrounded by guards. The place they had confined John was deep but had a high window in which one could look down into his darkened cell.

"John, are you there?" shouted Antipas.

"Vile one, commander of thieves, slayer of innocents. . ." spoke a voice in the darkness."

"Apparently you are," whispered Antipas. "I wish you well."

"For this you shut me up in prison, son of a dog, you wish me well? Perhaps in a well," he coughed.

"Oh, John, even when you choke yourself something draws me to you. Is there no end to your visions?"

"You are on a precipice, Antipas, and you will be dragged down, I can do nothing for you. Those closest to you are far away. You will never know their minds," spoke that raggedy voice.

I shivered. What did he know? I knew that prophets had reputations overblown, but what could he say? I knelt down in the shadows. I could see a darkness against the bricks which must be this strange man.

"It is done, Antipas. You cannot save me, and my going will be by your own hand."

"Never, I shut you in prison to save you from mob violence. It was all that I could do. My hand will not take your life," Antipas swore.

"Friends of the Herods do not ever walk without fear, but I am not afraid of oaths or madness, Antipas. I am prepared," spoke John.

Suddenly his eyes were visible in the darkness and he seemed to look straight at my shadowed form. "My head is yours, Antipas. It will be time soon, my visions are almost over."

"John, John, I cannot convince you," Antipas spoke, turning away. "He does not listen to me anymore, daughter, he has passed out of my hearing."

My breath came in gasps. "Let me leave here, the air has become suddenly close," my hoarseness nearly stifled me. He had called me daughter, the only time in months that I was not the center of his attention.

We moved back out of the tower and the sun seemed suddenly chill even at midday. "Yes, Salomé, it has been this way for the past 40 days. He has been intemperate, and preaching, but never resigned before," he sighed.

All at once his mood changed. "I cannot deal with mad prophets today, come sit with me, I need your hand."

I felt the change in atmosphere and almost fainted. What must I do? I must talk to my teacher, quickly, alone. "Father, I am sickened, may I leave you and lie down?"

His concern was almost touching but untrustworthy. "I will call a servant to attend you—guard, escort Salomé to her quarters."

I waved off the guard. "No, Father, I need to be alone." I stumbled back to my room and fell before the fire, exhausted.

•   •   •

"Now you must know what has gone before, Salomé," spoke the old woman. "You were only seven and did not see all of what happened when Antipas wooed your mother."

She won her prize, but the price was heavy. And this day, and this festival to come, seem to be foreordained, something beyond my years to fathom." She sank into the cushions by the fire and let her eyes wander. It was as if a trance had come over her, and a melancholy brooding. She breathed slowly, and this helped me to calm myself, though I was still frightened.

"When your stepfather first hired me," she spoke softly, "I was the most prized dance instructor of all. As a Babylonian teacher, I was respected, even when other women would have been talked about in whispers. Artists seem to be the one profession that can break tradition without being made outcast. And so I taught dance. At every festival I was welcomed as one who could teach young maidens, for though in middle years, I was still a virgin. I had thought to marry, but having no parents and no family in Judaea, there was no opportunity."

"Old One, in all of our weeks together, I have never heard your name," I queried. "Is this a part of your heritage, or is it long custom?"

"The name of my childhood I keep to myself, and the name I have adopted for the past twelve years is more of a sign of sorrow. I am called Mara, my child, the Bitter Sea, which cannot easily be made fresh again. Call me Aunt, or Old One, as you have been doing, they are more endearing than my use name."

"To return to your mother's story, and my sorrow—as she has taken it upon herself—is one of the strongest reasons for you being here with me now. Your mother was blinded by infatuation for Antipas, and could not see his cruelty."

"It was only after the past decade in court that she began to see him as 'great' in matters of state, but petty in his cruelty, and completely selfish in family matters."

"I have seen that from both sides, I think," I replied. "My mother has tried to influence him, even in small matters at times, but I have heard him getting only drunk and angry when she tries to subtly speak sense to him. At such times, I feel that I am only in the way, but when I try to pull away, he jerks me back to his footstool."

The old woman continued. "Her affair with Antipas, which eventually grew to their uneasy marriage, was flawed from the beginning. She, somehow, did not realize that she was a pawn in a play for power. He divorced his wife of ten years for her sake, as she could bear no rival. She was, after all, the heir to the Maccabees, and so her husband would be King of Judaea."

"How was this, Old One?"

"This story goes back four generations, to the time of Antipater, your great-grandfather, and Hyrcanus, the last of the Macabeean kings. Antipater was from Nabatea, the kingdom of Petra, south of Judaea. He had just helped Marc Antony in one of the perpetual wars against the Persians, and so was in a position to make a name for himself. Wishing to keep the old line of kings alive, and so bolster a Jewish sympathy in his rise as a client king, he married his son Herod, later the Great, to the old high priest Hyrcanus's daughter, Mariamne. This was in the face of massive opposition by the Sanhedrin, who supported Hyrcanus' brother, Antigonus, but Rome backed him, even when Marc Antony was executed, as the closest friend Rome had in Palestine."

"Herod had already had one son by a Petran wife, Antipater, his heir in Petra, but by marrying Mariamne, he became heir to the Maccabees, as only a daughter's son or husband could inherit the throne. Mariamne and he had two children, Aristobolus and Alexander. But he mistrusted Mariamne, and after the children were of age, he plotted to have her killed."

"His mother-in-law Alexandra appealed to Cleopatra of Egypt, but the letter was intercepted and Alexandra and Mariamne were killed. He married Malthace, a Samaritan woman, and had two sons, Archelaus and your stepfather Antipas."

"He married yet again, to a granddaughter of Hyrcanus, another Mariamne, always trying to keep the line of the Maccabees alive by the birth of a daughter, who would be the next in line after Antipater. From this Mariamne was born Herod Philip, your father."

"Herod the Great was a cruel husband, and saw intrigue, not unlikely, in everything, and, like all his previous wives, Mariamne died soon after your father's birth. The fifth wife, Cleopatra of Jerusalem, openly declared war on him, and when all was done, had involved his heir Antipater, Alexander, and Aristobolus, all of whom were killed."

"Aristobolus, in the meantime, by his beautiful wife Berenice, had had a daughter, and three sons. Your mother Herodias was that daughter, now the most eligible woman in the kingdom as the only daughter of the line. Whoever married her would have a claim to all the old followers of the Maccabees. As I said before, Antipas was Herod the Great's son by Melcene, a princess of Samaria, a non-Jewish wife. Antiopas' half-brother, Herod Philip, son of Herod the Great and the second Mariamne, had survived all the intrigues, and married Herodias, so he was now the presumed heir to the Maccabees."

"However, Herod Philip had no political ambitions and spent all his time in Rome, preferring a quiet life to a life of rulership. In that quietness, you were born."

"Antipas, feeling his chances were lost with Herodias, and to keep the peace on his southern border, had married Phasaelus Shaqilath, the daughter of Aretus, King of Petra, a distant cousin of his grandfather Antipater. Their lives were apparently happy, and she bore him two sons. But then Antipas went to Rome, away from his new wife, away from Judaea and Petra, and saw Herodias from afar."

"Antipas surrounds himself with weak minds, and Herodias deliberately held back her intelligence when she chose to seduce him. But she was the heir to the Maccabees, and so held a token of power."

"He knew that she would have to be his chief wife, yet he was married to a princess of another state, presumed to be his prime wife, and this would not do if he was to marry the heir to Judaea. He pondered this dilemma for over a year, while he remained in Rome being trained in Roman law for his new office. As long as he was married to Phasaelis, he could not marry another woman and make her chief wife, only by divorcing her could he follow his lusts. But Phasaelis learned of his betrayal, even in Galilee, and escaped into the desert with her sons before he could murder her, and so not have to go through with divorce."

"Even so, Herodias came to me to win his heart, no matter the cost. She despised her husband, Philip, as he was content to be a quiet gentleman without a throne. Now she needed to convince Antipas that she would be worth his ruthlessness, even if it caused a war. She was the prize, but now, all she can do is bend his will in small affairs, but the larger affairs of state, which she hoped to control, are completely beyond her."

"I was one of her few triumphs, for though I stay in the shadows, I can at least hear all the doings of the court, even when I am not named in law."

"I can understand the awkwardness of the situation from politics, but you spoke of cruelty, what could keep you here, if what you say is so?" I questioned. "My mother puts up with Antipas out of spite at this point, but what hold has he on you?"

"I taught Herodias a dance of temptation, a dance to woo, and to seduce, but she did not know the price of my instruction. "Four years prior to her meeting me in Rome, Antipas had hired me for his dancing girls. Though he let them learn, I was watched and he waited for me, finding me unguarded as I walked to my room one night in his warren of a palace. His guards turned a blind eye as he pushed me into my own room, stripped me, and raped me. With all my protestations, even when he could clearly see that I was at my moon time, he took delight in pain and my humiliation."

I winced, feeling her anguish, as the words spilled out over the fire. "But why did you stay, I still do not understand. Wouldn't Babylon be safer?"

"Where could I go, a woman with no pride left, who could not publicly teach anymore, with only the pension of the court to survive on? Antipas could not throw me out on the street—even he was not that careless—but he bought my silence only by a guarantee of survival. His rape injured my womb, and I have had increasing flows every month. Now, my moon time is weeks in duration, and only constant exercise gives me even a week every month without pain. I can find sympathetic Greek physicians here to at last keep me alive, but travel home, except with a doctor in tow, is beyond me. There was a physician in our entourage at Massada, but I took great care for you not to see my pain as it would have distracted from your training."

"How have you survived all these years," I gasped. "I have seen you at a distance for years, but I had no idea of your pain. You keep your head erect and walk with a dancer's grace. If this is in spite of injury, your stamina puts me in awe."

"It is," she spoke. "Twelve years is a long time. It is a hard life, living in the shadows, and not daring to appear at temple. The dogs can smell me coming, even with constant bathing, so public gatherings, except on rare occasion, are out of the question."

"Yet now there is something more to keep me, something that has made even my pain endurable, as it is coming to an end, or at least it feels so," she murmured. "I had given up hope, and felt as if I was fated to watch you, an innocent, be caught and raped, just as I was, without being able to do anything. And then the Baptist came, preaching disgust at Antipas, and Antipas—in some peculiar fit of sanity—respected him. I have watched for this past year since he has been in prison."

"Three months ago I was watching him from an upper window when he suddenly turned in my direction and spoke only one sentence, 'You will make it happen, my time is at hand. The axe is laid at the root of the tree, and nothing can stop its fall.' "

"No one else seemed to hear that sentence in quite that way. I questioned his disciples during one of my rare clean times, and they had only heard the words of Elijah the Prophet, a preaching that never stopped. Samaria must fall—meaning both Herod, as the son of a Samaritan woman, and Herodias—as an adulteress."

"This message his disciples heard, and the Zealots were arming, but beyond that constant murmur, there was nothing outstanding in his words to me. Somehow, my child, I feel that it is a purpose beyond my understanding that has brought us together. Antipas has become blinded in his lust for you, he forgets my presence in his life like a long-forgotten toothache. And though, as you say, he has noticed John the Baptist's change in preaching, it never occurs to him that his entire household is caught up in doings that he cannot imagine."

"I am afraid, Teacher, I only wished to protect my mother," I spoke, "and get back at him for his constant attentions—you are saying I had no choice in the matter?"

"Remember that young mouse in the wilderness, Salomé, caught up on an owl's wing? I have felt that way sometimes," she murmured. "It is only after years that I look back and see that a guidance beyond my own guarded my steps and kept me from utter ruin."

"Then I have no choice, and Antipas can be mocked and silenced only by the death of a prophet?"

"It seems so, but at least you have the knowledge that what you do out of what will be viewed in court as petty spite has an underlying justice from the start, and a hand far beyond your own, and starting years ago, has brought it to pass."

"But that must mean that your rape was fated to happen, and the abuse upon abuse that my mother has suffered are all to no purpose!" I grieved.

"Not so, my Young One, the years have taught me that a life must run its course and a lesson must be learned in the clearest way possible. Sometimes among many choices, none are without pain, and one stops asking why."

"But, don't cease to question, you will be years in finding your own answers. Somehow I have been given a few years with you when you are young, but you will live years beyond me and dream dreams I can not even contemplate. The world you know will vanish in fire and sword, but somehow you will survive."

"How do you know these things, Bat Mara?" I spoke. The words just slipped out.

Her voice cracked. "At great intervals my eyes are opened, just like the Baptist, and I see glimpses of the future, like shattered crystal. But you named me Bat Mara, Daughter of Sorrows."

"What an unexpected name, something I could not foresee." She laughed. "You have named me anew, a Kindly Bitterness—I will not forget it. Somehow we will see this one through, my daughter."

CHAPTER 4

The Dance

The Feast of Dedication had its origins in the rebellion of the Jews against Antiochus, a Greek governor who had violated the Temple and was bent on destroying all trace of Jewish worship custom. A statue of Zeus had been set up in the Temple, and pigs—sacred to him, and specifically forbidden to Jews as scavengers—had been sacrificed on the high altar. After many years of guerilla warfare, a group of Zealots calling themselves the "Hammers of the Lord," the Maccabees, had led an uprising that succeeded in deposing Antiochus and restoring Jewish worship.

The Temple had been rededicated but the oil available had only been enough to light all the lamps for a single day. It would take eight days for a round trip to the coast for more oil. Miraculously, the lamps were said to have burned for the entire eight day's journey.

The Maccabees had eventually given way, as I had learned, to the family of Herod the Great, my stepfather's father. Almost to buy his way in, he had rebuilt the now rededicated temple as a wonder of the world, with gold altars, hangings of scarlet and blue cloth, and carvings of the great winged bulls called cherubim on its walls. For this act his family was tolerated if not exactly loved.

It seemed ironic to many that the Feast of Dedication would be celebrated by Herod the Great's descendants, when the Herodian dynasty now eagerly accepted and mimicked all things Greek.

Be that as it may, Herod Antipas—usually just called Herod in court, but Antipas at home—this drunken son of the desert—was the Tetrarch of Galilee, for all intents and purposes the closest thing Israel had to a king. During this season, he even had the pomposity to wear imperial purple and invite the Jewish Council of Elders, the Sanhedrin, to a feast for the Festival of Lights, trying to outdo on this one day all the other religious festivals on the calendar in display of his claimed Jewish heritage. As he wished to invite both Jewish and Arabic elders, he moved the feast to Macherus, a day's journey from Jerusalem, and gave Bat Mara leave to gather any supplies she might need.

So here, on a winter's night, in a grand procession, Antipas, with me on his arm, and Herodias, a few steps behind, followed the High Priest and his entourage into the great hall of Macherus.

Bat Mara had taken her leave of me about an hour before the feast, going to direct the drummers and other musicians who would lead the dance. This one week was, by some miracle, her week without pain, so she was able to make a rare appearance in the hall. So that Antipas would not notice her, she dressed in a drab robe, and had filled out her appearance with rags so that she did not look or walk like the dancer he would have ogled. She stood at the far end of the hall in a cluster with the maidens, but near a door so that she could slip quickly away in case of trouble.

•   •   •

"Blessed art Thou, O Ruler of the Universe, who has kept us in life, and brought us to this season, and commanded us to kindle the lights of Chanukah," spoke Annas, the High Priest, as he strode into the hall with a torch, walking to the festival menorah. His son Caiphas had done the same an hour previously in the temple, but this was now his public show before the more influential of his cohorts.

"Bring the oil and wine, the bulls and fat, the lambs in honey, this is the feast of oil," spoke Antipas loudly, as if to outdo the priest. "I wish to celebrate this night of lights with dancing."

Sweeping himself into the hall, he mounted the steps to a divan, motioning me to sit before him on a footstool. A hard chair was pulled up behind the divan for Herodias, but rather than take offense, she made a great show of gratitude as she spread her gown and sat down stiffly.

I sat quietly, gathering my strength. This was my night of innocence, one of the last I might ever have. The feast would last eight nights, but I would only perform seven dances, and by the eighth night I would be viewed as far from pure.

I was dressed in pink, very pale, and had covered my hair with a white veil pulled back. I felt rather silly—this had once been one of my most flattering and talked about robes—and now it felt so frivolous for my dangerous mission. I smiled absently, but the drummers had already started the beat I knew would beckon me to dance, a gentle flutter underlying the feast. It would be hours yet. Nothing had been left to chance.

•   •   •

Dish after dish of exoticly spiced delicacies arrived, each more magnificent than the last. Most were either oily or at least brightly colored for this festival. I rapidly lost my appetite though Antipas continually tried to feed me. I had to be charming, but it felt very strange wearing a mask of flirtation now.

Between each course a different form of entertainers would present themselves before the multitude. Because the first course was gaming beasts, the first performers were dressed as hawks and hunters, chasing each other back and forth across the hall. The drumming behind them was a slow beat, with tambourines following the movement of the hawks. It was a merry chase.

The second course was oily breads and fruit condiments. For entertainment there were jugglers who tossed rings of hard bread in the air, getting a smirk even from the most staid of the guests.

•   •   •

The last course was spices, fruits, and light wine. By now Antipas was drunk on the heavier red wines served with the first course, and I was eager to get out of his way. I signaled the drummers, and Bat Mara motioned to a dark-robed figure with a huge woven basket.

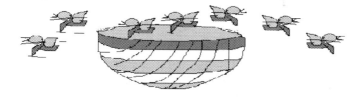

The dark-robed person strode from the corner with the dancers to a point before Antipas' divan and cried out, "L'Chaim, I wish you life. I give you Salomé and the dance of the sparrows." I recognized the figure—it was Tobias of Galilee. I laughed as I remembered that he had last seen me being hauled up in just such a basket at Massada. The basket was thrown open suddenly and a flock of sparrows flew out, flying upward into the far reaches of the hall. The tabors and tambourines sent a murmur through the crowd as I rose on tiptoe and danced to the mosaiced zodiac at the center of the room.

This was my dance for my mother, to remember her who birthed me and my connection to her—a dance of innocence. From tiptoe I collapsed to a heap upon the floor and gathered myself into a pink ball of fluff. As the tambourines fluttered, I, too, began to flutter—first one arm and then the other, as if a chick just hatching, pushing myself out of the egg.

A sharp crack brought me up with a start as if to signal the final breaking of the shell. I stretched myself, but still kept close, as if I was just learning to use my wings.

Though I did not creep, I bounced a few steps in a bent, almost squatting position, my arms stretched out straight but my eyes to the floor as if uncertain how to walk. I mimicked walking back and forth on a very narrow limb and my eyes began to wander. I looked at Antipas as if seeing him for the first time, a young child moved from pillar to post in the court intrigue.

I could see my mother's eyes twinkle, for the first time in many months, as she was charmed by this moment, even though she knew where this dance would lead through the nights following. For the moment, then, I would play the innocent.

Antipas looked puzzled. He was holding his wine well, as it was still early evening, but he was definitely fuzzy. This was not the flirtatious Salomé he was used to seeing, the one who pulled out of his arms, yet seemed to want to play with his affections. This was a young and lonely child. I could see the wash of innocence go across his face and he turned to look at Herodias.

She smiled graciously but I could see that her hands were still very tense. Antipas pushed himself to an upright position on the divan but his movement sent my footstool crashing to the floor.

This seemed to startle him out of his reverie, and instead of reaching for Herodias as he had been about to do, he motioned to a server for a dark glass of much more aged wine.

I continued my dance, fluttering about the hall, but trying to watch him for what he would do next.

Antipas stared into his cup. This was not what he had expected when I promised him a dance, but the hall was apparently quite charmed. He must play the good host, though his mood had soured. At my next turn around the hall I could see him sending the server to Annas, who nodded appreciatively, watching my dance with interest. Annas murmured something to the server and beckoned to Antipas. Antipas rose from the divan and walked over to Annas' grand chair. What were they up to?

My dance was almost over, and Antipas returned to his divan. I had paused by one corner of the room and received a single rose bud from a servant. With this I tiptoed to the center of the room, whirled a last time, and sank to my knees, extending the flower in his direction.

Antipas, knowing that this night's dance was over, signaled to Annas. Annas unexpectedly came forward, raising his hand in blessing. "L'chaim to you, daughter of Zion. In you a rose is blooming in the dead of winter." I blushed and fell silent.

•   •   •

My stepfather was angry, but controlled. "For this dance of a child I sent you off! What has gotten into you?" he bellowed. We were alone and it was late at night, as usual.

"This is not all I have learned, but I want you to be able to concentrate, Uncle," I spoke softly, not to anger him further. "I have a dance for each night, and each one is so different, I am sure you will be intrigued," I offered.

"This coming evening had best demonstrate that," he spoke testily. "You are a lovely woman, and I want my court to see that!"

"As you wish, Uncle," I spoke softly. "Now let me go so that I may be rested."

"You touched me tonight," he replied. "I did not know how lonely you were," he sighed. "Go, I need to think."

•   •   •

"Purple tonight, beloved, you are the daughter of Israel," came the command in mid-afternoon, delivered by a palace guard. I smiled secretly, adding another feather to my headdress. "I would be most pleased," I told the servant to reply. "Let Herod know I will wear my finest and the dance will be to his liking."

The hall was draped in purple paraments, as if to welcome royalty. The hangings were of Chinese silk, almost contraband in the Roman Empire now, ever since Tiberius had convinced the Senate to forbid men to wear it. And here it was in a swag over the hall. It shimmered in the light, and reflected in the golden candelabrum prepared for the feast.

Antipas came first into the hall, this time taking a seat on a stone chair, enough like a throne to give one pause. Annas came in second, to light the second lamp of the great sconce. Herodias came in third, dressed in Tyrean purple and black.

Fourth, I came in—as a signal honor to the hall with an announcement of my own—in a purple silk wraparound garment—only the finest cloth would do for this day. A silver comb with amethysts held my hair back. A fan of purple-dyed wood was in my hand, and a headdress shaped like a crane's fluff of raven's feathers completed my ensemble.

The first course tonight was peacock with a dark purple wine from near Mt. Carmel. The great bird was served in its feathers, which made a great sweep across the table. I thought about how people would pick at the flesh of this bird, and what my dance of the raven would bring to mind. I winced, and could barely nibble my food. The music of harps was the offering between the first and second courses. These were the great bards' ten-stringed harps, recalling David soothing the mind of King Saul. These were accompanied by jasmine incense which floated through the palace.

The second course was duck, preserved with salt from the Dead Sea. It was an oily flesh, but tasty. I tried to concentrate on it, feeling like a bird of prey as I tore it with my fingers. The second entertainment was a line from the Song of Songs. "We caught the foxes who fed on the grapes." Again, hunters and their prey ran through the hall, laughing as they went. I began to rise with the mood of the hall.

The last toast this evening was a mint drink from Persia. This was cloyingly sweet, with a vinegary aftertaste. For some reason it tasted good and served to clear my head from the wine of the first course.

At my signal, the drummers began to beat a stalking dance, reminding them of the foxes retreat earlier in the evening. I took a plate of grapes from Herod's table, and carried them with grand ceremony to the middle of the room and put them on a pillow in the center of the circle of stars there. I was brought a black shaggy cloak, made of strips of cloth. As I was draped with it I shouted, "I am Noah's raven. I bring news of sunset and shadows. I am not tame."

My form became sinewy, and my cloak clung to me like feathers. The outer edge of the cloak was shot with purple and black and caught at my wrists so I could spread it like wings as I circled the hall. I stopped, fluttered, took a cluster of grapes from the great mound and hid them in my cloak, as if secretive. I ran to Antipas, tossed them in his lap, and then ran off, turning back as if to watch. I again circled the hall, running to the center, and running out again, this time tossing a single grape into Annas' lap.

Suddenly I was joined by a flock of purple-garbed maidens, each of whom had a black mantle covering her hair. They surrounded me and would not let me out as I sought in vain to leave the circle. I loosed my hair from the comb and held it out, extended, as if a raven's claw. With intensity I had rarely known, my hair blossomed out like a cloud as I raised my comb to rake another dancer. She gave way so I turned to another, and a third. Each of them gave way, but as soon as my back was turned, took a bunch of grapes and hid it in her bosom. Over and over again we circled, with first me being surrounded, becoming ever more anxious, attacking, feinting, and breaking out again and again.

At length, I ran to my stepfather, and stood as if pleading for his help. I turned with the comb raised for the last time and the flock of raven maidens cowered, and then melted away as I sat down.

"You are indeed a wild raven, Salomé," spoke Antipas, "a fitting favorite for the Tetrarch of Galilee." I stared and kept silent.

·   ·   ·

"That was a dance of intriguing insight, Salomé," spoke Antipas as we left the hall. "You show favor to those who are powerful, and shun all those who would strip you of your pride. Am I reading this right?"

"You are wise, my Uncle. A streak of madness may keep some enemies at bay from bewilderment."

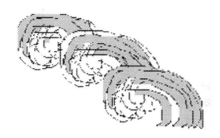

The next night the theme was Galilee, and deep Lake Chinnereth, the source of the Jordan, kept fresh by its many springs. They called Lake Chinnereth the Sea of Galilee in sort of half self-mockery, but storms even on its waters were not to be trifled with.

The halls were hung in blue, and fresh plants were everywhere. They must have kept some very warm and humid hall to keep them beautiful as the weather turned cold. I was dressed in an icy blue, reminding myself of the snow of Hebron and the deep blue of the heavens.

As this was Antipas's night to show off his own Tetrarchy, he was not quite so pompous, but was dressed in a simple Grecian garment with blue and white trim. Even in his late 40's he was a striking gentleman. But the smile covered such a small heart for so well proportioned a body.

Annas, in blue and white as well, with the breastplate of the priesthood across his chest, lit the third lamp of the menorah to start the feast.

The first course was fish, for which Galilee was famous. Fresh, or salted with spices, or simply cooked in butter, this course was an exercise in diversity. The entertainment was of acrobats, who tossed each other in a net, like leaping fish. They stored all of their equipment in a boat that had been set at one end of the hall. A long woven rug, also in blue, flowed across the hall, as if a stream cascaded from the recesses of the palace.

The second course was of almonds, pine nuts, and raisins. Dried fruits from the Galilean hills preserved well. I thought of the Song of Songs, "comfort me with raisins, for I am sick from love." A foreboding rhyme, at best, for me in this night of sorrow.

The final toast before the dance was accompanied by servants with rose water in basins to wash the hands of all who were present. I stood, now wrapped in a midnight blue cloak with my white and blue shift only appearing from the waist down.

As the tambourines played like rain on the rooftops, I began to sing at a slow murmur, scarcely heard. I danced with broad steps, as if striding from rock to rock to keep out of the mud. Finally, I stood on a raised white step just beyond the sea of blue.

I bowed to my stepfather, and then gave my deepest courtesy to Annas. "Sing, O heavens, shout O earth, roar O sea, and all that fills you," I canted, following an ancient melody. "I call you to witness the beauty of holiness, Kadosh, Kadosh, Kadosh. I swayed and sang a song from deep in my lowest register, a cry of abandoned children, a song to the thunder and the lightning to hear my cry, a wail to the Maker of the Heavens to look with favor on this humble servant.

The reeds and pipes followed my wail as it floated, almost like blue smoke, curling around the feet of the guests. This was not a song of sweetness and joy, but one of deepest sorrow, a sorrow of a land and people who were troubled. And yet the song was filled with love for the abandoned land,

and as if in prophetic trance I began to dream of the waters under the earth welling up to restore the lost to favor.

I heard myself call to Antipas for my mother, mind to mind, but the words would not come out, all that came out was a wail for an abandoned wife. Would he hear, or was he deaf to anything but himself?

A hush had fallen across the hall, this was not the refreshment the guests had come for, but it froze them in their places. I motioned to the servants to pass among the guests and give them an opportunity to refresh themselves. The hush grew deeper as not a single guest—including Annas—was not moved. Antipas breathed slowly, as if under a great burden.

As if by instinct, I sounded a cymbal and the reverberation caused everyone to start talking at once. The spell of sorrow was broken and people could breathe again. I was drained, but knowledgeable that at some level my stepfather had heard. What he would do was unknown to me, but I had done my duty.

I walked silently to my room that night and slept without dreams.

•   •   •

Dawn came up crisp and crystal in the garden. Most of the plants had died down but there were a few hardy perennials that seemed to wait for the last of the frost before they could be beaten down. A lone cedar held sentinel in a corner, the only tree not affected by the swiftness of the seasons. Tonight was the night of affirming life in the midst of this subtle dance. I felt I should see what life I could find in the winter and try to use it in my meditations

I had risen early and sat on a bench carved out of a single slab of marble. A skilled artist had carved roses into the armrests, and they seemed almost alive, as the marble was a whirl of pinks and blues. As if in answer to these forever frozen flowers, a gardener was out carefully clearing dead branches away from the living roses that grew in an arbor at the other end of this small space. Only a few green leaves showed which branches were dead and which alive.

The same could be said of me. I felt frozen in time. My emotional senses were searching for that green space my teacher had told me about. It seemed to be deeper than I could go at this moment. I looked for moss among the rocks in the pool, but though the water was fresh, the winter chill had reduced even the algae to a barely discernible rime.

Last night's dance had been a garden in a torrent of rain, what could I do tonight to portray mother Hevah, life beyond death and sorrow. The water murmured from the spring and tumbled down the rocks.

It was early yet, barely past dawn, and sounds from outside the city walls could be heard. Cock crows had passed at the sunrise, but even calls from far away could be heard in the still air. By some freak of the wind, I heard a young lamb call to its mother. The late lambing season was upon us, and the hills were full of sheep at night. There was my image, a shepherdess among the lambs, caring for the smallest child. I thought of Antipas, and how I had adored him as a child, running to catch up as he swept through my uncle's palace at Caesarea Phllipi. I played in the garden often, and was always muddy, in a rough woolen garment to keep off the chill and not mess up my court clothes.

Somehow, he always had a kind word for me. But now the wolf in him had come out, with no time for lambs. There seemed to be very few soft spots left. I pitied that lamb on the hillside and contemplated what I should do.

•   •   •

The fourth night. Green. This time the palace imitated En-gedi, the gardens near the mouth of the Jordan. King David had written about them, describing their perpetual springs which kept them flourishing even at the driest time.

The plants from the night before were present, but this time they were arranged into almost a jungle of growth, filling the hall with fragrance. I thought of Nubia, and Eden, black and green, and I was robed in both, a black camisole like the night sky, with a great green full-circle cloak.

Antipas had settled onto his divan again, and I had been given a couch of my own. His favorite must have the best. Herodias was at least comfortable this time, with a cushioned seat near a pillar so that she could view the play to come. The drummers were hidden behind tall ferns, so that their music came like echoes out of the night.

By now, more and more of the court functionaries had been eager to come to the feast, for word had gone out that my dancing was unusual, to say the least. Antipas was all smiles, as he had never expected this feast to be the complete talk of the town.

All the lamps had been turned down for this moment so that the hall was in darkness. A cauldron with burning coals had been set in the middle of the hall and I was seated near it on a black footstool. I threw a handful of copper sand onto the coals.

The sparks flew green, just as the sun had flashed that day in the desert. "Sunrise!" I cried, and the lamps were uncovered. I rose as the beat of the drummers grew suddenly furious and my cape whirled in my own wind. "I bring you Eve, Mother of the Living!"

I shouted to the hall. Covers were thrown back and the sound of birds filled the place. Their cages had been kept covered throughout the feast so that they would be silent but now their clamoring filled the air. A monkey sprang at me from its trainer and I responded by springing through the hall, from pillar to pillar, gesticulating to each attendant, imitating the monkey. At my signal, other dancers ran about the room, throwing green patches of cloth everywhere, as if to imitate springtime in a moment.

After gibbering about the hall, I returned to the center. The music died down so that only a lone shepherd's pipe could be heard. The hall was expectant. From the reeds, a lamb was pushed forward. I held out a sprig of straw and it cried plaintively as it shambled toward me, nuzzling at my hand. "By cool pastures and still waters," I spoke, "I am shepherdess, and guardian of my flock."

Just when the quiet had touched the hall, a howl came simultaneously from all four corners of the room. Gray-robed figures dressed as wolves lunged to the center, growling. The lamb quailed. Rather than be frightened, I stood my ground, holding the lamb close and continuing to sing my shepherd's song. My voice grew louder and louder, echoing about the hall. I waved a fan made of straw toward the wolves, as if calming their cries. The fan started quickly but then became languid and slowly entrancing.

The wolves at first leaped and continued to attack but then, one by one, they slowed until they all stood still. Then they fell to the floor and curled at my feet. "The wolf and the kids shall lie down together," I called.

Leaving the lamb with the wolves, I glided across the hall, and in passing a table, took a sprig of herbs. Stopping before Antipas, I held the sprig to his mouth. "The wolf and the lamb shall lie down together." His eyes grew wide, and he chomped hungrily at the sprig. I whirled and returned to my couch. A chuckle from Antipas bubbled into laughter and the crowd cheered.

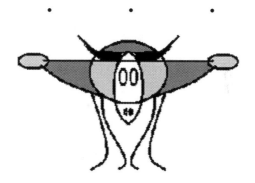

"Bat Mara, I am very confused," I spoke to my teacher by the fire. "Sometimes my stepfather is mad, sometimes very perceptive, and the mood is harder to predict each night."

"That is the difficulty of this dance, Salomé," spoke Bat Mara, touching my cheek. It wakes every mood, shakes them up, and it takes its toll on the dancer as well as the intended focus. It was difficult for you to learn, even in preparation. The performance is almost an unlearning process as each dance strikes at the heart."

"The night coming is the dance of the ox, Bat Mara. Is that why it has become so hard?" I asked.

"Partly, my daughter. You are at the midpoint of this sacrificial dance, and only you and I and your mother and the drummers know where you are heading. Tonight's dance will be difficult, because all others will see it as the welcoming dance of a stranger to the harvest, and read no further. Antipas will see deeper, but it is because he is meant to. Even Annas will be distracted from its true purpose."

•   •   •

The fifth night's focus was grain, an offering of thanksgiving for the harvest. Antipas was used to using every device during this one holiday season to display his Jewish heritage. Bat Mara, being one of the chief retainers, had known the rhythm of this holiday for long before this dance cycle was prepared, so she had prepared me well to know what to do and when.

Though my dances had been spectacular, each story was one well familiar to many of the guests, in the order presented, and it was only my additional flair for theatre that made this feast outshine any other Feast of Dedication in their memory.

The guests, therefore, were expecting the familiar story of hospitality in the book of Ruth, and they would not be disappointed. The floors were covered with rushes, and the hall was draped in yellows. Baskets of grain were at every door—barley and wheat, millet, and on this occasion, wild rice from Babylon. Bat Mara honored Babylon even here.

In this dance even my mother took part, having the long familiar role of Naomi. At one end of the hall was a great statue, representing the Baal of Moab, the God of sacrifice that Ruth had served in legend apart from the preserved story before deciding to follow the God of Israel and follow her mother-in-law into exile from her own country.

A fire was set in its belly, representing the many first-born children sacrificed to it, one of which would have been Ruth if a disfiguring blemish had not been found on her at the last moment. The dancers threw many figures of straw into the fire, all anonymous children lost to history. One figure was dressed as I was, and passed from hand to hand through the hall, from dancer to dancer down the line.

As my little doll reached the fire, Herodias stepped forward and stopped the chief dancer. "Look, this infant is blemished, it is not worthy for this event, let me take her away."

She took the doll from the last dancer and ran to the center of the room where I was hidden, lying flat under a cloak. She whirled about, hiding the doll under her garment and then reaching down and pulling my cloak around her. As if a child suddenly grown to adulthood, I rose from beneath her skirts. "I am Ruth, and my God will be your God, my mother."

Herodias returned to her seat near a pillar and I whirled the cloak around me. "Behold the threshing floor of Boaz," I shouted, stooping down and taking a headdress in the shape of a cow's head from the floor.

The dancers, who had been standing still, ran to the doorways and lifted the baskets of grain and began to dance with them. Male attendants ran with torches around about the hall as the drummers beat a furious dance. I bent over and began to slowly shuffle, making a spiral in the grain at my feet. From the spot in the center I walked as the music grew wilder and wilder, going ever more slowly.

The guests' eyes became riveted on me, as they realized that I ignored the music, and kept only to my stride. I was an ox, a servant, one usually unnoticed at the edge of a hall. Like Ruth, I was as a foreigner, a stranger, not fitting in with the dance of the multitudes.

The dancers continued to gyrate, distracting some guests by sheer force of arms, but for the most part, all eyes were focused on me.

I stopped as the drumbeats came to a halt. I was before Antipas's divan, and I had traced a spiral which wound five circles about the hall, one for every day of my dance thus far. I stood with eyes bowed. "I am orphaned, and need a kinsman who will be my guardian and raise up an heir to my house." I carefully took off a sandal and threw it on the floor before my stepfather, the ancient appeal to justice.

Antipas was thunderstruck. This was not the coquette, nor the raven, this was the orphan, and I had appealed before the court of his peers. He took the sandal from the floor and heaped grain upon my head, a sign of acknowledgement and pity.

Annas eyed him slowly as this night he sat close to him. "Do you know what you are doing, Antipas?" he whispered.

"I am not certain, but this child has confused me and I seem to do what I must."

• • •

"What am I to you," spoke Antipas in his rooms after the feast. "You give me affection, and yet you turn on me in the great hall." He was drunk and not at all happy.

"I am what you see before you, the daughter of your wife," I spoke.

"This is not the Salomé I have known before," he groaned.

"I am many things, Father. Must I satisfy your every whim," I pleaded.

"But you are so beautiful, and you make me feel so young." I felt his breath on my cheek. "Even when you appeal to me, I remember Boaz took Ruth, he did not merely safeguard her. I want you." He took my head in his hands.

I turned from him as he attempted to kiss me. "Father, no, no." His hands were all over me. I squirmed. Would I have to face this madman now? No wonder I had been prepared for this moment. "Father, wait, wait. I will give you much of what you want, but wait."

"I want you now, Salomé. It is not enough."

"You must wait!" I somehow pushed myself just beyond his grasp. "Not yet, I am a virgin."

"Then I shall have the best from you, then!" He rose from his couch and reeled after me. I fled across the room toward the door but he reached it ahead of me and blocked my way.

I saw a shadow from behind the door rise up behind him and bring a club down on his head. The figure was slender but strong. Antipas collapsed.

"I am wrapped in darkness tonight, do not fear," the shadow whispered.

"I-I" I stuttered.

"No, do not say anything. The guards are coming." He vanished behind a pillar.

"My father was drunk tonight, could you put him to bed. He seems to have hit his head." I put on my best plaintive manner as I pulled my shift around me.

The soldiers were not surprised. They did not speak but only nodded and bent to carry Antipas to his couch. I inched out of the chamber as they went about their work and fled to my room.

•   •   •

Now I was furious. Perhaps that was the whole reason for the dance of the ox, to set me up as a puppet so I would know what it felt like to have another follow my whims. I shuddered. My teeth were on edge, and it was very hard to concentrate.

Bat Mara gave me an herbal concoction to settle my nerves. "My child, you were fortunate to escape where I did not, but it only shows how necessary this dance has become. This will calm you for the morning," she spoke as she put me to bed, "but by midday you must begin to prepare yourself."

At noon I began to prepare for the role of Sheba. I carefully darkened my skin with oil, as the tale of Sheba's journey was well known in the court, and Sheba had been known for her ebony skin. My hair was reddened with henna, and I had it carefully braided into the Sabean curls famous in Egyptian carvings for a thousand years.

As the heat of the bath steamed around me, I began to meditate on the figure of the gold lioness I had carried with me to the bath. The Lion of Judah was famous as a symbol of Israel, not often did they think of the lioness, who was the real ruler of the pride in the wild. I stretched and yawned and reached for the cat muscles from my training. This evening's dance was one for my pride, and my encounter with Antipas only drove it more deeply into my soul.

This was the fight for my own womb, my own personal dignity, and it would not be taken from me.

●   ●   ●

The sixth night was a night of wealth. Antipas had pulled out the best fabrics, Egyptian linens, and cedar chests, all bound in gold. Gold goblets were at every table, saffron from Hindustan was served with rice, spices from Arabia scented the curtains. Opulence was on display here. Heavy gold ornamental tables were carted in with brass bowls filled with Roman, Greek, Babylonian, and Egyptian coins. Figures of copper, bronze, electrum, and gold were at every corner.

As if the last evening's encounter had never happened, my stepfather smiled broadly at every one and every thing. He was decked in a linen gown threaded in gold. Herodias had coins in her headdress, clothed as an Arabian queen with an embroidery of yellow roses worked around her hem, her red hair billowing about her shoulders.

Even Annas recognized the need for finery and had sashed his temple robe with a belt of leather and electrum, leaving the gold to Antipas.

I was in a crushed cotton shift that puffed about my waist in many plaits. My bodice was tight and accentuated my figure. I remembered some Cretan figures I had seen in

Tyre and had modeled myself after them. Though propriety demanded that I not be bare-breasted, the bodice had no sleeves and had been carefully molded to match my figure.

Only the barest ring of leather about my neck held the dress up. Over this barest of figures I wrapped a cape of fur, the orange shade of a lioness of the desert. My hands wore long-sleeved gloves, buckled to my forearms with cabochons of topaz. The fingers were open and my hands were painted with copper powder, shining in the light of the torches like claws unsheathed.

For the first part of the feast, I sat on my usual tuffet at Antipas's feet. He would occasionally caress me and try to brush back my mane of fur, but I gently yet firmly put his hand aside and gave him some sweetmeat instead, attempting to be the soul of courtesy. I remembered that John had called him an old fox, and he seemed to have dressed to deliberately match the part. His beard was wiry and had been curled for the feast, and his red hair, matching my henna, shone in the amber lamps of the hall. I fed him chicken carefully, trying not to identify with the bird.

A brass cymbal reverberated through the hall and I took my leave of my stepfather to join the dancers. I pulled the cape around me and enveloped myself with the spirit of the lioness.

•   •   •

I led the women out a side hall so that we could be announced as new visitors. A brass trumpet sounded, echoing through the palace. "Sheba, Candace of Ethiopia, requests audience with the Lion of Judah," intoned the Herald.

Antipas rose from his place and called, "The Lion of Judah is eager to see this Queen of the Desert and the Forest."

Dancers covered in orange cloth, wound tightly as not to move as they spun, sprang forward with finger chimes.

They bounded as gazelles before the wind. Nubian warriors with spotted clothes moved forward with large leopard-furred shields as if to chase them from the hall for the sport of it.

They scattered, forming a wide arc around the hall, warriors and gazelles forming a rustling sea of shields and twining limbs.

"Out of the eater came forth meat, and out of the strong came forth sweetness" I spoke, growling as a lioness of the pride.

"I wrested with the Lion of Judah, and bees made a nest of his hide," spoke Antipas, answering a riddle as old as Israel, Samson wrestling with the lion.

"I am darkness, and the desert road," I continued. "I rush where I will, and only the beasts of the field know me by my scent. Humans have lost their jungle ways, and so I can betray them if they are not watchful." I paced to selected tables in the hall, raking my false nails across them, grating the ears like a cat scratching its favorite post.

I lunged at many guests, particularly the Gentile ones, and they sank back, unwittingly playing the part of frightened goats to my lioness.

"Riddle me this, O Great One," who should rule the trees, the cedar, or the brambles."

"The cedar would be wise to rule, as the bramble will destroy all with fire from its heart," answered Antipas in the ritual answer from the preaching of Elijah. It was strange to hear a Herod be a prophet in his own house.

"You are wise my king, but there are yet more riddles to be learned," I swaggered, and slung a chain of coins curled around my hips, throwing my cape to the ground. The cape drug the floor like the tail of a lioness. I fell to the floor, creeping as a stalking beast. The gazelles bounded out of my way, and the warriors bristled. The cymbals and finger chimes shimmered like grasses in the breeze.

On a table at the far end of the hall was a vase of gilded roses, yellow like sunrise, crafted out of gold and wax, but hardly separable from the real roses that were planted in a vase next to it. I covered the table with my cloak, hiding the real and false ones. As I lifted the cape, the hall could see that one of each was missing, hidden in my arms. I crept again across the floor, holding my prize until I was at the center of the hall.

This time I spoke to the hall from the circle of stars. "Which is more truthful, the art of the wise, or the wisdom of artifice." I held the two roses before me. "Even Solomon could not say, but needed the help of the bees from his garden to choose between them. What say you, assembled guests?" The crowd murmured, many of them were foreigners and this was a riddle game they did not know.

"I am a rose of gold, thorny and brazen, you have beside you a golden rose, one with no thorns." I flexed my fingers as if to extend my claws. My mother sat beside me, still as marble. "What say you, lion to my lioness," I challenged Antipas.

"I am a bee, seeking honey," he spoke, knowing the ritual words. "I will know the pollen of truth." But his eyes were narrowed and maddened and clearly holding back temptation to wrestle me to the floor, even before the crowd

"Then you shall know the true rose tomorrow, my wise judge." I shouted the ritual response in fury and swept from this hall.

•   •   •

For the first time in all of Antipas' nightly attentions, I refused the messenger when he came for me at close to the midnight watch. "Sheba must have her night of rest" was all I told the hapless servant. I suspected he would be beaten as the bearer of bad news, but that could not be helped.

I peeled my robe off as the cold sweat had all but painted it on me. So this terror I felt was a prelude of what was to come. The lesson of unfaithfulness was hard to deliver as it made me as the messenger seem worse than a whore, but how else could my stepfather be shamed before all of his friends.

Most of his attentions in court had never physically passed beyond public propriety, but his words—his words had known no bounds. I had heard that the gossip had branded me already his bedmate, joining him in mocking my mother with my new-found favor. Only this previous night showed anyone differently, and only then to those who had perceptive hearing, often lost with the taste of wine.

•   •   •

The dawn was red. We should expect a storm. Woodcutters noted the approaching weather and came to the city in droves. Anyone within a two-hour ride of the city could be guaranteed to sell all he could bring to stoke the fires. It would be chilly tonight. What a night for lust and war to be partners.

I woke early, restless, but knowing that this seventh night was what I had been preparing for. Though Chanukah ran eight nights and days, the last night was the white of innocence and memory, a dance I would not be performing. I sat and stared as the water clock turned to the third hour of this fateful day.

"I am the Rose of Sharon," I thought from the Song of Songs. "The maiden in full ripeness of youth." Tonight would be the feast of that Rose, the red of marital love, a renewal of the covenant of Israel. I prepared for the bath, one of several with progressively more fragrant oils, a private mikvah for the Baptist.

I thought of his ranting and raving, and his strange sense of perception. After my encounter with him, Bat Mara had talked to his disciples and they all seemed moved at his plight, though none were willing or able to speak to Antipas. None of them were aware of this night to come, though from what I had heard, he had, even up to last night, spoken of that cryptic axe at the foot of the tree. As I started the second washing, I felt watched in my bath as if by some unseen force. I felt hunted, and hounded, almost as if a servant were just outside the door, trying to beg my attention. "Who is there?" I called, certain of a spy. There was no reply, but the curtain across the door moved slightly.

Carefully rising, not showing emotion, I gathered a cloth around me and stepped out of the basin. I could hardly breathe, lest I show fear.

Was that a breath I heard, gruff and raspy, or was it just feverish imagination? "Watchman," I called to the hall. There were feet down the hall and a voice behind the curtain.

"Yes, my lady."

"Is there someone there with you? I saw the curtain move."

"None but I," but his voice caught. I was fearful. Was my stepfather watching my every move?

"I must go out. Will you get me another cloak, this one seems to have fox fur all over it." I spoke, hoping my watcher would get the message.

"Yes," the guard spoke curtly and turned away, walking with determined strides, making a great noise. I suspected I heard stealthy footsteps in the hall, but I dared not pull back the curtains to give the lie to the poor watchman's story.

"Your cloak, Salomé," spoke a voice I knew to be Tobias through the curtain. I breathed. Safety—at least for the moment.

"Could you wait for me there?" I questioned. "I need to walk in the garden, but I am not dressed."

"Certainly, my daughter. I am not rushed."

My face was scrubbed clean, and I felt refreshed. I drew back the curtain and touched Tobias lightly on the shoulder.

"You look splendid as yourself, my Young One. Why must you always wear so much paint, you are a much better woman than that!"

"I cannot tell you, Tobias, and that is hard on me—more than you can know. But one without knowledge cannot be blamed for being unaware." I took his arm.

"Let us go out to the battlements instead," I apologized. "Tobias, I need to feel the wind."

We climbed a stairway to one of the guard posts. I carried a jug of warm drink for the soldiers, for which they were grateful. This was one of the few places I could escape during the day and be safe, for Antipas had to trust the day soldiers, and could not bribe them. To have a palace in Jerusalem, or in the Decapolis, an essentially Roman captive province, one must observe proprieties, and one was a certain lack of choices during the day. At night, they could turn the other way intentionally, but the day was too open for obvious bribery.

"A sparrow comes to the rooftops," smiled Georgio, one of the garrison. "Certainly different than a lioness," I smiled. Even the soldiers had heard of my dancing. Georgio had known me since early childhood. He was from northern Circassia, and with his blue-black hair he was quite striking.

The wind blew through my hair under the mantle, and I breathed the scent of snow. "O, let me be clean of him at last, even I must die for it." I prayed.

•   •   •

I returned to my room and began the third mikvah at dusk. This water was steamy with musk and myrrh, nard and jasmine, a combination guaranteed to incite lust and madness. Oddly enough, it was also the spice mixture prepared for burial, and I felt as if I must bury my entire self alive to get through this night. Tonight I would be Jezebel, Samaria's Wrathful Rose of Ashteroth, not the gentle Rose of Sharon. What a night for a prophet to come to a dance.

As we lined up to enter the hall, Antipas was dressed in an imperial red toga. He was "an apple tree among the plain and fruitless trees of the wood," I thought, continuing the rhyme of the Song of Songs. His fruit, however, was poisonous. "Let me not taste it," I prayed.

My dress was a long silk winding cloth, nine yards long, scarlet and wine red. This I wrapped tightly on itself, accentuating my figure so that it was unmistakable. As a last touch, I capped myself with a sheer veil of spider-web gauze, with a circlet of rubies. Herodias had dressed modestly, ever more clearly to mark her contrast on this one night to the hall.

Though her robe was red to match mine, it was cut in the style of a Grecian matron, and made of linen, completely unlike my courtesan's cloth. This was Wisdom come to share the feast with the Whore.

At my waist swung a potpourri of jasmine and musk, as if I had not drenched myself enough. My windings were split nearly to my thigh. From Herodias' bodice swung simply a bunch of cloven apples, and her skirts were long and shapely, accenting her figure, but that of a woman of station, not one who had to strut her finery before the world.

Everywhere one looked one could see red. Cloths on the table, apples in every bowl, even the gold and brass seemed red as they reflected the hall.

My footstool had a scarlet pillow. Antipas' divan had been covered in rose petals. Someone—clearly not he—had placed a single living golden rose on Herodias' chair.

Cherries, apples, raisins, all fruits of love were the last course of the feast. Antipas fed me cherries and sought to paw me, but always with a careful eye to the hall. He dangled a cherry in front of me and only my taking it from his fingers to my lips would quiet him.

"You are Jezebel, remember, Salomé, you have no thought for marriage, only the love of the marketplace, the jaundiced, the jaded," I thought to myself. "It is your office of state, the Whore who knows which minds are ensnared by lust."

I caught my mother's eye and moaned inwardly. She heard my thought and showed tears, but knew that until this last dance was over that there was nothing she could do.

At last the feast was done.

·   ·   ·

I rose and went to the door. "I am the Rose of Sharon, and come seeking my truest love." I spoke the words of innocence but my voice was husky.

"Who would rise and tell me where the true rose is to be found," I sauntered across the hall, bells now jangling at my waist.

I began to move as the drummers beat a dance of lust. I swayed and enticed and danced no longer the maiden, but the street-wise courtesan.

"I call to the wise on the street corner, but they do not listen," I continued, quoting an ancient proverb."

"I am the Rose of Sharon, the lily of the valley." I mocked the words as I spoke. Purity was the last image I conjured up.

Antipas rose to the occasion in more than one way. "As the lily among the thorns, so is my beloved among the blossoms."

"Comfort me with your apples, let me savor your raisins, for I am sick for love." I quoted a bride's dowry blessing as I stared at my stepfather and threw back my veil, but it meant far from innocent words.

I moved to the center of the hall, dancing around the circle of stars ever faster. I could hear the sound of the whip. Bat Mara was at her work to induce this last paean of temptation.

"I come to you seeking the true rose, and to make a request from the master of the garden."

Antipas was almost slavering. "Anything for you, the true rose," he gulped. "I must have the scent of your petals."

"You make a request of me for your answer? A novel response from the master of wisdom," I mocked. "I am the maiden and I need a dowry. What gift can I expect from one who is already a bridegroom."

"I am your slave," spoke Antipas, as if bewitched. "The maidens of the field are no match for you, even the roses in my garden are faded like the winter sun, and can be cut down."

Herodias rose quietly and moved away from her seat. Her face was pale, even though she had expected such an insult from her husband on this night.

This ritual mockery was almost at an end. "I need a small gift, something insignificant. A token of your affection."

"Ask, ask!" he shouted, and the crowd added their jabs. "Ask, ask!" the men were driven mad. Antipas stood and was about to move forward.

I rose, and the whip cracked. I held my hand forward to halt his movement. "One moment before this rose is plucked, my lord. Swear before the hall that my request will be fulfilled. My small gift." I laughed.

Antipas was hungry, and his hands were trembling. "Anything, anything, up to your mother's place in court."

"You swear by my footstool?" I condescended, making a mockery of a holy oath.

"I swear, by you, my Rose of Sharon, what good are footstools," kicking mine aside.

"You swear by my headdress?" mocking his crown.

"I swear by my wealth," turning over a bowl of coins.

"You swear, before all your guests, that my small desire will be fulfilled, for your grand desire?"

"By the hall, and by the fire, I swear," he laughed.

"My small gift, my Lord, is but a token. I wish a certain delicacy on a platter, only one morsel."

"If it is to be found within the palace grounds, it will be fetched immediately," he cried. "It is my birthday, and I am feeling quite generous."

"I hope you find it to your taste, great lion, for it fits only a royal feast."

"Speak your desire, then, and the cooks will bring it. I will command it by my own hand."

"Hear his words, o people, I call you all to witness. He swears by footstool and wealth, by fire and hall, his words will be true." All the guests nodded in assent. They found this banter fascinating.

Antipas was getting hotter. He had loosened his robe and had thrown off his cloak. The sweat of desire poured from him and I could smell him even across the hall. "Anything, Salomé, command it."

"Then send a cook with the sharpest knife, my lord. I wish the head of the Baptist on a platter."

My stepfather fell to his knees as if gored. "No!" he wailed. "You knew—Elijah!" He cried bitterly. "By my own hand I have sworn, and I cannot take back the oath."

The hall was silent as the guards moved swiftly to the task at hand. Within moments, a dish was brought and placed in my hands as I stood like a statue in the feast hall. The platter was covered with a golden bowl.

"You have this as my maidenhead, my lord. A fit morsel for the King of Brambles," I shouted in bitter triumph. With a kick, I slid the platter across the room, where Antipas hugged it, like a beloved child, to his chest.

I strode from the hall, my hands dripping with gore.

•   •   •

The hall was silent, and dressed in the white of mourning for the eighth day of the feast. Antipas and Annas sat in silence, or so I was told. Herodias, Bat Mara, and I stayed in our rooms, careful to stay out of sight.

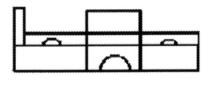

CHAPTER 5

Winter in Jerusalem

The return to Jerusalem was subdued. It had been a week since the death of the Prophet, and yet Herod was still in a foul mood. Mother and I had kept to ourselves, staying as close as possible to our quarters but now after seven days the prospect of spending another day in close air was stifling.

The guard had just changed for the third hour watch so the sun was no longer on the horizon. A light snow was beginning to fall and it swirled around the steps of the gate to the court of the women. Vendors of hot meals were surrounded by steam and other hearty folk, including a few beggars, were out. I wandered from stall to stall, not really interested in buying anything, but needing the exercise and the air away from the palace grounds. A blind beggar sat at the gate of the Temple. In a whimsical mood I bought a skewer of meat and left it near him. It would not do for me to touch him, but he seemed to be more lonely than usual on this day of snow. "Peace be upon you," he spoke. "You are a kind good lady."

"How do you know who I am?" I spoke with some surprise.

"I am blind, not deaf, little sparrow, and I hear you speak with the vendors almost every morning in the summer. We poor are not without our gossip, but we tend not to mention it to you unless you ask." He smiled with that lack of squinting that comes from one born blind.

"It seems that I must watch myself everywhere," I sighed.

"Not so, little one," he whispered. "Bat Mara has spoken of you as one who can be trusted, and we are to ignore whatever scandals come out about you."

I was pleasantly surprised to discover that Bat Mara's care stretched so far. Now I knew at least one source of news that could be trusted when palace walls became too inquisitive.

I reached into my dress and pulled out a coin. "Take this for your friendship. What shall I call you?"

My father's name was Timotheus, a weaver from Tyre. He never got around to giving me a Hebrew name, so they all call me Bar Timeus, the son of Timothy. This is my station, so you will often find me here, as long as there is some sun in the sky to keep me warm. It is chilly today, but it is often better for me to be out for the few who must be shopping than to come up empty-handed for my begging."

"Well, Bar Timeus, good health to you, and expect a little something on occasion. Sleep well."

I wanted to get something cheery on this day of snow, perhaps a bauble for Shoshanna, the steward's wife. She had kept us in basic foodstuffs during the last few days of Antipas' tirade, so she deserved something in exchange. Besides, it would give me the chance to bargain with the beggars, a skill lost if not exercised daily.

I passed out of the Court of the Women and down a side street. A guard watched from a battlement and nodded his head slightly as I looked up. I was bundled up against the chill and felt almost shapeless but apparently could keep the eye of a soldier entertained on a cold morning.

I sauntered a bit just to give him something to consider, and tossed a coin into the air, letting it fall where it might.

The coin rolled by chance down a gutter and managed to go some yards without stopping, finally ending its spinning at a tie for camels next to a small shop. A wide array of cloths were hanging from dowels, marking this the store of a tallis-maker, a weaver of head cloths. These ranged from the long winding cloths I had worn in my dance, to simply turbans, enough to cover the head with a touch of color. One caught my eye—a deep purple, shot with blue, a rare combination as the colors were difficult to obtain, and often reserved only for the very wealthy.

"I see you have good taste, good lady," spoke a creaky voice.

"If this is what it looks like, it is rare to find such workmanship in such a quarter. Why has it not been stolen?"

"It is but the fourth hour, excellency, and I had just this moment hung it from the cloth rack. Feel its texture, it is a rare weave."

"It is. I had not expected this so long after the caravans have left. They are not due back until spring." I glanced at the few camels in the stable of the inn next door. They were grey with age, and clearly weren't worthy of a trip beyond the village across the valley of Hinnom, much less to Jericho or beyond.

"I keep a few cloths in hiding and put them out a few at a time for discriminating customers who come out on cold wintry mornings," spoke the creaky voice, chuckling under his breath.

"You are a wise vendor, always the select few, so the price stays up. I will give you three drachmas for it."

"Three drachmas? I am an old man, a sesterce at least."

A sesterce indeed, a week's wages for a soldier, this vendor knew his fabric well, but for a sesterce he could be bribed. Who was this man?

"Perhaps four drachmas," naming less than a tenth of the price quoted," the weave is rare, but not a king's price."

"You would rob the poor, I keep so few of these sashes," he cringed with emphasis.

"O wizened one, I respect your age so I will not accuse you of thievery, but I have a dozen of these at home. Four drachmas and a few small coins from my purse for the fringework, and not a temple shekel more." I named the temple shekel for emphasis, a coin worth only as much as the priests could extract for it any given day.

"Bat Mara has taught you well, Sparrow. She must give you begging lessons," he chuckled. "I will not try to trick you, four drachmas it is, and I will throw in a silk tying cloth with it."

I carefully weighed out the four drachmas, balancing them in his scale so that he knew that they were all unshaven. Thievery was so common, that without a scale, a vendor could be robbed blind as Bar Timeus with coins that had lost all value or were merely alloyed to mimic gold, silver, or even bronze.

He bit the coins to make sure they could be bent, "silver they are, and pure," and weighed them carefully. I have a shipment from Tarsus next week, would you like me to set something aside?"

"From Tarsus, the caravans have stopped running until Purim, who is coming to visit you from Spain?"

"Not so far as Spain, your excellency. He comes from the Tarsus in Cilicia, in the Taurus Mountains, where the tribe of Benjamin still survives. My old friend Shmuel is coming for his son Saul, my apprentice."

"I wondered about him, the one with flaming red hair?"

"Yes, always into something. But this is a sad time for him."

"How so?"

"Even with all the riots here, we thought his family was safe in Tarsus. We received word that Saul's mother died of a fever, and Shmuel is coming to mourn his wife at the Temple."

"That is sad news. "Where is Saul now?"

"He went to Caesarea with another weaver to meet his father at the docks."

"When will they arrive?"

"By the next Sabbath at the latest, you will find Saul adorable, but be respectful, he will be in mourning."

"I will try to bring him something special from the kitchens, then. Good day to you. Who shall I remember to Bat Mara?"

"Tell her Mattathias the Tentmaker. She will remember me from when she began dancing. I was her first friend in Jerusalem."

The watchman called out the next hour. It was now high noon, and food would be served in the kitchen if I hurried. We may have hidden in our quarters while Antipas sulked, but that did not mean we starved.

"Shoshanna, I have brought you a new cloth for your troubles."

"Sweet sparrow, I do not need bribery to care for you. What color is this one?"

"Blue, like your eyes. It will set off your coloring well. Your henna against the cloth will look like a spring sunrise and I am so tired of winter."

"As are we all, my dear, was there any disturbance in the street today?"

"Not that I was aware of. It was quiet, almost peaceful."

"Then it must be the calm before the storm. Shusa has sent out for provisions for a council with Pilate, and that means trouble. I would keep close to the walls for the next few days, we may have to leave suddenly."

"Leave, it is dead winter! That would be difficult."

"True, young one, but you are the royal household, and so must be protected from unrest. There have been messengers all night talking about something in Samaria, and Pilate is not at all pleased."

"Pilate is involved, then I better stay in my quarters. If he has been called, then the soldiers may be on short watch."

"True, and this time even Georgio has been called to council."

"Georgio! My mother's bodyservant. I better just pack and be prepared for anything."

"It would seem so. Pack the winter needs as we may be going to Galilee."

"That will be quite chilly. The palace is not well heated. That means the wool. Well, forget fashion now, is there anything to eat?"

"Yes, I have sliced cheese and baked several loaves of barley bread. Eat well and keep yourself warm. The hypocaust will give you hot water tonight, but they are pulling off the fire slaves tomorrow to prepare for anything."

"Thank you for the warning, Shoshana, I will at least be clean before I go. It may be a week without a bath, and oils only go so far to cover the stench."

I remember going to my rooms and trying to choose carefully what I should pack. Bat Mara was there before me, and many of the most beautiful things were still hung in the closet. Only the most drab, unshapely, and unflattering clothes were laid out.

"We will be traveling dangerously, my dear, and even the best laid routes are full of rebels."

"I have heard nothing of this. What has happened?"

"Over a thousand Zealots have died." She named the radical sect which wanted to overthrow the Romans.

"A tower near Samaria fell on them as they rallied and they blame deliberate weakening of the walls by Pilate's henchmen. Far from cutting them off, this has only spurred the remainder's rage."

I shuddered, maybe John's words were not really aimed against Herodias after all. I felt suddenly remorseful.

"Bat Mara, was this what John meant about the tower of Samaria?"

She read my thoughts. "John's words have many meanings, but part of them were addressed to you. A prophet's words never have only a single truth."

I packed to keep my thoughts focused. "Where is Mother?"

"Herod, for some unknown reason, has called her to the council. It seems he wishes to imitate Pilate, who never makes a decision without his wife Procula in the background. She never speaks in public, but privately she is said to be a shrew."

"Bat Mara, whose gossip is that?" I smirked.

"Only Shoshanna's, but she is preparing the food for the council so there may be some truth in it. It at least gives us something to talk about on our way to Galilee."

"Our way—you are coming with us?"

"There is no reason to keep myself hidden anymore. The dance is over, revenge from Antipas would be meaningless. All those who need to know my story know it, and at least you are, for the moment, untouchable. Herod tires of courtiers daily and may remember you again."

Herodias walked in at this moment and spoke, "wise words, Bat Mara. Salomé has been remembered and is expected at tomorrow's council. Procula was there this evening, and though she finds me detestable, and cannot stand Antipas, she took me aside as Herod and Pilate were at close quarters. She spoke almost timidly, as if I might bite."

"I have heard the same thing about her. I'm surprised you have no scars yourself."

"Not from her, though her tongue is quite vicious, I am told. This time, however, she warned me that no road is safe. It seems that she herself had been in Caesaraea and had been brought to Jerusalem by night, by the way of the Jordan."

"Why that is almost four day's journey out of the way. Is there that much unrest?"

"More than you can imagine. It seems that John's death has set even Samaria astir. I cannot fathom that one man's influence could go so far. I thought people hated him, particularly the rich, but now even influential teachers are beginning to wonder if they treated him badly. I do not know where we can rest out the storm."

"Well, most of your clothes are now packed, as we have been preparing behind you. Do we leave soon?"

"I had intended so, but now you have been called to council tomorrow, so we must delay. But three days at the most."

CHAPTER 6

Council

"You are summoned, Salomé," spoke the messenger. "Wear the most conservative robes, as we audience with the governor."

This was news. I had felt hesitant to return to court at all, as Herod was a wounded lion in his grief. But I had no choice, he had governing to do, and he needed ears in the court that no one would question. I hastened to the courtyard to meet the soldiers who would escort Antipas and me to Pilate's forum, being held in his private apartment in the Upper Palace, the far wing of our quarters in Jerusalem. Although connected by many corridors, it was faster to go outside the palace to another entrance, and with the unrest, we must be guarded at all times. My venture into the market had not gone unnoticed, and I would now be watched.

On this day in particular, I welcomed even Roman occupation, as the unrest was daily getting closer to bringing all of Jerusalem into an uproar. I was still unmarried, and therefore a prize for any ruffian, either as ransom bait, or as a booty of war. To this date, I had moved in a world protected, always under guard, either Antipas or Pilate left to keep the peace.

Peace. Looking back at that time of troubles, I wonder how I could have thought such things. Everywhere one looked was abject poverty or corrupted wealth—at least near Jerusalem.

In Galilee there was some mitigation as the trade routes crossed there from everywhere, but this winter in Jerusalem had taught me to be wary.

As I was carried in the divan to the palace, we were overtaken by a horseman dressed in red, a centurion fresh from the coast. This must be an emergency indeed, to not spare a horse.

We were escorted into the palace, almost at the soldier's heels, and were announced. From the corner of my eye I could see him, clearly exhausted, He was a leader of sorts. He must have been or he would not be a centurion, a captain over a hundred. But Judaea was in constant turmoil and it took a special kind of poise to be stationed here.

I whispered to the guard who escorted me, "who is that young one, the one barely bearded. He looks familiar, but I cannot place him."

"He has the look of your father and your mother in him," he spoke, "as he is your uncle, the son of your father's half-brother, and your mother's brother." His name is Agrippa, and he is the youngest prince of Tarsus."

"Tarsus, another Benjaminite? He is a Hebrew?" I was startled, first a weaver and now, apparently, a prince from the same place.

"From his mother, as are you. You Jews are flung all over the empire, and are in many families of Rome, sometimes quite wealthy, but young Agrippa comes by his citizenship by public service," spoke the guard. "He was sent to Rome after his father's murder. Your stepfather spoke for him, and he has become a favorite of Tiberius."

"How so much to be so high so soon?" I continued quietly, though very interested.

"He has just returned from Rome, which is why you have not met him before, as his mother, your grandmother Berenice, married your uncle Archelaus and lives there, or at her villa in Vienne, far off in Gaul. He is a soldier and goes where he is ordered. Pilate is having him watched, to ensure that his heart does not become divided, but generally I have found him to be a good soldier."

I fell silent. I had begun looking for a protector against Antipas, but one who would not ruffle too many diplomatic feathers. It would not do to speak with him in court until we were formally introduced, but keeping inquiries discreet might avail me a great deal.

Uncle, I was so young, and you were a stranger. Did you know I watched you from that moment? It would be scarcely seven years before you became my sole protector, but the spark of trust was planted early.

·   ·   ·

The Upper Palace in Jerusalem was remarkably airy for having high walls. It was built in the Roman villa style with open corridors that relied more on architectural features than curtains for privacy. Though the outer walls were sealed, a space at the top with narrow windows allowed the breeze into the house, and inside were several areas open to the sky surrounded by rooms on two floors.

It was into one of these open spaces that our entourage was led. Rather than hold this discussion in the public judgment hall, Antipas had specifically requested a private audience, and as there was the danger of riots, Pilate diplomatically agreed.

Antipas was announced and was led by soldiers to a small anteroom. I kept to his heels, and though the guards said nothing, it was clear that they were a little nonplussed to see a woman, even veiled, at this private audience. I kept back in the shadows and said nothing.

When we were led into the banquet hall, I saw that Pilate, also, was not completely alone. Standing next to a column was his wife Procula, unveiled in his home, and quite striking. Procula, I had heard, was Emperor Tiberius' daughter, and so, as a Roman matrona, a power in her own right.

Why would she be here? I was intrigued. My mother had spoken of Procula, but only now, actually in a Roman judgment hall, did I see why she was so jealous of her. It was clear that she was not a fixture to be ignored, but a person to watch, almost like a hetera—those Greek courtesans who had taken up homes in Caesarea and Tiberius.

They were patronesses of arts, and entertainers, but what was Procula? Perhaps this was why my mother felt so shamed in her own hall. I must ask her on my return home as this was the first time I had been "officially" allowed in Roman territory. I had seen, and been surrounded by centurions much of my life, but as a woman of the palace, I had only just come of age to enter society. Why did it have to be this occasion?

•   •   •

"Hail Caesar," spoke Herod. "I present myself to you with news, your Excellency."

"As one 'friend' to another, is it, Antipas?" denied Pilate.

Both Pilate and the Herods were "friends of Caesar," a rare title in the Empire. Pilate called him Antipas to distinguish him from his father Herod the Great, and Herod

Philip, Herodias' first husband, both of whom he had known when he first arrived in Judaea as Procurator.

"It is rare that you have been so insistent to address me at home. Why the subtlety now?"

"This uprising borders both of our territories, as it is in Samaria. Both you and I need watchful eyes in the borderlands," replied Antipas.

"I see you brought your watchful eyes with you, Antipas. I had heard rumors that your daughter had grown lovely, but she is more than expected. Where have you kept her?"

"With the women, usually veiled," he lied glibly. I had had the freedom of the streets for several years, but he pretended not to know of my excursions. He could not be that daft, but I left it alone.

"You remember my wife Procula, do you not? As this concerns what eyes and ears may not see, you should know that she has my complete confidence." Pilate spoke with a nod to Procula. Procula remained silent, but it was clear that she did not have to hide in shadows to observe. Very like a hetera. This bore watching.

"I will not give offense, I come to speak to you about rebels and Zealots," Antipas continued.

"You are their Tetrarch, Antipas, what do you suggest?" murmured Pilate.

"Most are rabble, but a few are hotheads and perhaps an example would be sufficient."

"Antipas, I have tried to put this people down in any way that I can, it does not seem to matter. The least you can do is not interfere when my soldiers move against them."

My stepfather pondered. "I will say nothing, as long as the soldiers keep to only those directly arrested."

"There are many eyewitnesses, and most of them will speak up, as they know the penalties well, Antipas. Do not think I will be light on them, or on any of your kinsmen."

"Your father slew his sons on a pretense. You are currently friend to the Emperor. Be sure to stay that way," concluded Pilate.

"I see," responded Antipas. "Then there is no mercy?"

"None." spoke Pilate. "Agrippa, you are in charge of the garrison at Samaria, do your duty with the rabbles."

"I obey," Agrippa replied. "What is concerned?"

"Take the first 300 and crucify them on the road between Jerusalem and Samaria. One every hundred paces or so should space them out nicely. Do not take them down until they are quite rotted."

I held back a retch. This seemed to be the Roman "taste of justice." And Agrippa was forced to commit it. How much more would he be tested? That he would grow to be a man of peace could not be anticipated from what he was forced to do in his early years.

"Herod, it is fortunate that you agree, as this young centurion has come with news from Rome for you."

My stepfather's eyes narrowed. What could concern him from Rome? Tributes were paid annually, and Caesarea, the coastal town, where Pilate's residence as Procurator was located, was the seat of all government.

And Pilate had addressed him as Herod, not Antipas, carrying the weight of Rome even harder, as Rome had installed the Herodians, not Jews. To carry on such a conversation in a private residence in Jerusalem was unprecedented.

"I bring news from Tiberius," spoke Agrippa. "It seems that there has been unrest among the Bactrians—and you are first in line of defense."

Antipas frowned. "Bactrians, they stay in the desert on the other side of Parthia!"

Agrippa continued. "You are friend to Caesar, and the trade routes from Parthia and China end in Galilee and Syria. My stepfather Archelaus was quite mad, and lost his territories but your brother Philip, rules Syria and needs a partner in Galilee. All roads must be watched."

I watched my stepfather more closely, what would he say. I had not paid much attention before in court, but if Procula and my mother could watch, and occasionally influence, here was my first opportunity.

"What does Rome require?" Antipas spoke tersely.

"An increase in the garrison at Gedarenes, at the least, and regular reports to both Pilate and Tiberius concerning all Parthian trade," Pilate intoned.

"How large a garrison?" Herod queried, "Gedarenes is large, but not Caesaraea."

"A legion will be stationed in Galilee within the year, with its headquarters in the Decapolis. Gedarenes has been chosen as one of the chief stations."

Now I knew why Pilate had consented to this meeting. Rome was becoming wary of the East, and Galilee was the weakest point. The Decapolis was a large cluster of city-states east of Judaea with Gederenes near Galilee as its largest city. It was both Roman and Parthian, with a mix of both governments in an uneasy truce, and Galilee, Peraea, and Samaria, all three of Antipas's territories, bordered its scattered holdings. What was Tiberius up to?

The rest of the evening was spent on inconsequentials. Antipas had turned over the selected 300 leaders from afar, never questioning the judgment of Caesar. I listened as carefully to what was not said, as to what was. There was no mention of tribute from Galilee to Rome, no mention of any new appointments in Judaea.

Pilate was determined to speak little and do much— without consulting Antipas. Would Antipas do the same?

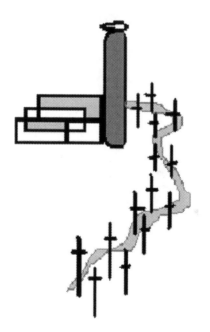

CHAPTER 7

Fire

The days wore on and midwinter was upon us. The riots that were predicted with the mass crucifixions were intense, but put down so brutally that the city was in a state of shock. For more than a week no one ventured outside, but I finally could stand it no longer and went down to the kitchen entrance to the palace, hoping to find a way to go out without notice.

Chusa, the steward, was putting together a list of the many items needed. He smiled in my direction, though I had worn as nondescript clothing as I could find, covered so that no one could easily recognize me, even the soldiers who had ogled me before. "Sparrow?" he spoke, as he always called me. "What do you think you are doing?"

"I am weary of being pent up, and need, even if through these clothes, a bit of bustle," I responded.

"So you think to sneak out of the kitchen door, rather than be carried in a sedan chair?" Chusa inquired.

"Yes, in a chair I see nothing, and they announce me," I pouted. "I want to see some of the market before everything is gone."

"Ah, ever the bargainer are you," he observed.

"Remember to ignore your palace manners. The merchants pay no attention unless your language is spicey. They may not see your face, but they drive a hard bargain." advised Chusa.

"Bat Mara has trained me, you know, I will do as you wish, and twitter like a bird, lots of spice." I chattered.

"Make sure you come home to roost, then, and keep out of trouble." spoke Chusa.

The city air was crisp with winter. A swirl of birds were clearly flying away to sunnier Egypt. I breathed deeply, clearing my lungs from the closeness of the palace.

I knew the back streets well, and wandered back to Mattathias' booth, prepared to act like a fishwife if I needed to. Finally I spotted what I wanted, a green veil shot through with silver with silver coins hanging all around it. Yes, green in the middle of winter, that would suit my mood. It would not do, of course, to go directly for what I desired.

"Is there nothing you have left here, merchant, it seems only bare patches. I cannot buy these cast-offs."

"My merchandise is less than perfect, as I hide it from prying eyes. Here, my eyes are squinty, what does this seem?" He held out a scarf of Parthian silk, rewoven from imported threads until it was almost transparent. I gulped.

"I have seen better in my laundry. Is there nothing of springtime in your wares?"

"Perhaps yellow? Or maybe red? They are sunrise colors?" mocked the merchant.

"I seek a deep green," looking deliberately toward a patch of browns and blacks.

"Then go down the way, I cannot help you, there is only this old rag here, I must let it go for only 50 talents."

For 50 talents I could have bought his shop and half the market. Was I being too brazen. I was not about to give him that satisfaction. "Ten dinars," I spoke, naming the price of a sandle. "See the fabric is torn!" The fabric was solid, the weave was deliberately open. The merchant dithered.

"I will let it go for perhaps 100 dinars. The palace women would pay no less."

I chuckled. Palace women indeed. "I say 50 dinars." The cost was enough to buy the bolt. I knew his merchandise well. Bat Mara had shown me many bolts of cloth from Persia, carefully pointing out the weaves, their uses, and their workmanship.

He bantered. "It is a hard bargain you drive. For sixty you have may have that cheap trim."

"The trim, there is scarce enough for a veil," I bantered back. But no matter, sixty dinars, if you throw in that rope." I pointed to a linen rope about six cubits long.

"You rob me, my sparrow," laughed the merchant, winking. "But let your mistress know that I will remember her."

The code word was there, so I knew he recognized me. Only my servants knew my pet name around the palace, and selected merchants were told "mention a sparrow if you have news." Chirping indeed. The banter again was allowing me to walk freely without disturbing anything. "What are you called?" I queried, as if a stranger. "That I may tell my mistress?"

"Mattathias the Weaver, of the Street of Tanners." he replied.

I smiled, acting as if I did not know him. Half the weavers of Jerusalem were named Mattathias, so I would not be selecting one for special treatment.

When all the Greek trappings were taken down, all the curtains had to be rewoven, and Mattathias, my ancestor, the new King of Judah, had turned to his countryman for help.

All the boys born to the weavers in the next years seemed to have Matthathias as part of their names, and though it had been seven generations since that time, still the name persisted. Those young boys' grandchildren were old men now, but there were still too many of them without further identification. The Street of Tanners was long and broad.

I queried again. "You spoke of sparrows, good merchant. What may I say to my mistress? Do they nest well? It is not yet spring." I spoke in code.

"The sparrows are fled to the coast, and only the ravens remain," he spoke. "Some of us watch the birds before we return home. May we have safety?" His coded words asked for sanctuary for his tradesmen. So far, they had not participated in the riots.

"Do not feed the ravens, and perhaps my mistress can help," I ventured. This was to warn him not to take down the bodies by night for burial.

"The birds will fly before the week is out," spoke the merchant.

At this point, his flame-haired apprentice edged forward. "I watched the sunrise this morning, Master. It was red and cloudy," he ventured.

"The boy sees much and speaks little. Sparrow, this is Saul, just back from Caesarea. He went there for the purples and to bring his father to the Temple.

I blanched behind my veil. A boy of thirteen, and two old men, caught up in the middle of a riot? This would not do. I rearranged myself to take the cloth and rope.

"Tell the boy to come to the kitchen entrance to the palace at sunset," I said abruptly.

"There will be food for him there, and a gift from my mistress."

I went to the end of the market and wandered back, acting aimless. Just one more palace servant buying cloth. Sunset, the coded word, which even a young boy knew, meant three days. Quite a bit of news. We must be prepared. I had almost regained the kitchen gate.

"Fire," someone shouted. "Someone, please come!" I moved out of the way, as a flame shot up, only yards from where I had been standing. What had happened?

I could not see for the smoke for a moment. I was glad for my veil or I would have coughed in it. Which booth? No! Not that one. Mattathias' merchandise was gone. Was it accident, or planned? Would we know? I fled inside the palace.

•   •   •

The fire burned quickly but was soon out. There was a well in the market so the merchants banded quickly and managed to douse the flames. I heard from Chusa that Mattathias was injured but would survive. What of Saul?

"Was there a young red-haired boy found with him?" I inquired of one of the guards.

"Yes, his apprentice, he is hovering at his bedside."

"Guard," I spoke, making a decision. It seemed that Mattathias had won his bargain. "Take this two sesterces and go to the marketplace. Buy what you can, mix the cloths, but make sure to hide the higher-priced fabrics inside the bundle. Then go to the dyers and buy a pot of purple."

If you run out of money, come to the palace. I cannot let a good deed cause disaster." My sesterces would buy what was left and people would think it greed.

The guard bowed. This sparrow had a bite to her. I waited in the kitchen, and he returned with many bolts of cloth, some quite old and moldy, but some shot with silver. Greed was the last thing on my mind. My plan must be done discreetly, as to not shame a good merchant. What to do?

"Is there an old cart in the palace, something we haul wood in?" I inquired.

Chusa thought a moment. "Yes, it is broken now, but can be fixed in a day if you want it."

"Perfect. Take this bundle from the guard and wrap it with some old rags. I do not wish our friend to suffer. If they think me greedy, maybe he won't be noticed with a rickety woodcart. He must leave by sunset tomorrow."

I watched the guard. Chusa might be able to pull this off. His face was known, and maybe the merchants would take a hint. How to signal this right? I took a needle made of bone and wrapped it deliberately in green silk thread.

"Guard, take a servant and this cart and find Mattathias. The needle is for the young boy. Tell him the sparrows must fly north before the Sabbath."

Now I must find my stepfather.

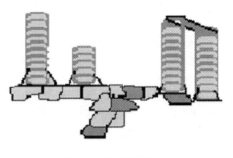

CHAPTER 8

Philadelphia

Antipas was unusually sober. He had no wine on his breath, and he was keeping a grip on his temper, shouting only to be heard above the din of the receiving room. Even he was not inured to crucifixions yet. He had spent the better part of the week advising caution to the most agitating of his hangers-on, but to no clear avail. Though he was anything but an observant Jew, except when he was being watched, he did his utmost to keep peace in Galilee, which was his province, though he stayed more often in Jerusalem. Constant traffic between the provinces, and especially to the Decapolis, kept anything— even Pilate's cruelty—from being anything more than a nine-day wonder; however, Antipas knew he needed to leave Jerusalem, and take at least his close court with him.

I sat at his feet, at my customary place, now much more modestly dressed than before. Antipas was mollified by my presence, but he seemed distracted. "Georgio, announce that court will close in one hour. Only the most urgent disputes will be heard."

"Most urgent disputes," I wondered. As if 300 leaders weren't enough.

"There are merchants from Parthia," announced Georgio, "to speak about trade."

Tell them I am wearied, I will speak to them next week in Philadelphia, but there are too many more important matters here, what else?"

"The fire in the weaver's quarter, it has caused grumbling," continued Georgio. "The merchants fear for their safety."

"They should, Pilate's soldiers are keeping double watch starting this evening. Pick the first ten merchants and give them a safe passage warrant, I can do no more," commanded Antipas.

I was glad that I had given warning when I did. Some merchants may have taken the hint, these clearly had not. "Daughter," Antipas spoke softly, "we must go to Philadelphia within the week."

The Decapolis was a part-Roman, part-Persian outflinging of the Empire east of both Judaea and Galilee, called so as it had 10 major towns. Philadelphia, one if its larger towns, was directly east from Jerusalem, across the Jordan in a fertile valley. Antipas often fled to it when unrest in both Judaea and Galilee became too much. He kept a home there, and with sufficient messengers, was able to keep control of affairs in Galilee, even from a distance.

The town was well laid out, with both Greek temples and Roman amphitheatres. Away from Jerusalem, I was even allowed to go in a sedan chair to the theatre. Most unusual for a Jewish princess, but when not in Judaea or Galilee, I could learn much more even in a shrouded chair than staying in the villa, or so I thought.

One morning, as I had finished breakfasting and was putting on my overgarb to go into the main villa, I heard voices coming from the outer chambers. Their accents were Babylonian, very like Bat Mara's, so I wondered who they could be.

I peered through the lattice, as I was not yet in my veils. There were several merchants in Parthian garb, and one person in a bright yellow robe with a purple sash. His hair was very short, unlike the beards of the Parthians, so I knew him to be both a eunuch and a monk, and a warrior monk at that.

The silk road went many miles beyond the Roman Empire, I knew, but what was a warrior monk doing so far from his mountains. I dressed eagerly, and tried to come as quietly through the gate as I could, trying to be an "invisible" woman in the courtyard.

The voices whispered, "will he listen, do you think, these negotiations have been going on for months, and still no clear trade agreement," spoke the figure in yellow, in a combination of Aramaic and Farsi. He seemed to be the one in command. The word "negotiations" was definitely not the usual Aramaic phraseology. Bat Mara had taught me a few words in Farsi, as she was from Babylon, and this word seemed to carry a deeper implication than "negotiations". It felt like "treaty" or "diplomacy"–highly unusual for merchants. What were they up to?

I went into the chamber where Antipas and Herodias kept room for receiving. Even at retreat, the world would not stay away, and Antipas set one hour after noon to receive visitors. These seemed to be the merchants he had directed to meet him in Philadelphia.

Antipas had me sit on his footstool and wear my veils around my face rather than across it. This rare sight of a woman's face in a receiving room brought a smile from the man in yellow. "So you keep the custom of the Parthians, Herod? Not many will listen to women's voices."

"The faces of my women I keep always before me," he spoke. "Is this not so among your people?"

"Tibet is many miles from here, and passes through many lands, how do you know our customs?"

"I listen to my dreams, and my night thoughts, and sometimes even the voices of my women." I thought of Bat Mara and her position at court. Through hidden means, Antipas indeed knew many things beyond his borders.

"Then you know of our horse lords, and some of our merchant captains?" the monk ventured.

"Indeed, I wish to breed my horses with some of yours," Antipas pursued.

"Horses. . . and their baggage?" he murmured.

"Their baggage would be most welcome," spoke Antipas cryptically.

"But will you keep the highway open?" spoke the monk.

"Gedarenes is open to you, you know that," continued Antipas. "The fair is approaching, within the month, however…."

"Then we will meet you there with our baggage?" ventured the monk.

"Bring a sample of your baggage, and we may yet breed true," spoke Antipas, "but do it quickly, Rome is moving."

I pondered these words. Gedarenes was on the east side of Lake Chinnereth, in the hill country, and was a merchant town. It was the crossroads of the East, with the highways from Egypt, Parthia, Damascus, and even China converging. I must listen closely. Baggage could be anything, from wealth to weapons, but with a monk from Tibet it could only mean one thing, Bactria. Bactria, as Rome had brought word, was restless and looking for friends—and enemies.

Bactria, in the back of the mind of every Greek-speaking provincial, was a haunt. Its warriors were fierce, and it was the only land to fight off both the Greeks and the Romans. Nurses would frighten small children with stories of the Bactrians riding in at night and killing everything in sight. No one was safe. Were my ears hearing right?

"Parthia welcomes the friendship of the Herods, and Rome" spoke the monk, as he and his merchants took their leave. I shuddered. Antipas could not be thinking of rebelling against Rome, he only stood because of friendship with Caesar? I chilled and fled the receiving room taking refuge in the women's quarters.

My mother noticed my restlessness. "What troubles you, sparrow?"

"My uncle is unwise to risk so much. As if the rebels weren't enough, our lives are in peril."

"Our lives are always in peril," spoke Herodias. "Persia and Bactria have had an uneasy peace for over 300 years. Bat Mara has warned me that the Jews of Babylon always keep themselves ready to flee at a moment's notice. Even the scholars are not immune. She learned to dance, but always to keep a light foot ready to go with only a veil."

"And Antipas seeks their help?" I cried.

"Antipas toys with things beyond his control. He is like a cat, he must always have his mouse to play with. As you have escaped the net, now he must toy with his province. The Romans are watchful, so he may not win, but always be careful. They will let him breed horses, and play his games, but they are not without their spies."

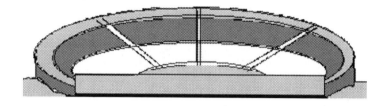

CHAPTER 9

The Theatre

We stayed in Philadelphia for a month. This was a far cry from Jerusalem, where the Temple overshadowed all the great courts on its high hill, and so pervaded all of life. In Philadelphia, Rome ruled, and Greeks played. Philadelphia was a "pleasure city" of the Empire, where gladiators fought at the Colisseum, and there were several Greek theatres. Here I was a princess, but not "in state." I could occasionally go out in a divan chair to the theatre, and this time I would only be going with a small escort.

Georgio had requested to accompany me this time, as the play was about his homeland. It was the tragedy Medea, about a princess who was abandoned after she had given up her kingdom and her crown to an adventurer. The first part of the story took place in Colchis, where Georgio had spent his youth. He had told me the story from his countrymen's point of view, as the ancient kingdom of Colchis was now the conquered Roman province of Georgia.

The Caucasians had been fashioners of jewels since ancient times, and they washed their fleeces in the rivers to catch the gold dust from the high mountains. Over time, these golden fleeces were a temptation for Greek pirates, who raided incessantly until one of them captured the princess Medea. I watched the play with interest.

All the female parts were played by young men, as no woman could appear on stage. The wigs were convincing—as was the garb—and the masks they wore, to fix expressions of delight or sorrow, tragedy, or blessing, were striking. With a turn of voice, a young man became an old woman, crying at injustice, or the deep voice of a god, declaring judgment.

Unlike the stadium, where the crowds seem to thirst for gore, death never appeared in flesh at the theatre. One heard a herald cry, a chorus moan in wails, one of Medea's children would run across the stage, fleeing from her raised knife, but you never saw the blood. The child's screams were imitated by tambourines and bagpipes, off stage, abruptly falling silent at a single thump of a drum. But no blood.

How like, and unlike, my dance. The symbols played in my mind. The Greek play, even from the Hellenic point of view, saw the story of Medea as one of abandonment. First, Medea would abandon her homeland, sacrificing her own brother to fend off pursuers. Then, she would in turn be abandoned by Jason, who after promising his kingdom to their two sons, married another, leaving her in poverty. In revenge, she slaughtered their sons, and presented their bodies to Jason before fleeing in a chariot drawn by dragons.

I pondered this play. Georgio was not far off the mark with how I was feeling. Was I a new Medea, starting a tragedy earlier, or was there some way of escape?

Across the isle was a sedan chair, covered in Arabian tapestries. A hand reached out and beckoned for Georgio.

He approached the divan as if he knew the occupant. Who could this be?

"Sparrow," he spoke softly. "There is someone you must meet, if only for a moment. She watched your reaction to the play, and feel that you and she have something in common. Shall we move to a more private space?"

I was intrigued. Who could Georgio know who would not have approached me at the compound? I nodded in agreement, and the two sedan chairs moved into an alcove close to one another and a common curtain was thrown across them for privacy. A hand, covered in bracelets, pulled back the curtain. I saw an older woman, clearly from the desert, yet holding herself with dignity.

"Your excellency, this was the only way we could ever speak. I am Shaqilath, and I could have been your grandmother."

I gasped. Shaqilath was the mother of Phasaelis, my stepfather's first wife, and she had every reason to hate me, yet here she was, begging my audience.

"I, too, have watched the theatre, and found my heart touched by the plays. For me, it was the story of Helen of Troy. Through no fault of her own, she became the plaything of the Gods, and launched a war we are still playing out, more than 800 years later.

"Is Phasaelis that wife? Is Herodias? What role shall I play? Perhaps I am Cassandra, seeing the truth no one will believe."

She opened her hands and stared at them ruefully. "They say lines of care can be read for truth, but mine are too crossed by sand to be clear. I never knew what I would do were I ever to meet you, but now that you are here, I feel that we understand each other, even if we meet but seldom. We are both women driven by circumstance. I am older, and now have many responsibilities. Your stepfather's divorce freed my daughter to rule my own kingdom after me with my brother, a chance she could not have had, had she remained married. He will never know, but I thank him, even for his adultery."

"You thank him? But your husband and your son are at war on your daughter's behalf."

"Yes, and for the past ten years I have held that grudge, commanding the generals myself to go to war. But now, it is enough. The man who spoke most clearly, the prophet John, is now dead, in the very fortress of Macherus to which my daughter fled from your stepfather's anger. Our private war is ended. Herod will not know, but because of you, there shall be peace between our kingdoms, though not yet. My husband and my son will not rest until Antipas is defeated, but I felt I owed you a warning."

"Why me?"

"You spoke truth in a way he could not ignore, and that women have seldom been chosen to deliver. I wonder, will we be remembered, or like Cassandra, will our words be written on the wind?"

"Lady Shaqilath, I shall write you."

"Not yet, there will come a time when it is safe, but for now, just speak thought to thought, and I think we will understand each other, even in our separate palaces."

The curtain was withdrawn. I was alone again in my sedan chair. I heard her chair depart. After a moment of silence, I beckoned for Georgio.

"How did you know?"

"I have been with Antipas' palace for many years, both in Rome and here in the Decapolis. Shaqilath and I were friends from afar, and I could not see her daughter murdered. It was my hand that warned her to flee, and Antipas has never known who thwarted him."

A friend indeed. I had never known how many had watched my footsteps. Spring was stirring, and the snows would be leaving Galilee. It was time to go home.

THREADING
THE MAZE

Synopsis

The return to Galilee changes Salomé's viewpoint to that of a spy in her own household, learning of a bargain with a Chinese tradesman over silk. Her teacher is healed by a storyteller, she learns healing from a Cyrenian doula, and respect for another's gods from a Phoenician priest of Baal. She journeys to Capri for a trial and finds herself betrothed to an uncle she has never met.

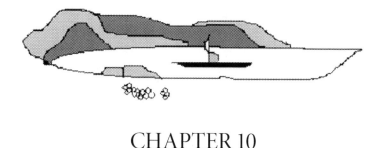

CHAPTER 10

Galilee

Home. Galilee's hills smelled of roses, filling the night with soft dreams. It was hard to keep morose, even with palace intrigues. I lingered in the moonlight watching over the wall to the gentle waves on the great lake. One could imagine it as a great dancing floor, what would it be like to walk on such a glassy sea? That would make a storytelling. I grew sleepy and took to my rooms.

The next morning I sat in the garden and spied a finch, twittering after seeds. How many miles away was Massada, and yet here was this finch. Was there something I should be listening to? Small seeds, hundreds of them, scattered here on stony ground. I wondered how they had gotten there— they'd never grow. I must ask the gardener.

Leah, the gardener, had been part of the Galilee palace in Tiberius for years. She had helped lay out the fields, and even the guards treated her with respect. I queried her where all the seed had come from.

"Ah, your excellency," she spoke. "I have the maidens scatter seed each morning. It keeps the birds happy, and keeps them away from the wheat fields. They know we won't bother them here."

I laughed. "Even the wheat on dry ground bears fruit then?" I ventured, remembering an old proverb.

"It does indeed. In this case it sprouts wings and flies" spoke the woman, smiling. "Have you heard the new maggid, sparrow?"

"Maggid—storyteller? I queried.

"Oh, yes, he comes from a small town west of here, and he has captured people's imaginations. His stories are simple, yet they seem to reach beyond our troubles." She smiled.

"We don't need any more zealots, that's for certain," I spoke in earnest.

"Oh, no, mistress, he speaks only of peace—he even talks to Roman soldiers," she continued.

"Now that is unusual. Then he's not a rabbi?" I ventured.

"Oh, some call him rabboni, but he's much more a maggid, his stories come from nature, not Torah, though he seems to have been trained well. His touch heals they say."

"And a wonder-worker to boot, not another John!" I shook my head.

"Well, he seems to be a cousin of John the Baptizer, or something, but he certainly is not a wild man, if that's what you mean. He dresses well, wears the proper tefillin, like any good teacher, and goes to synagogue quite proper, but more often he's telling stories," she affirmed.

"Doesn't he work? Even teachers of the law need a profession?" I queried.

"He's quite a good mason, they say, he helped lay down the marketplace in Nazareth. And he's good with his hands, shapes a good plow, though he's not a blacksmith. He doesn't shirk work. Maybe that's why people listen to him." Leah dusted off her hands.

"So he works while he talks?" I murmured.

"Sometimes. He will sit and repair a net while talking to the fishermen. He'll help the farmers weed while he talks about sparrows, and he'll pick up a stone and help the herders repair a fence when he talks about towers. He breaks bread with everyone, women and men alike, but does so in such a way that no one takes offense."

"Is he married?"

"I think so. There are at least two rather wealthy women who are clearly taking care of him, but one is much older, I think she's his mother. People defer to her judgment, but I'm not from Nazareth. The other one you know."

"Really, who is that?" I puzzled.

"You call her Bat Mara," Leah declared.

"She said nothing. I must talk to her about this."

"Well, she must have her reasons, as she seems much more peaceful than only a few months ago." Leah continued. "Your dance took a lot out of her, and she had been filled with such darkness."

"She did not accompany us to Philadelphia, and I knew she needed time alone, but what could have happened?"

"That, my sparrow, you will have to take up with her."

•   •   •

I found Bat Mara picking at a piece of fabric with a fine needle. It was a tapestry from Babylon, with multicolored threads forming a picture of lions. Though a small piece, barely enough for a cushion, it must have cost a year's wages. Yet, here she was, picking at it as if were an old scarf.

"Bat Mara," I said breathlessly. "You look different, what has changed you?"

Bat Mara took a pin out of her hair, letting it fall around her. It was long and black, shot with silver. She smiled.

"This is rare," I thought. "I have never seen her not looking pinched and sad." And her hair, it had always seemed mousy before, now it was lustrous.

"Ah, my child, I thought never to see such a day," she smiled. "I can repair a cloth of gold, and it does not matter."

"What are you talking about, Bat Mara? Leah told me something happened, but she refused to say what."

"Look at me, sparrow. What do you see?"

I thought carefully. I recognized the garb, but something was different. Brown and rust—always. But wait. Though it was a dark brown fabric, it had always been rusty as well, stained before with her perpetual flows. Now it was clean cotton—there was no stain. "You're healed!"

"Yes, my sparrow. I no longer need my physicians."

"What happened?" The more I looked, the clearer the differences. And I had only been away from her a month.

"It was the Teacher." She spoke, using the word "rabboni."

"The maggid I heard about? He did this?"

"He said I did it. He took no credit, though I know I touched him."

"You touched him? That could have gotten you killed!" I declared. "This is Galilee!"

In Galilee, even more than in Jerusalem, the sick were often either abandoned or at the very least, kept behind closed doors. With executions in public, there were already enough sources of disease, and people did not wish to be reminded. The Torah code of uncleanness for women on their flows was strictly enforced, and Bat Mara had been an outcast, even at court, hidden away. She was wealthy, but that made no difference.

"Something told me to listen to the gossip," Bat Mara slowly began. "Women talk to women, even if I have to officially 'not be seen'. And all the stories of Yoshua began to come back, even to the palace. They said he was John's cousin, or maybe even John come again."

"Has Antipas heard this?"

"He only began to teach in the last few months, so word is only filtering up to the court now. I feel fortunate that I heard so soon," continued Bat Mara. "Apparently he was fairly ordinary until after John was killed, but then he began to speak much more in public. And then he, apparently, healed a Roman!"

"What, that must have been news!"

"Yes, that was what stirred my attention. Wandering healers I have heard of before, there are a few in Babylon. But they don't often come into town, and they are usually more concerned with the court than with the countryside. In this case, there was a centurion who was a friend of the synagogue."

"He was doing his job of checking out potential troublemakers when his servant took sick. His servant was Jewish, a slave he had bought from a merchant to pay a debt. And so he came to the synagogue to see what they could do. The rabboni had just taught that day on Elishah and Naaman the Syrian, reminding us that sometimes it was foreigners who were healed. And here came Aurelius, the centurion."

"Leah had been working in the garden," she continued, "when one of her maidens came running. "Come quickly," she said, "Marcion was healed.""

"Marcion was the sick slave. He had been at death's door, and nowhere near the synagogue."

"What happened? Was it the Teacher?"

"He wasn't even there, he told the centurion to go home."

"Back up. What?"

"Aurelius had come to the synagogue for help, and Yoshua told him, 'go home! Your faith has saved your servant.'"

"Now the centurion had just come running back to the synagogue to give thanks. His servant was healed. And the maggid wasn't even there!"

"Something told Leah to go and get me and take me to the village at once. I was in pain, but I didn't care. You weren't here, and at this point I felt as if everything was hopeless. I had saved you, but my womb was still bleeding."

"How did you manage it, didn't people try to hold you back?"

"I just started walking, saying to myself, 'I just have to touch him.' I don't know why, I have never been so brave before or since. The dogs were barking, there were people everywhere, but I just walked into that crowd, as if there were no one there at all. I didn't cry 'unclean' as I have almost every day of my life for the past twelve years. I just walked and reached out my hand. And then it happened."

"What!"

"I touched his sleeve, and it was like a bolt of lightning. I felt my womb grow very, very warm, as if I had suddenly flowed all the more, and then it stopped. For the first time in more than a dozen years, it stopped. I could feel no flow. I backed up immediately, and I slid through the crowds, unnoticed."

"How? What? No one stopped you?"

"I took about twenty steps, and then Yoshua shouted! 'Someone touched me!' "The crowd laughed, 'of course someone did, you just healed Marcion,' " they spoke all at once. 'Don't you remember.' "

" 'No, it was someone else, I felt power leave me,' he spoke. At that I stopped walking."

"What did you do?" I gasped.

"I came trembling, both with terror and with joy, bowing low to the ground. Nothing made sense anymore." 'I touched you,' I said. 'I had no choice.' "

"Then he smiled, and lifted me from my knees. 'Go in peace, daughter. Your faith has saved you.' "

"He called me daughter, and I am near twice his age. But then I remembered, to you, I am Bat Mara, daughter of sorrows. Was he a prophet, to know my inner thoughts? That was scarcely six weeks ago, Salomé, and I still tremble. I spend no more money on physicians, and I can even sit and smile in a courtyard with an expensive piece of fabric."

"Though I cannot travel with him, I have decided that my payment to God will be to pay for his lodging any time he is in Galilee. It is the least that I can do. I am wealthy, and he is a laborer, in hearts, as well as in the stoneyard. The laborer is worthy of his hire."

I pondered. This old woman had lost almost my entire age from this bleeding, and in a moment it was gone. Would my life, or hers, ever be the same?

CHAPTER 11

The Bazaar

Late spring had come, and the time of the horse bazaar was nearing. Antipas spent time in Gedarenes every year, looking over the horses. Since the time of Solomon, the Parthians had bred creatures of perfection, and the marketplace here went back to that time. The Greeks, the Syrians, the Scythians, everyone looked to the Parthians to bring the horses of central Asia to breed the imperial horses used throughout the Roman Empire. Far from being a single breed, they were a mix of Arabian and Asian, bred for hardiness, even in the mules. To be a soldier, one must sometimes be months on the road, and horses were more valuable than the gold used to pay for them.

And so Antipas came, with his entourage, to the bazaar at Gedarenes. This time, however, he was also there to officially welcome the Romans, not a task that he seemed to be relishing. He bristled as he spoke, he had been the friend of Rome, and now he felt the heel of Rome. It was not a pleasant prospect.

The city of Gedarenes was built on a cliff, where birds wheeled down to the water. The city graveyard was built on the hill, and the poor often camped out among the stones during the yearly fair. The bazaar stretched halfway across the headland up to the borders of the walled town.

Gedarenes spilled over from the Decapolis into Galilee, right in the middle of the heights of Hebron.

Hebron, green hills filled with cedars, with cool nights. These weeks in springtime were the gates to the sultry winds of summer, with desert storms, just the time for the yearly market, when both young lambs and young foals could be bought for a bargain. But not so the yearlings. These, if the breeds were true, were haggled over for hours, and even auctioneers became bewildered.

Mother and I had gone to the marketplace, this time in our large sedan chair. We had to work through go-betweens, but looking through the screens was fascinating, here in this crossroads of at least five cultures.

"Look at the carpet-makers, Salomé," spoke Herodias. "The Parthians make the best weavings in the world, and each one tells a story. Sometimes it is a horse on a hill, or a well with strange one-horned goats from the hills of the Kurds. They make the brightest colors from simple weeds, and I always watch for a new pattern. When they weave the silks into the camel's wool, it makes a sheen that you can see across a room. Let's see if we can find a new weave. Georgio, direct the carriers to that shop."

The carriers let down the chair as we wished to bargain directly. We pulled back the screens, as we were now fully veiled, with only our eyes showing. In Philadelphia, we could walk with the veils around our faces, but in Gedarenes we had to follow the customs of Galilee. Now it would be our hands, and voices, with a squint or a wink to bargain beyond words what could not be communicated by gestures.

The weavers were busy at their looms, both women and men, the women with coins all over their veils, their cymbals jangling as they moved the shuttles and tied on each of the colors.

A new picture was slowly forming, one of reeds and ducks on a field of swampgrass among willow trees. Herodias waved her hand with a gesture with two fingers.

Two gold talents! This was indeed a find if she would spend that kind of money. I dreaded to see what the merchant would say.

His hand formed a three that changed to one, and then four. I was puzzled. What was he getting at? Herodias hands shifted and she spoke softly. "Two." Again, the merchant formed a three, and then a one, and then a four, but this time, ended with two.

"Three talents, your excellency."

"You drive a hard bargain," she spoke through her veil. "Are you certain of the time?"

"Yes, Antipas came through here just after dawn."

I was completely baffled. The numbers made no sense. Three talents? Dawn? I had my own code in Jerusalem, was this my mother's?

"Good merchant, three talents for a simple weave?" spoke Herodias.

"It comes from Babylon, and the ducks are made of silk," the weaver responded.

"Ah, my teacher will enjoy this then. How soon till it is finished?" she queried.

"By the end of the fair, two weeks, after the horse auction," spoke her merchant husband.

"I will send for it, be sure the duck's bills are bright!" she asserted.

"We will find the threads for it, peace be upon thee," spoke the merchant.

By this I knew the bargaining, or whatever it has been was at an end, at least for this weaver. We climbed back into our chair, and moved on through the city streets, pausing to let the crowd push through in a tight place between stalls. Herodias motioned for the carriers to put us down and walk three paces away. Since we were enclosed in a safe place, the guards could discreetly watch from a distance.

"What was that about, mother?" I spoke in a whisper, puzzled.

"I asked the merchant if anyone had come to the marketplace to meet with Herod. 'Two' meant Antipas would meet someone."

His hand formed a three that changed to one, and then four. I was puzzled. What was he getting at? Herodias hands shifted and she spoke softly. "Two." Again, the merchant formed a three, and then a one, and then a four, but this time, ended with two.

"The merchant said '3-1-4', which meant three Parthians, one foreigner, and then all of them left, with Antipas along. The repeat with the second '2' meant they left the market."

"All of that from numbers, how did you know?"

"I have learned that I cannot pass notes in a crowd. If I hired a scribe, Herod would confront me as 'influencing the market' so all I can do is send signals. If a merchant sees a 'two' it means I'm hunting for my husband, no matter what else comes out of my mouth."

"And three?"

"The merchants know that whatever I ask, the price must be higher than I bid, or else. I cannot be known as one who will not pay for information."

"That's a year's wages for a rug!" I spoke astonished.

"I see the merchants once a year, and they travel everywhere. When I saw the ducks, I remembered Bat Mara talking about them as they nestled in the reeds near Babylon, so I knew that these merchants would know any strangers.

When they responded, I knew that my factors had chosen wisely," she informed me.

"I will not often teach you all the code, Salomé, but just this once, particularly since you saw these merchants in Philadelphia, it was worth letting you know."

"Then you know about the sparrows?" I smiled.

"Who do you think taught them the code?" she winked. "I must be perceived by Antipas to simply be a hard bargainer, and you must be safe in the weaver's quarter, but it keeps me knowing the sources of information without betraying them."

"I spread the seed around, just like in the garden, so even the ravens know where to feed," she continued. "Women in a market can talk with their hands, in front of their own husbands, or even a guard, and what no one hears, they can't repeat, even under duress. The numbers change, from year to year, only the 'two' remains the same."

"And the time? What did that mean?"

"It means Antipas wishes to be relatively under wraps here. If one arrives just after dawn, only those buying food for a household breakfast will be out. The yearling colts are also brought out to exercise before being put under shelter in the heat of the day, so this gives the chief traders a time to see all of the merchandise without the sweltering sun interfering."

"But it's spring, the sun is not that hot, even at the ninth hour!" I protested. The ninth hour was mid-afternoon.

"The colts are run through their paces, and by midafternoon they will be fatigued. It is best to see them in the morning, before they are drenched with sweat," she concluded.

"Any more information, Mother?"

"Just the ordinary. The rug will be finished by the end of the market time, after the horse auction, by which time Antipas's bargain will also be sealed. This time, if we watch for the opportunity, we may find out what the 'baggage' meant, daughter," spoke Herodias.

Herodias motioned the carriers to return, and Georgio took the rear point to both guard us and guide the sedan chair to the forum. In every major Greek and Roman town, there was a central market area, sometimes with a collonade. In the middle of this market area was a pedestal, with words enscribed in Aramaic and in Greek. In this forum, the inscription simply read "Gedarenes. Parthia." All east of here was Parthian, all west of here was Roman.

Under the collonades were stone tables, some with braziers set on them, where traders would cook choice chicken or lamb parts on skewers. We could see a few guards we knew sitting at one of the tables. Behind them were the entrances to the Roman baths.

One guard came out of the baths and walked to a table, getting one of the soldier's attention. With a Roman salute, the second soldier went to the door of the baths and went in. The first soldier sat down.

By this we knew that Antipas had chosen one place we could not go, but at least let us know that he was well watched.

Herodias hissed in frustration. "No ears under water—yet!" she mumbled defiantly. "Antipas is an old fox," she stated. "But this hen will ruffle her feathers despite him."

CHAPTER 12

Pigs

Herodias made a trip daily to the bazaar, seeking news of Antipas, but no matter how inquisitive and persistent she was, she never got more than a glimpse at the strangers whom we had seen in Philadelphia.

On a hunch, she sent Georgio to the stables at dawn, simply to watch. With a pouch of coins he deliberately jangled, he left our compound, and we had to wait impatiently for his return.

While we waited, we busied ourselves with palace gossip. The local servants were more than happy to let us know anything they heard, as even one coin from Herodias purse was more than they would see from other sources, and they could go and bargain for something rare, if only once a year.

It seemed that in the past season, a pestilence was rumored to have swept through the region, leaving some of the men with a brain fever that made them delirious. As it had come at the same time the Romans had garrisoned a new group of soldiers in the barracks, everyone blamed them for bringing it on, though in this case they had come to rebuild the aqueduct for fresh water into the town. The shards of the construction had fallen into the wells, and the water had become polluted.

The Romans worked day and night to clear the debris as heavy rains had mixed sewage with the well water and corroded the lead pipes. The men who worked with the Romans, unfortunately, had taken sick from drinking from the wells before they were purified.

The Romans, wisely, had drunk only wine the entire time. The Romans were not at fault, but there was much grumbling.

Until the wells were cleared, the women, who had normally gathered at them in the mornings, were forced to stay indoors, and so they exchanged news, and sometimes overheard things that would normally have been beyond their hearing. In this we were in luck. We had been right to send Georgio to the stables, they confirmed, as there were unusual goings on. Saffron-robed traders had been seen, and it was all the gossip of the harems.

"I've seen them walk by without making a sound. They're like cats!" The Persian women were terrified of them. They told us in whispers that whenever they came to town back in Babylon, the woman did their utmost to stay out of sight. They were under the pay of the Bactrians, and any women not watched tended to disappear. And Antipas was bargaining with them. This was dangerous. What twist could he possibly be turning in his mind?

•   •   •

We waited impatiently for Georgio to return. At last, almost at sunset, we heard the jangle of his purse, much lighter than before. He motioned silently for Herodias and I to follow him outside. This was most unusual.

In the yard was a colt of raven black, a deep color rarely seen. He invited me to touch it. "He's gentle, as he has been whispered down."

"Whispered?"

"Yes, a rare gift, they don't treat them with a lash, but with a soft touch, and, apparently, a secret language. These rare horses almost understand human speech and they will work on reigns or knees alone. But that is not why I brought the two of you out."

"I was walking by one of the Greek stables at sunrise. The colts were being brought out to exercise in the early morning dew. It was breathtaking. Such lines of strength. And me with few coins…" he smiled.

"Out of the corner of my eye I thought I saw gold. I turned to see a flash of saffron being quickly covered up under a dark robe. What is this? A monk, whispering with a linesman?"

"I looked for some excuse to get closer. Several of the trainers were walking toward the stables, and one of the grooms was rubbing down the most beautiful dark-coated yearling I had ever seen. I walked over to him, fortunately only steps from the linesman, and spoke loudly. "I'm looking for a horse for the Tetrarch. He wishes an Asian breed." If this didn't get the monk's attention, nothing would.

The cowled figure turned. "Your eyes are sharp, Hittite," spoke the stranger in Assyrian.

"Not I, wanderer", I returned in the same language, "I come from Colchis."

"But your speech is from Asia, not the taint of the seamen," he replied in Georgian.

"You detect my parents in my tongue," I spoke politely. "But I was raised in the legions."

"A rare one, with a gift for tongues," returned the monk, shifting his accent to Farsi, "are you conversant in Persian?"

"Let us not bargain in secret!" I shifted to Greek.

The monk laughed, "but this is Syria!" shifting to Aramaic.

"Enough of the language lesson, warrior" answering in the same tongue.

"I see there are no secrets from you, then, legionnaire!" he spoke in Latin.

"My robe is Roman, but do not mistake my loyalties, I am here from Antipas," shifting back to Aramaic.

"I have already spoken with him today, is this some new bargain?" he spoke warily.

"No, just confirming the location."

"He agreed on the graveyard, is that not true?"

"How will we know you do not cheat us?" I spoke.

"I know the pig farmers. They dig for truffles there," spoke the monk."

"Only one well versed in this area would know them, and not a stranger. Expect a messenger there, then."

At this the monk turned away, and vanished into the bazaar. I tried to follow but he was too quick for me.

"You are fortunate, mistresses, that Antipas trusts me not to divulge what I should not. You need to know as you are his queen and his daughter, but it goes no further." "However; there is more to my story than this monk." He continued to speak as if in recounting a dream, unfolding a most unusual story.

•   •   •

The soldiers had been sent to the graveyard for their daily inspection of the slums, and in this case, to ensure that fresh water was made available to the villagers camped there. Antipas and Archelaus together had agreed on a building campaign to ensure the aqueduct would be fresh and now, after 10 years, they were finally getting Roman cooperation.

As we had learned, the water had been poisoned by the leavings of the foundry, and the pipes of the aqueduct carried the runoff into the public wells. The men of the villages, thirsty from work, had drunk the water and become sickened, delirious, and then raving. The legionnaires were blamed. The sickened workmen, now wandering and raving, slept in the graveyards—like ghosts—who had to be wakened in the mornings.

The duty stations were rotated, so that no single soldier would be singled out by the bandits, who had taken it upon themselves to sleep—like the madmen—among the stones, and ambush any particularly hated soldier.

In addition, as part of the building plan, a grove of oaks had been planted there, sacred to Zeus, and a temple was planned for the area, as this was a Greek-speaking area, albeit for all the Jews in it. Pigs—sacred to Zeus—which were kept both for food, and to seek for truffles, roamed the hillside and had to be kept away from the graves. This combination of sickened workmen and perceived Greek uncleanness put a stamp on the area of constant unrest and religious zealotry.

On this day, of all days, Yoshua, the storyteller, had been in the marketplace. He was well aware of the story of the poisoned wells, and yet he did not wish to antagonize an already tense situation. Apparently he turned the story on its head.

"Remember the waters of Mara," spoke Yoshua, "where the sweet wood drove out the bitter? Here the God of heaven must help you find sweet earth!"

The crowd stirred. One particular man, who had been quite a skilled laborer, had wandered into the bazaar and was raving. Yoshua stopped him with a word.

"What is your name, friend?"

"My name is Legion, for we are many!" he replied.

"In this you speak the truth, for you are not alone, and you speak for many," spoke the healer.

"But we are poisoned!"

"Do not worry for what you have taken in, but of what you spew out."

The man stood dumbed. No one could believe their ears. Was this storyteller a friend of the soldiers?

"I give living water to those who are thirsty. It will clear your mind. Drink!"

The message was an old one. Truth from the Torah was like a stream in the desert. But in this context? It seemed shallow.

"The God of the heavens and the Earth will heal you."

"What do you mean?" the man blinked.

"Even the unclean know where to find fresh water," the teacher spoke again.

"The pigs? I must follow the pigs?" spoke the man.

"Do you wish to think clearly again? The pigs will guide you. Don't eat them, just trust them. Remember Naaman the Syrian. Here the Syrians will heal you—the outcast."

Yoshua was strange. He constantly taught that healing came to everyone, especially foreigners. What was he asking for?

"The pigs are wise. Follow where they dig," he continued.

At that moment, a swineherd from the temple of Zeus came in driving a flock of young piglets, but they broke free and began to run up the hill right toward the graveyard and the oaks. They dug, and dug, and the pulled out a thick mass of truffles.

"Eat," spoke Yoshua.

The man obeyed. He heaved, and spit up, a great mass of black and bile. But then he blinked. His eyes cleared.

"You are a magus, not a mageed," the man spoke.

"No, it is the power of God in every living thing," returned Yoshua. "Even the lowliest, and the most unclean know how to find healing. Your mind has been poisoned by the waters, I have had to find sweet earth to clear it. The truffles have leached the poison from your mind. Even the lowliest roots of the trees, found by creatures you cannot eat, can heal. I am not a magician, just one who tells stories, and listens to the Spirit in the wind."

The priest of Zeus had watched the Jewish teacher and was in awe. "Will even the Greeks listen to this man?"

Georgio continued, "My mistresses, I do not know where this man comes from, or what may be coming, but even as you listen for spies from Bactria, other things you do not anticipate are happening."

Bat Mara had been right. This storyteller would bear watching. "But what of the monk?" I was impatient. "What of the monk—the man in bright robes?"

"He was also there, apparently talking with a silk merchant. Apparently Herod has set spies throughout the marketplace for any of these monks, as they are the only ones who are reliable ambassadors to Bactria. Antipas is trying to corner the silk trade, at least in this area. It seems an odd thing, that simple threads could be more powerful than horses."

Although I was young, I had been in the marketplace all my life, and found it the one reliable source of news. "Georgio, you may have hit on it. Whenever Mother would send me to the marketplace, I was always told to go to the cloth merchants first, as their ears stretched farther."

Herodias smiled. "You have learned one of my secrets, daughter. The threads of the world carry news as no other messenger. And Herod is trying to buy the source. That will be an adventure worthy of a devious mind."

Georgio spoke. "You speak in riddles. Why would Herod care?"

"When I was young, Georgio," spoke Herodias, for once admitting that she was over 30, "silk was worn by every high-born male in Rome as a symbol of status. The togas shone like pearls in the sunlight. In the 4th year of Tiberius reign, the trading of fabric began to literally unravel the market. My father lost a villa over a gambling debt, all for the price of a single bolt of cloth. My uncle's closest friend, Tiberius, newly arrived as the second Emperor, chose to show his wisdom by curbing the trade with China."

"People thought him odd to forbid the wearing of silk by the men of the Empire, but it effectively put the trade into the hands of the favorites of the Emperor, closing the market to all but the shrewdest investors. Tiberius had to have a source of funds that reached everywhere, what better than the threads of the craftsmen."

"And now Antipas wants that trade?" queried Georgio.

"Yes, and as a 'friend of the Emperor' he accomplishes two tasks at once," mused Herodias. "He ensures that he has the ears of the farthest ambassadors from China, and he gets to speculate in the most volatile market and ready source of funds. Trying to move the end of the trade route from Petra to Galilee is quite an accomplishment. He may be a king yet!"

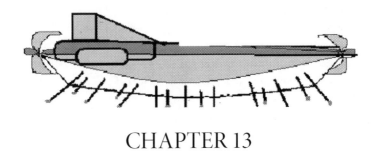

CHAPTER 13

Silk

The Assyrians had long-established trade routes with the Han Dynasty of China and wove tapestries from raw silk and, when they moved westward to become the Syrians and took over Tyre, brought their knowledge and secrets with them. Both Persian and Chinese silk found its way to the Senate of Rome and there was not a household that did not have at least one weaving. Now that we knew that he was watching the silk trade as much as the horses, my mother Herodias and I became watchful for any changes in the cloth markets.

The horse market had now closed, but the weavers continued their trade throughout the year. The pits of the dyers could be seen from our villa dotting the hillside like enormous flowers throughout the summer. The weavers of the great circuit of land around Lake Chinnereth called the Galilee used the many mineral salts from the Dead Sea as mordants to make deep blues, green, yellows, and reds that were famous throughout the Roman Empire.

The one color we never saw, however, was purple. This color was reserved to a guild of its own, centered on Tyre, some 60 miles away on the coast, the shipping port where the purple guild added their murex dyes and following the old Phoenician traders, established outposts in Alexandria, Cyrene, Tarsus, Massilia, Napoli, and Lydia. Antipas watched this market most closely, as it was tied to the Emperor's banking pursuits.

Herod Antipas had been summoned to Rome many times during his training as a tetrarch, and the ships in which he traveled were often these cloth merchant vessels, with enormous sails, bearing tapestries from Persia, and cloth from Babylon and beyond.

A messenger arrived at the villa in Gadarenes during the audience hours. "Your excellency," spoke the messenger, "I bring greetings and a summons from Rome. A ship awaits you at Tyre."

I overheard these words, with some consternation, from my seat in the court, clearly visible at Herod's footstool.

The herald continued, "Your nephew Agrippa is in need of your presence before the Senate."

This news from Rome was trouble, though I could not say why. The centurion spoke no further words, simply gave the summons to the Senate.

I inquired after his wife, Cyprus, for guidance but discovered that she had left a week ago with him on a courier ship. Families were not often invited on these state visits, so there was something in the air I began to wonder about.

The next two weeks became a flurry of activity. As the horse market had closed, there was now a fallow season during the summer during which Antipas could be away from the Galilee on court affairs without losing his edge.

Leaving the palace in the hands of Shusa, the steward, he gave orders that Herodias, I, and a company of about two score selected servants would go with him to Rome. At least ten of these guardsmen were Roman legionnaires, ever watchful, and Herod was distrustful of them.

In addition, the ships were being prepared at the Syrian port of Tyre, also used as a slave market, but most of this special crew were soldiers, not galley slaves. To ensure privacy, therefore, Georgio, our personal servant, was put in charge of the household effects and we prepared to set sail.

Herod and Herodias took a private quarter in the main point vessel, a 4-tiered galley ship called a quadreme, which acted as protection for the rest of the merchant fleet. I was given a small cabin on the same vessel, at the rear, above the drummer's station.

This ship had been specially refitted with a private quarter in back of the battering ram but otherwise was clearly a fighting ship rather than a rather lumbering merchant ship. The flotilla of merchant ships, as they billowed behind us, looked magnificent as we sailed at dawn.

As the sun began to climb and the seacoast became gradually more distant, I began to think of Rome, and my father, Herod Philip, now working with the Senate, along with Agrippa. I pondered what I would say to him, now that so many changes had happened. My parent's separation had been difficult (I had been only five at the time) and I had not seen him since. He was still alive, living peaceably in his villa and I had been assured that we would see him once court matters were finished.

All that changed, however, once we were at sea. The merchant captain's orders had been kept secret and were delivered to Herod only when we were at full sail. We were to go directly to the imperial court on the island of Capri, near Naples, an unusual summons, reserved only for "friends of the Emperor."

Antipas' bearing immediately changed as if the weight of administration had fallen off his shoulders, and he became expansive at this news, sure that his dreams of rulership were finally to be heard.

Mother and I looked at each other as we were informed, pondering the merchant vessels laden with cloth, and both of us became deeply troubled. Something was amiss, yet nothing could be seen on the surface. I saw a manta ray float up through the crystal waters beyond the pier, and then descend, vanishing into the depths. The shifting moods of Herod were like that manta, clearly seen for a moment, and then becoming invisible.

We sat on the deck of the merchant galley and watched the waves go by. We remained in sight of land following the southern Mediterranean coastline, so we still had many days to go.

At least two weeks would be spent at sea before we put into the port of Cyrene for supplies before crossing to Syracuse and then to Capri. The port of Alexandria floated by in the night as I watched, the Pharos lighthouse fires winking out as we passed a dune.

In the morning light, I picked at a shawl with a bone needle. The threads I used were fine, and could go three times through its eye. I bemusedly looked at the ropes holding the sail, woven of camel's hair. Bat Mara had told me a parable of her teacher who compared rich people to camels. Easier, he had said, for a camel to go through the eye of a needle than for the rich to become righteous and enter the Kingdom of Heaven.

Well, the needle's eye would certainly have to be large, as even the camel-hair rope took very special tools to weave. I chuckled, thinking of the great dromedaries leaning down to go through one of the gates of Jerusalem called the Needle's Eye.

A simple story, yet it stuck in my mind. Threads wove my life together, I bargained for shawls and learned of zealots.

My mother commissioned a tapestry, and the fabric itself became a bone of contention.

The rich were like the cloth they wove, intricate, confusing, full of knots. The thread came loose in my hand and the whole picture became unraveled. I would have to start anew, this time tying off at each point. Was that what Herod was doing? Making sure that each stitch was in place before he appeared in court?

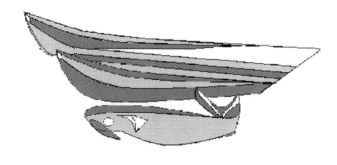

CHAPTER 14

Cyrene

Tyre was far behind. Alexandria was now a week behind, and we were now coasting into Appolonia, the port of Cyrene in Libya. Dolphins were playing beside the ship, seeming to welcome us into the harbor. Their laughter echoed my own. I was eager, even though we would only stay two days to replenish supplies, to see the marketplace there.

Antipas maintained a factor in both Appolonia and the larger city of Cyrene, as the region was reknowned for horses. Bat Mara knew it for its trade in medicinal plants and had sent me on a mission to the marketplace, should I find the time.

The Jewish community was large, maintaining a quarter of its own, and the mosaics of the agora were finely detailed. Something told me to watch everything as any place Antipas maintained an agent was significant.

Under the Ptolemy's, the Jewish community had thrived, winning special concessions from the Greek empire, but now that the community was a Roman city, they were considered second-class citizens, and this uneasiness was evident, in subtle ways, in the attitude of the dock workers toward our arrival. Herod Antipas was a Roman ruler, but he was also a Jew, and we could feel very watchful eyes at all our movements.

The Greeks had left their stamp with temples to Apollo, Zeus, and Demeter. Even with the unfriendly eyes, I was impressed by the architecture, as this was the first city I had seen with such a mix of styles.

A navy memorial, with a carving of a dolphin bearing a merchant ship riding the waves was clearly visible as we were carried to the outskirts of the city, some 6 miles inland. The valley of Cyrene was green, protected from the desert to the south by low-lying hills and maintaining a cool breeze at night off the waters of the Great Sea.

Agrippa maintained a correspondence with the Jewish leaders of the city, so Antipas was expected to meet with them, which was the only reason for our taking the time to come inland rather than staying at port.

After we settled ourselves, Antipas awaited the arrival of the local Jewish council. The rights of the Jews had been slowly eroding and legal obstacles against land ownership and some of the normal professional courtesies had begun to lose weight. As I listened, I learned that a new community of Jewish freedmen (former slaves) were becoming more vocal and were looking for a voice to present their case to Rome. Antipas was hoped to be that voice.

"Your Excellency, we know that you have the ear of the Emperor," spoke the factor. "We have long maintained your factor here, and we do not wish to make your life difficult. However, your property is at stake." The city councilors have not allowed us to buy more land for your stables, and it is because you are Jewish. Can you not advise us in this matter?"

Herod stroked his red beard. "Have you proof of this prejudice, other than murmurs?"

"It has been slow in coming, your Excellency," spoke the leader of the local Sanhedrin. "The changes have been subtle, and it was only when a combined force of the natives of Cyrene, some Roman citizens, resident aliens, and farmers began to question our money-lenders that we realized the extent of the prejudice. We are but one quarter of the city, and the others now seemed determine to trim our holdings."

Herod was silent for many moments at this revelation. "Bring me a tally of my holdings over the past five years so that I can see for myself where changes have happened. I will study it as I set sail."

Though I did not see his tallies, my own eyes in the marketplace showed me that an uneasy distance was being maintained. Our money was still accepted, Greek drachmas could be spent anywhere, but we often were not shown the best cloth unless we insisted. My banter did not work here, and Herodias did not have pass codes, so we had to bargain with words, with no information transmitted.

In contrast, Bat Mara had been right to send me to the apothecaries. The healers were priestesses of Apollo, and the community of women did not maintain the prejudices of their husbands. I was now 16 and my cramps each month were significant. Poppy oil had helped, but I now needed something stronger.

"How may I assist you," spoke the herbalist. "I have been a doula for many years, so the ways of young women are not strange to me." The words came out of a face that was wrinkled and orange as a dried apricot.

"Do you have lotus blooms here?" I had heard about them from Bat Mara, who had acquired them through her physicians.

"Egyptian or Libyan?" she queried.

"What is the difference?" I replied, puzzled.

"Egyptian lotus oil is made from the blossoms and though it soothes the pain, it is temporary. Libyan lotus is from a different part of the plant, and can be taken in small doses in a tea over a week's time. Sailors use it to prevent seasickness, very similar to your cramps."

"Sailors? Then the stories are true of Ulysses stopping here?"

"O yes, this was his island of the lotus eaters. The city grew around the spring of Apollo in this temple, and we have maintained a temenos for women for more than 500 years."

"I seem to have wandered into a myth, then?"

"No, the old tales always contain a grain of truth, even when as small as a lotus seed," the old doula smiled.

"I will remember you to Bat Mara with kindness."

"Bat Mara? You know of her, we have not heard from her in some months, is she in good health?"

"She is my nurse, and is now quite well." I told her of her sudden healing.

"Is this teacher from one of the mystery schools?" she inquired.

"Not that I know of, he seems to be completely of Galilee." I responded.

"He reminds me of Aesclepeus, using what others find poison to heal the sick. Are you certain he has no training?" she continued.

"I cannot speak for him, as I have never met him, and Bat Mara has been quiet of late, but I will ask her to correspond with you. I had no idea her letters were so watched for news."

"We will look forward to them, good lady," she continued. "Here are the seeds, dried to a powder, take them slowly, too many at once will make you unable to think," she warned.

"I will be careful, Bat Mara was always drinking tea, now I know why," I smiled.

"Peace be upon you, your Excellency," she dismissed me with a wave.

As I sat back down in my sedan chair, I was suddenly cramped. What was this? The sickness of women was upon me and I turned back to the doulas. "Help me," I moaned.

The old woman beckoned to the servants on my chair and they carried me back into the healer's precinct. "What is this?" queried the doula? "Are the cramps heavy?"

I moaned incoherently. She laid her hand on my forehead. "Sea fever", she concluded. "Drink this" she held a cup to my lips. The brew was bitter, and I wanted to spit it out.

"No, if it tastes bitter, then it will drive the poison out," she instructed. "When you are well, there is no taste to it. The potion contains salts as well as willow, so drink it all down."

"Your cramps this month are combined with fever, but since they have just come on you, we can stop the fever before it spreads, your soul is strong at this time, though your body is weak. Use that strength of womanhood in your prayers," she spoke. "Your Mother will hear you."

"My mother?" I puzzled, "but she is back at the factor's home".

"No, when you are ill, you will learn that is the Mother who heals. She guards the tents of Israel, and contends against illness and death."

I pulled out a talisman, still weak. "Do you mean Leah? I was given this as an infant, and it is a ward against the desert wind."

"Yes, and no, Salomé" spoke the doula. "Your mother, Herodias, taught you well, to remember the foremother of all the Jews, Leah the healer, but no, this is the God you carry within, who when you are brave is your Father, but when you are weak, and in need of healing, is your Mother."

"Then the stories are true of the mothers of Israel?"

"O yes," the doula murmured, cooling my brow with a cloth. "The glory hangs over the homes of Israel, like the smoke over the Temple, and ensures her daughters that she is first in the home, and in the heart, before she shows herself in the deeds of the Temple."

"This teaching, long known to the Mothers, is why I questioned you about the Mageed. He seems to speak of the Temple of the heart, not the Temple of the Herods. Send us word if you hear more, you now know why we listen in the marketplace."

CHAPTER 15

Tophet

As I was carried in the sedan chair back to the factor's villa, my bearers took a wrong turn and I found myself next to a columbarium. Urns—more than a hundred of them—were arranged near an altar with a blazing statue of Baal.

Though I had seen a similar statue in Tyre, I had always heard that it marked a "tophet", as the rabbis taught it, an "abominable thing," a place of child sacrifice. As I peered through the curtains, I saw a young family, a mother with three small children, dressed as for a wedding, bring a child wrapped in swaddling clothes, and give it to the priest to be burned. The children were laughing. I shuddered, why would families take their young ones and throw them to the fires? And laugh about it, and even dance before the altar. Only the most perfect children would die, and walk willingly into the flames. I remembered my dance, and the statue of Melech, the God of Moab.

And yet, Abraham had been asked to take his own son and offer him up. Was there something I was missing?

Flowers grew in abundance around the cemetery, and the altar was well kept. The season was high summer, and with the symbol of the Cyrenians being the phoenix reborn from the ashes, I pondered what it might mean.

When we arrived at the women's quarter, I asked to speak to a eunuch of the harem. Eunuchs often were hired by women in seclusion to conduct business so that a propertied woman would not be seen on the street. He found my request most peculiar.

"You wish to speak to a priest of Baal? You are a Jewish princess, this is most unusual!"

"I will likely be ruling in Syria, where there are many religions. Though I am young, I am not blind, and I do not wish to deceive myself. What I have seen disturbs me, and I would rather hear, even through an interpreter, the truth."

Herod was sequestered with the factor for the afternoon, so there was still sufficient time, as the temple of Baal was quite near. So that there would be no scandal, I was carried veiled in a rented cart to the public square near the factor's home, and I spoke to the priest through an interpreter while remaining in my chair.

"Holy one," I used the neutral term, "my carriers took me by a back way in error and I found myself next to a 'tophet.' People of my religion have been warned of your practice of child sacrifice. I wish to understand."

"Your excellency," he spoke in Latin, in which I was barely conversant, bowing to the ground. "We fear that you have maintained a slander caused by ignorance. We only return to the Gods what is theirs!"

I listened carefully to the interpreter. "Returned to the Gods, what language is this? You slaughter children, perfect children, or that is how my eyes see it."

He hesitated, and thought for a moment as to how to best phrase it. "No, your excellency, the children brought to us have been without blemish, it is true, but they are premature or have died suddenly, found without breath in their cradles.

My lady," he continued, "children of the sea, unless they are strong, often die of pestilences within the first nine months after birth, before many of them are out of swaddling clothes. Even with the care of our herbalists, they die young. Our belief is that they are taken back by the God to come back again stronger."

"As we are the people of the Phoenix, rather than bury them, we return them to the fire that they may carry that strength into their next life and be born able to brave our world."

He sighed. "They carry our prayers with them, and so, like the animals of prayer, they are given to the altar, not to the earth."

"But your mothers do not mourn," I argued. "They seem happy when they bring them and they bring flowers."

"Our prophets say that the fires of heaven are a sweet offering, as do yours. What could be sweeter than a child returned to the arms of its loving Father. They go to be reborn stronger, and so we rejoice and dance with them."

"But there seem to be hundreds of urns, are all your children sickly?"

"No, your excellency, but a pestilence swept through this region less than 20 years ago, and the children were the first to die," he shook his head sorrowfully.

"No family was without a loss, and with a population of over 10,000 men, many with multiple wives, the fires were going night and day. Our physicians know enough that you do not keep a body above ground for more than a day or it spreads sickness, and our fires glowed in the night as we returned the children to the Father."

"Then each urn is of a child who died suddenly?" I queried.

"Yes, we honor each child separately. We do not make mass graves." He bowed deeply.

I stumbled on words to relay through the interpreter. "I must think on this. I thank you for your information, holy one. May you help others rejoice."

"Peace be upon you, good lady," he spoke in Aramaic, bypassing the interpreter.

"Peace be upon you, holy one, how do you come to know our language?"

"I studied in Tyre for many years, and only recently came to Cyrene. Herod's factor is well known to me. Although I am a priest of Baal, I have studied your own holy scrolls and commentaries. Our library is quite extensive."

"How did you get a holy scroll?" I gasped.

"Many years ago, a synagogue was burned in northern Syria during an invasion of the Persians. There were no survivors. There was a library there, and the priests of my order took it upon themselves to preserve them. Only recently have we found opportunity to find scholars among you who would not fear if we returned them to your keeping. I am fortunate to have read them. Your Talmud is one of the most fascinating commentaries on the human experience I have seen. One scroll spoke of your beliefs that the dead return, in the next generation, to the families that they have left behind."

"Yes, we often do not speak of it, but many of our folk believe that. I sometimes wonder if I am Salomé Cleopatra, my great-aunt, as she was known for her shrewdness from an early age. She died in a palace rebellion before I was born, but they say I favor her."

"We are not often given to know, my lady. Perhaps we shall speak again," he stumbled, bowing low, "when you are more in charge of your own affairs."

"Peace be upon you," I deliberately said in Latin, dismissing him by drawing the curtain.

Was this how a princess acquired her knowledge? I had found factors, priestesses, a queen, a young apprentice tailor, horse traders, and now this priest—all seemed to have a perspective on their surroundings, simply by living—that I could not have in my somewhat circumscribed world.

Whomever I married would have a very hard time keeping up with me, as he might never know whom I might be speaking to behind his back. Spies were everywhere— they might as well be mine.

•   •   •

Helen of Troy, Ulysses, and now the Phoenix, I felt as if my life were a play, and the script was already written. I thought of Shaqilath, and wondered what court dispute she might be resolving at this moment. The Lion Court was not that different from our own, yet she was a ruler. What would that be like, to be listened to, rather than invisible in court?

My mother's eyes gleamed in the moonlight as I shared with her my queries with the healers and the priest. "We rule, even when we must be silent" she spoke tenderly. "I must show you something I hide even from Antipas."

From around her neck she pulled a fine thread of silver. "This was a gift from your father upon our marriage. It is light as a feather, almost unnoticed, its links made by the silversmiths of Damascus."

When we were first married in Syria, I thought him ambitious, and so I thrived on his attentions. We came to Rome to be trained, I as a matrona, and ruler of a household, he as a client king of the Empire. His holdings from your grandfather were significant, though small. They are still some of the most beautiful in Hebron, and they look out over a stronghold."

"I was charmed by this necklace, Salomé, simple yet strong, almost unseen, but seeing everything. Though I chose to leave him for his brother, I somehow had to keep this necklace, a symbol of his way of maintaining a distance, and ruling over the small, even hidden things, which is the way of women in the Empire. Who would have thought that a man could so clearly perceive our thoughts?"

Herodias gently strung the necklace around my neck. "And now, for you, the ways of women have come, and we must begin to prepare you for marriage. You will not choose your husband, nor he you. It will be a matter of much thought, as you are an heiress without peer in Syria. A gentle man to quiet a colt, or a strong man to face a fury, I do not know which will best temper your steel."

I finger this necklace, still around my neck after 50 years, and think of my two husbands, one old, one young, two different temperaments. Would I have understood so clearly had I not watched my mother in both her pride and her quiet moments as she sought to prepare me for a life of court?

I wondered about my father. I had not seen him in 12 years, would he know me? I was only six when I left Rome, and his villa was but a faint memory. I had been moved more than a dozen times over those years, shuttling back and forth between Caesarea Phillipi, Jerusalem, and various cities in the Decapolis. Could a husband give me stability?

My mother was a matrona, yet her life was far from stable. I fingered the necklace as I thought. "I should ask him for advice, but will he give it?"

CHAPTER 16

Syracuse

We set into the port of Syracuse to replenish supplies and offload our cargo of cloth, tapestries, dyes, and oil. Syracuse had long been the crossroads of the Great Sea, dating back to Greek, Phoenician, and Cretan empires. As was usual, we sent out runners for the factors to meet with Antipas in a private audience to determine how well our imports would be received. We were to stay in the home of one of our local merchants, and we anticipated good accommodations.

As we traveled from the port up to the villa we could see elephants working in the fields. These were dwarfed elephants, not the great war steeds of the Indus and Phoenicia. They were scarcely taller than our horses, and kept for their endurance in building log enclosures for livestock markets for which Syracuse was the chief center of the Empire. Here in Syracuse and in Malta they were bred for their size, and were the gentlest of beasts.

I remembered the stories of the Greeks bringing the great beasts against Jerusalem during the Maccabean revolt,

133

and they were still remembered in legend laying siege to the city, but here they were treated almost like dogs, not war machines.

"Mother," I spoke. "Do you think we could convince Herod to let us have an elephant in Tiberius?"

"That would be a hard doing, Salomé," spoke Herodias. "He prefers to breed horses and trade silk, not beasts of burden and ivory. Do you have any idea how much those beasts eat?"

"But they don't seem to be taking more than a horse would eat in hay. I wonder if they need anything special to keep them small?" I replied.

"I will inquire, perhaps a breeder knows," observed Herodias. "One never can anticipate what use it might be."

I think my interest in animals started at that time. These beasts were exotic, certainly not the sheep, camels, and horses of Galilee. Learning their history enabled me to watch markets of Indian goods as well as Persian. One never knew when fashion, or friendship, would change and a new trade route would be needed.

I thought of Shaqilath and the Lion Court at Petra again. The Nabateans were the gateway for both Han and Indian traders, and they were friends of Rome, not vassals, a unique position in the Empire, where all other kingdoms were under the iron heel of the legions. I wondered how long it would be before I could write her. The questions in my mind were endless. "I must talk to Georgio alone," I thought. Perhaps he could send word.

The Jewish families of Syracuse dated back more than 500 years. When Israel was restored under Cyrus, many Jews had already settled in other lands, and though they knew that Judah had been restored, they had already put down roots and had no desire to move, but instead to trade with the families who returned, bringing with them, at that point, the friendship of both Persia and Assyria.

Many years had not changed those families, and they retained ties to Persia, and Babylon, despite all the Roman Empire tried to enforce. Syracuse, and the whole island of Sicily, were often at odds with Roman policy, and worked behind the scenes. If you wanted anything done to anybody, you could find someone in Syracuse to accomplish it.

I kept my eyes and ears open, and listened carefully at the factor's audience, as this time I was openly invited to listen.

"Aretus' factors are shrewd, your Excellency," spoke the factor. "Though you are at war in Judaea and Galilee, he is careful to treat you as a favored customer abroad. Our fees for guides for the caravans from the Indus and Mogadishu have been lower than in years."

"Does he take our coinage?" queried Antipas, "I had heard rumor he was only taking drachmas."

"From us he will take whatever comes to hand, drachmas, sesterces, even Persian coins," continued the factor. "He knows that Galilee is a crossroads, and that you never know which money will be used. The money changers have been doing a brisk business. We are expanding and may need to set up a new bank in Cyrene to take the lending offices."

"Now I understand Cyrene's worry," reviewed Antipas. "Your largesse is causing trouble in their city. We are expanding our banking, and that expansion is seen by our competitors as a direct insult to the non-Jewish quarters of the city. Be very careful, success in one city does not necessarily translate to good policy in another. Alexandria may be a better choice. Our families have been influential there for thousands of years, and Cleopatra helped to put my father on his throne. We do not forget. What news of Lugdunum?"

"The villa is being built, your Excellency. Archelaus' old architects have picked a site well watered and have set aside a hillside for your compound. Will you be inspecting it soon? The kitchens and calidarium are almost finished."

"I hope to go there once my business in Capri is complete," Herod spoke, calculating rapidly. "Perhaps two months."

"I will send word by courier ship, then," concluded the factor. "The builders will work overtime to have the private quarters ready for your arrival," spoke the factor.

"The reception hall may still not have a roof by then," he chuckled, "but you will have a place to receive guests."

I contemplated this news. A home in Lugdunum? I knew that the Herods maintained quarters in almost every area of the Empire, but had not realized that we were building a new home in Gaul.

"Mother, did you know of this?" I whispered to Herodias.

"Antipas and I have discussed the possibility. We know there is trouble in the Galilee, and if his plans within plots within treaties do not work as he would hope, this gives us a place to escape. He speaks to his factors as if this is simply an expansion into Gaul, but he never leaves himself without a retreat. Listen carefully to the next visitor, as she is expected."

A woman in heavy veils was guided into the hall and the hall was cleared of all the normal courtiers. I was intrigued. What could she bring that would require such secrecy, and why would I be admitted into this conclave.

"Pandora," spoke Antipas, "what a pleasure to see you."

"That is the name I have chosen for this occasion, your excellent majesty."

"I understand you bring me a gift, an appropriate name for the occasion. A box of troubles no doubt."

"You did pay me well to do my profession, do not squabble over niceties, your Excellency. I keep quiet and ensure the silence of your enemies."

"Does the Cretan ambassador sleep well then?"

"He slumbers well enough not to be wakened for at least a week. You did not ask me to give him to Persephone."

"Lady Death's embraces will have to wait. I simply needed him not to be awake while I steal a course of favors out of his entourage. If he is not aware, he cannot be blamed."

"Then my box of dreams pleases you?"

"Well placed, my friend. Your fee is placed with the usual factor under vintage wines. The Syracuse vineyards produced a very heady brew that year."

"Several guests will be sleeping for a while, I did not single out the ambassador."

"It is well, then. My escort will see you out?"

"No, your Excellency. If you do not see me leave, then I was not here."

Herod chuckled, "guard, please bring in our next visitors."

While the next visitors, several farmers and a cobbler, were led in, the woman lost her way in the entourage.

The visitors bowed low, "Ave Herod," they spoke. They also bowed toward we women, an unusual honor.

"I hear the summer wheat is close to harvest," spoke Antipas.

"It is, your majesty," spoke one farmer." and we are about to plow a new crop of barley. Sicily is so mild we have three harvests a year."

"Do the harvest beasts work well for you, then?"

"You bought well, your majesty. They do the work of four horses or a team of oxen and do not tire easily," spoke the second farmer.

"My daughter Salomé has expressed interest in one. Would they do well in Galilee?"

The third farmer spoke up, and it was clear that the others gave him deference. "The winters are mild there, it is true, but they are beasts that prefer warmer weather. Philadelphia or Trachonitis for the winter, but the summers they could live in Caesarea Phillipi," the farmer spoke.

"As they are small elephants, they will not eat more than a horse, and they can live on straws and grasses that a horse cannot digest."

I smiled, and dazzled the poor farmer. I took a coin off my headdress and tossed it to him.

"You have a talent for pleasing a young woman."

The farmer stuttered. "Your highness. I-I-I."

"I pay for quality, and I want a breeding pair."

"What will you name them, your highness, it is your privilege."

"Since I seem to have been wandering in legends, what is the name of the monster of the rocks north of here. The one with snaky arms."

"Scylla, and her mate Charybdis, the whirlpool."

"Done. I know they are gentle beasts, but I am not, and it will keep me mindful. When can I meet them?"

"The beasts breed slowly, and though we have a young bull ready, the doe elephant is not mature enough for another six months."

"We will be returning before the winter, I have heard, by six months they should be old enough to travel."

"It will be done, your highness."

The farmers retreated and the cobbler was brought forward. Herod laughed, "I need new boots, my good man. I hear that it is newest fashion in Rome and Capri."

The cobbler blanched. "I can make you good soldier's boots sir, you want them to wear. I don't make dancing shoes."

"Can you make them black?"

"Please, sir, I do not wish to insult the Emperor's favorite, brown, or blue, or calf skin, but not black."

"You are wise. I wish to appear my best to the Emperor, not be an insult. How fares Tiberius?"

"I am simply a cobbler, sir, and it is not my place to judge."

"You may speak freely here. The ears of the court are not in our villa."

"He is old, your majesty, and much dissipated. He has flashes of wisdom, but he is paying no attention to Rome. There are many enemies, and many of them in his own household. He has always judged his household and his servants fairly, but he is now under a bad influence."

"How do you know these things, a simple cobbler," spoke Antipas.

"Soldiers pay no attention as I fit them for boots. I listen as they laugh, and jibe, and complain. We make the best boots here in Syracuse, so I was asked to make a very special small pair of black boots. The man who wore them was small, but his personality filled the room. His eyes are squinty, sharp, and malevolent. I kept my mouth pursed and full of pins so that I would not be tempted to talk back."

"I am fortunate that you are my cobbler, then, I would not wish to be misled," observed Antipas.

"No, your majesty, I have been told that you listen to servants, where others do not, and that this has kept you alive in very trying times."

"I am harsh, and cruel, and given to temper, all true, and yet I listen to my servants and favorites more than others. My father was a violent man, and he did not listen to his household. That will not be my mistake."

Herodias and I glanced at one another. How much of all of our doings did Antipas know, and how much not. Were all of us spiders weaving a common tapestry, or would we be tangled like moths and left to dry?

The court ended and we were led to the women's quarters.

"Mother, who was that woman 'Pandora'?"

"I have seen her unveiled only once," Herodias spoke, "and that was because I was in a hall unobserved. She changes her clothes and face and appearance as quickly as an actor. She has at least five names that I have heard. She is a strega, a dealer in potions."

"A poisoner, then?"

"Bluntly, yes. But not always poison. She is a brewer and an apothecary. She knows that a little will soothe, a lot will kill, and the most potent weapon is misdirection. It has kept her alive. She is from Gaul, which is where Antipas first encountered her, visiting my mother. Archelaus, his brother, was insane, but he knew how to persuade. A draft here, a potion there, convinced his enemies that he was shrewd, even when he was simply mad. You may need her in the future."

"I . . . what?"

"Our life in Galilee rests on a knife edge, and any weapon we can use for misdirection, I fear, must be used. Herod had a sleeping draft given to the Cretan ambassador so that he would not be able to bid on some rather fine spices from India. We are trying every way we can to be prepared."

"The king of Petra's armies are getting stronger every day and I fear for our safety. We are staying on his good side away from Judaea, but my existence is every day an insult to him. My ambition was to be in the center of power, and Antipas seemed the best way out of Judaea and into the Empire, but it has cost us dearly."

"Then my father?"

"Your father is a wise man, and has stayed in Rome, away from the troubles of Judaea. I could have had a quiet life, if not an adventurous one, had I stayed with him. Now it is full of cobwebs, and silk, and excitement, but I wish you to be safe. That is why I brought you on this voyage. You must see all sides of our life, the good and the bad, and right now, there is much evil, and you have been sheltered. I will not make that mistake again. I will teach you every tool I know, the passwords, the market speech, the tailors to trust, the weavers to shun. But you will find your own voices, and mine, I fear, will soon fall silent."

She suddenly laughed. "Now get out of the court clothes, and into something heavier. We must go see an elephant."

"You are serious?"

"Yes, you must meet Charybdis properly if you are to be trusted."

Taking a guard with us, we inquired which fields were worked by elephants. The chariot ride was smooth and I remarked on the roads.

"These are some of the oldest roads of the Empire, your excellency," spoke the guard. "The workers dig ten feet down to the bedrock, and build up layers of rock and earthwork before laying down the paving stones. This road has been ridden by more than three generations of horses, laid down in my grandfather's day under the old Republic, and is still as new as the day it was built."

Both the threshers and the plowmen were out today. The threshers would go through the fields systematically piling up the shafts, gathered by the gleaners behind them into bundles.

Once the gleaners had passed, and all was stubble, the plowshares, dragged by elephants, would turn over the soil for the next planting. In this way, three crops would be yielded, the early wheat, the summer millet, the fall barley.

Syracuse was unique in using elephants for this labor, at least within the Empire, though I heard that elephants were the chief builders in India.

We arrived at the elephant compounds and were introduced to the keeper. A mahout had been assigned to the young bull, and he would be traveling back with us in a few months. He was a young man, barely in his teens, younger than I, and was very thin.

"Vishnu, her highness Salomé Alexandra," introduced the keeper.

"Namaste" spoke Vishnu, bowing with his hands folded together.

"He blesses the God within you," spoke the keeper. "His family has kept elephants for a thousand years and he speaks their language."

"Their language, they are intelligent?" I responded in awe.

"Elephants are the wisest animals on earth," spoke Vishnu. "They remember their keepers and those who are kind to them even when years have passed. I have been taught their speech from infancy. What is the name you have given my young bull?"

"Charybdis," I replied.

"Yes, of course, the whirlpool god. You will laugh at this, please stand back." He led the young elephant to the bathing pool to be washed and we stood at a distance. The elephant reached down his nose and sucked a great deal of water, spraying it in all directions, like a fountain.

"A good name, I see," I laughed. "He drains the water like a whirlpool and then blossoms forth like a flower."

"Namaste, Charybdis," Vishnu bowed toward the elephant.

"Namaste, indeed," I responded.

"He will know his name when you return, your highness," Vishnu spoke. "I hope our companionship will be a pleasure to you."

We returned to the villa laughing at the elephants to find Antipas quite anxious. He smiled, but it seemed forced. "We must leave in the morning, I have received troubling news, and must be prepared. I am not certain whether I will be praised or castigated at court, and either way makes me nervous. I want to know that the two of you are safe."

Our night was spent repacking our household so we arrived weary to the ships to finish our journey to Capri, and the court of Tiberius.

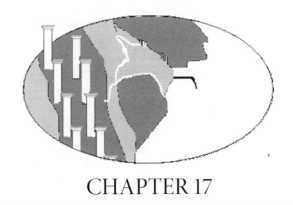

CHAPTER 17

Capri

I will never forget the fog. It sank into my bones and chilled my clothes. We had arrived late at night after a storm, and even the lighthouses were faint. The clanging of bells were all that kept our boatswain from the rocks. Capri is a very tall island, with many caves, and several harbors, but all were shrouded in ghostly shapes as we pulled up to the docks. We had come into the smaller harbor Capri Piccolo and were due to be ascending to Mount Tiberius in the morning.

The road through town was mysterious, one column disappearing before another came forward, as if a procession of the silent dead went by. The scene remains in my memory, even when other happier moments have faded. The road turned this way and that, with the horses and carriers barely able to keep from slipping off the side of the road. The rain made the surface slippery, and no one was willing to rush for fear of an accident.

Villa Jovis, Tiberius villa to Jupiter, set high above the city of Capri at the very peak of the mountain, had become the seat of Roman government as Tiberius had become terrified of rebellion.

He kept to himself, and was rumored to have riddled the foundations of his palace with galleries descending to the sea as an escape and to hide his passions. However, he would, on occasion, invite "friends of the Emperor" to private hearings.

Therefore, Antipas was beside himself at his upcoming hearing. He called and dismissed servants a dozen times looking for just the right blend of austerity and polish. I was dressed in the silk he could not wear, and my mother was dressed in the purples of a Grecian matron. She had been to the palace before with my father, but this was the first occasion with Antipas.

We spent the morning in preparation. The fog of the night before remained dank, and it was easier to stay indoors until we were escorted up the mountain. We drank warmed wine and waited impatiently for the clouds to lift.

Around noon, the combination of fire and sun cleared the city and we were able to look out on the magnificent harbor. Our quarters were set back on the hillside so that we could see the full arches of both harbors, between which nestled the city of Capri. Hundreds of pillars—the ghosts of my dreams—were set in lines in every direction, forming long promenades full of markets. The sea was like sapphires in the sun, and boats filled the harbor.

We were to be presented on three occasions: once at Augustus' villa, the Sea Palace, second, at Villa Jovis, where we were housed, and third, the formal judicial court also at Villa Jovis. The succession of events would allow us to meet all the current palace hangers-on, and, Antipas hoped, allow him to form a clearer opinion of what he would be facing.

My eyes searched out my uncle Agrippa, who had come to our quarters to escort us to the first reception. Had it been six months since I had seen him? His red hair clearly marked him a member of our family, and he and Antipas could have been twins, but his face was unlined, and did not hold the scowl of a fox for which Antipas was often mocked. Agrippa was open-handed, and was known, even as the youngest of the Herods, for his wisdom, honesty, and generosity, often to the point of recklessness.

Agrippa smiled, "We have many cousins in Syria, why do you seek a patron in Rome?"

"She must learn the role of rule from someone who does not have the prejudices of Galilee. Women are not used to public spaces there, and my daughter has a rare gift of perception."

"I will think on this. Meanwhile, I will speak to Georgio about which families to introduce you to, particularly the women of station. We will leave for the Sea Palace in an hour, and that reception will be an occasion to be seen."

The Sea Palace had a garden that looked to have been constructed by giants. Great bones from some ancient creatures, seeming carved of living rock, were erected, making one believe that someone had found the Cyclops who were supposed to have erected the standing stones that were found throughout the Empire. I could not seem to walk a single step without wandering into legend. Whether these were great horses, or the bones of men, I could not tell, but they were huge beyond any creature I had seen walking on land. "Good uncle, what are these great bones?" I spoke to Agrippa gently.

"They were found in the bedrock when Augustus' palace was erected. Legend has grown up that these are the bones of dragons, the last of their kind, who died long before any men came here."

"I wander in dreams, my uncle. Do legends come to life?"

"In this place, many fantasies seem to take living shape. But you are now a young woman of station, and I must fulfill my duties to your Mother." Agrippa took my arm and escorted me to an old woman. She had the look of the Herods but the red hair was now striped with grey and she wore it up, gathered into a regal bun. He bowed low and spoke, "Mother, I wish to introduce you to your granddaughter. Salomé, your grandmother, Queen Berenice of Syria."

"Nonsense," said Berenice, at once putting me at ease. "Do not be so openly ambitious. My husband Archelaus is dead, and his lands are now in the hands of Pontius Pilate. They name me Queen out of courtesy, for marrying him, but all the land I have is in Vienne, Lugdunum, and in Rome, nothing but a single villa in Syria." She stopped with the lecture, and turned to me, "Salomé, I knew you when you were only two, just before Archelaus died, but you moved to Galilee before we could ever know each other. Welcome to the family quarrel." She patted my cheek affectionately.

Agrippa chuckled, but then turned, and asked me for his arm. Antipas had now joined us, and they now escorted all we women together. Agrippa with his mother on his arm, Antipas with Herodias, and I, unexpectedly, coming in as if they were escorting me, the youngest, and apparently the one being most carefully presented, myself, his niece, Salomé Alexandra, Princess of Galilee.

I did not expect the attention by which I was now surrounded. Each family of Rome was represented at court by its patron and its matrona, respectively the head of household and the chief female, whether mother or sister.

The patron was represented in the Senate if landed, or if a newer family in the House of Plebians, still containing families that had been around Rome for more than 300 years but had not bought themselves into the state houses. The matronas formed a sub-society of their own, and these were the women to whom I was introduced.

The Julians, the Augustines, and now the house of Gaius Claudius had many branches. Tiberius' daughter, Procula,

Pilate's wife, was already known to us, so the matrona we were first introduced to was her aunt, Antonia, the niece of Emperor Augustus, daughter of Octavia and Mark Antony, called Augusta, her Wisdom, for her rare perceptions. Now an aging matriarch, she had been the favorite of Julia Claudia, the third wife of the Emperor, Procula's mother, and had quarters of her own at Villa Jovis. Agrippa left us in her care for the moment.

Antonia wore many jewels, and carried herself like a courtesan. She spoke softly, "I can understand why you have sought me out. Procula was Tiberius' child of love, not legitimized until after her mother's death. Tiberius was determined to settle the question of Judaea peaceably, and as Empress Julia was Jewish, he thought to marry her daughter to Pilate, the new Procurator. He sought me out for advice, as the one who had taken Procula in when her mother had died. Pilate was hot tempered, but she seemed to be a match, and was willing to follow him to the ends of the earth. I have often wondered if another young woman might come into my care."

I was amazed. Here was the last remaining matriarch of the Augustines, willing to listen to someone from a far province, and she knew my father, my mother, their estrangement, and if anyone might know who might be my best protector, she would at least have the connections to make it happen.

"We have the family of the Herods and Hyrcanus in Galilee, the chieftains of Syria—Agrippa knows many of their princes. I know you are Jewish, but this will not be a barrier to a good marriage. Many of your people are well known here in Rome, even if they are neither Senators nor Plebians."

She smiled and her aged face showed many lines. "Many minor houses may have a patron who may be a good choice. Has your father chosen anyone?"

"I have not thought on it, your Wisdom. I had only hoped to escape from Antipas."

"We would be surprised if you did not, your mother has been most forthcoming about your recent troubles. You are not the first young woman to have a favorite murdered to escape a bad situation."

"But I felt so alone."

"Though not quite as openly, I do not know a single woman of station who has not had to contemplate just such an action, whether publicly or privately when she is suddenly out of favor— or as in your case, too much in favor. You are only the most recent, but you will not be the last."

"Are there no good kings, then?"

"They are rare as hen's teeth. Agrippa is one of the few that I hold no marks against—yet, though I have heard recent rumors. He has not yet succumbed to madness. Not all hope is lost. Berenice, you know your son well, does he treat women fairly?"

My grandmother Berenice's hair shone like bronze in the hall. "My son is one of the few I can consult with. He keeps his ears open, and his mouth shut. Men gossip as much as women, but they cover it in bravado. I have learned to listen to every merchant, every courtier, though sometimes their opinions are so wild that they actually are truth. I have heard gossip that Bat Mara, your dance instructor, is now healed, is that true?"

"Your ears are long in Galilee, who told you," spoke Herodias, who has not seen her mother in several years.

"Georgio, who is the best misdirecting gossip I have ever known."

I chuckled. Georgio seemed to have been involved in palace intrigue in three courts now. Who would have thought it?

"Now about your marriage," spoke Berenice, "I know of one Herod who would be safe, and that Antipas would not object to. He is in Rome, now, staying with your father."

"Who would that be? I thought I knew all of the Herods."

"He is Herod Philip," spoke Berenice, "the same name as your father, Salomé—and you know him. He was the last of the children born of Salomé Cleopatra, your great-aunt, just before she was killed. He is often away from Galilee, as he travels with his court throughout Syria, but he remembers you fondly. You were born the year he celebrated his founding of Caesarea Phillipi, and you grew up as a toddler in his home. He is a tetrarch, the same rank as your stepfather, and a closer friend of Rome than Antipas, so Claudius can find no fault in him," she advised. "And," she chuckled, "he is currently in Rome, staying with your father." She turned to Antonia. "Your Wisdom, would you agree?"

Augusta Antonia counted off on her fingers. "One, he is a Herod, so keeping the name in the family. Two, he is known in Rome to be loyal to the Empire—better than Antipas by far. Three, he is far enough away, even in Syria, that you will not be blamed if something goes wrong with Antipas' hopes."

At this my ears perked. Did Augusta Antonia know something that would change my fate again?

"Antipas is not honored in Rome. Tiberius has always liked him, and can find no fault in him, as he is just as cruel and rapacious, though Tiberius keeps his secrets in his dungeons. Here in Capri, at the Emperor's court, they match minds, so it will take a great deal to remove him, but evidence is mounting. Rome is independent of Tiberius, and the Senate has a way of choosing scapegoats—and Antipas may be the keystone to a wider rebellion. You, my young one, must be protected. Herodias, do you anticipate what is coming?"

"I am not surprised," responded my mother. "Antipas is my husband, but I protect myself as much as I am able. I was trained, like you, to be a matrona, and so always in charge of my own household, even when my husband goes to war. I will stay with him, regardless, I have no choice, but I would hope to find a way of escape for Salomé."

A way of escape, I pondered. I was not sure whether I should rely upon this gathering of harpies, or not. I had thought myself unique, driven by circumstances to an unlikely revenge, and yet here, in the midst of the Empire, I was considered ordinary, and not particularly out of place. How should I choose my way? I wished for Bat Mara's serenity, yet I knew that I would have to find my own peace. I wondered if her storyteller might have something to say. The poison of the waters now bubbled in my own soul, and the wine tasted bitter.

I turned to Augusta Antonia. "Your Wisdom, though my situation is far from unique, I still feel unclean from having brought a person who told the truth to his death."

Antonia paused, "you are a young innocent, and that is healthy. If you always think that you are alone, however, it will drive you mad. Our stories, like yours, are filled with lessons of women who are driven beyond their limits. You must learn to set your limits high. Kindness is rare when you are a ruler, savor those moments."

"Are there other young women in your charge?" I queried.

"You come of a line of strong women, Salomé. Berenice and Herodias have made good marriages here in Rome, and I have guided them when I am able. If you find yourself in a strange city, seek out the Vestals, they will be able to help you."

"The Vestals, but they are perpetual virgins, what could they know of my situation?"

"Not so, from the age of 12 to the age of 18, many young women seek out their halls for protection. Even if betrothed at birth, they need to be trained in poise, respect, and the ways of women. Only a few stay within their halls, most become matronas, but always remember the temples that taught them," spoke Antonia.

"The company of women is one of the few places that the men cannot enter," she continued, and the one law we kept from the Etruscans was their sacred precincts."

"But Vesta is Roman."

"The hearth has been kept holy, whether the woman within is Demeter, Kore, Hestia, or Shekinah."

"Shekinah? Your wisdom, what do you know of our faith."

"Young Jewish women seemed to be drawn to houses of power, and have had an influence in the Empire far beyond their numbers. Conversations between women raised in your Temple have been particularly enlightening. The presence of the power of creation first in the home and then in a man's world has always been the way of things. Scholars are not the only ones to tell stories."

"Then you keep the same customs."

"Similar, though not quite the same. The temple of Vesta performs the same function your laws call for, a place for widows and the aged to always find food. The laws of the Empire provide sanctuary in her temple, and the doors are never shut. Only at great intervals have the Vestals risen up and closed the sanctuary."

"How do you know such things?" I wondered.

"When Empress Julia was pregnant with Procula, I sought out the Vestals. Though she was Tiberius' favorite, he has his whims, and his favorites, and I wanted her to be secure. Only when he offered to legitimize her child, whatever its sex, was I willing to return to his side in the last months before her birth—and stayed with her until her death. Now

I am Augusta Antonia, the matriarch, not something I ever expected in this troubling time. I see many things and keep Tiberius informed, despite his new favorites."

She laughed. "Julia was notorious, and Tiberius caused a great scandal when he was forced to marry her, and divorce his wife of many years. Augustus was determined to see her safe as his only natural daughter, regardless of her history. She was now a widow, and he did what he could to provide for her, requiring Tiberius to marry her as the price of his adoption.

My uncle, Emperor Augustus, doted on me, and I could do no wrong in his eyes, but it was very difficult to have him so abuse Tiberius. I have remained a friend of Tiberius, and so guided him to officially legitimize Procula, but I have not always been successful in my conversations. Claudius, Tiberius' son, does not like me, but in an act of defiance, Tiberius keeps me returning to Capri on a regular basis, though I have a house in Rome. He is afraid to venture from the island, but I hear everyone, and entertain all sides. I am careful, but he has many enemies, and needs an eye that can see them."

I was bemused. Here was an aging woman, who had a life of court and scandal behind her, trying to protect me, a young woman from the edge of exile—what a rare gift.

"So the temple women will protect me?" I queried.

"If you are ever without protectors, do not hesitate to seek them out," Julia continued." You are gifted in finding ways not to be seen, and something tells me that you may need some connections into the women's courts in years to come."

How often I have pondered this advice. Women live their own lives, circumscribed by laws, customs, and communication barriers, but Empress Julia and Augusta Antonia had somehow overcome them all, even if Antonia felt she lived her life on a knife edge.

"What can I do to be prepared for marriage?" I asked my advisors.

"Learn all you can before you marry, afterward you may not be allowed."

"Make sure to have your dowry and your own property—a young widow is never an easy thing to be," interjected Berenice.

At this Augusta Antonia interrupted. "If you marry Herod Phillip, you will need to have a ceremony both by court and by custom, by Roman and Jewish law," she spoke.

"Be sure to get both a ketuba, and a Roman decree of marriage. You will be consort in a Roman province, and it is best to have your rights protected by Rome. I have a flamen who can walk you through the wedding vows of a Roman matrona. I am sure that Bat Mara knows several women whose ketubas you can read. She is an elder of many years wisdom."

The ketuba, the marriage contract, was a matter of some negotiation, as Jewish women, unlike many others, other than the matronas of Rome, were expected to be able to survive on the dowry they brought to the marriage if, at extremis, it fell apart, or they were suddenly widowed. Women, sometimes, could hold a trade, particularly if their husbands were scholars, and therefore bringing no funds to the household to feed the children.

The book of Proverbs was full of examples of virtuous women who invested in the market, wove cloth, and had their own honor before the people. Thank the Holy One that a woman was not expected to fulfill all the requirements of Proverbs or she would never rest. The weavings of women seemed to be included even in this negotiation of a marriage contract.

I had learned from my mother that the one ruling queen of the Maccabees, Salomé Alexandria, her grandmother's grandmother, after whom I was named, had created the ketubah.

She was the wife of Simon Judah Aristobolus, the King of the Maccabees. When he died, she married Alexandra Jannai, his brother, a man 20 years her junior. Judaea was at war, and Alexander left her to rule the country, and when he also died, he shocked everyone by naming her his choice of heir.

At 64, she took her life experience and left a stamp of justice. When she recalled the Sanhedrin as a ruling body, she created the marriage contract to ensure that a woman could survive alone. She was known as a ruler of peace, who used diplomacy and statecraft rather than weapons of war to survive in the turmoil as the Romans and the Greeks fought over the small nation of Judaea.

And now the man I was to marry was known as a man of peace. Would he treat me gently, and teach me the ways of statecraft like my ancestor Salomé, or would I have to use guile, like my mother, to survive in the family of the Herods?

CHAPTER 18

Tiberius

I thought I had become immune to pain until I saw Tiberius. He was old, and tired, and fearful. I was seated with the women at court, in an area reserved for those high-born, and as this was an official hearing, I was forbidden to speak, though I might observe. Tiberius walked haltingly, as if something was weighing him down. He was older than Antipas by about 10 years, but he looked much older. He was balding, as many of the Roman men, and he tried to carry his weight of authority, but because I was observant, I could see that he had become watchful, and world weary. Among his entourage was a much younger man, with high black leather boots, who seemed to strut as he walked.

Through whispers, I asked Antonia after him, and she spoke, "that is Claudius, but all the soldiers call him Caligula 'little boots' from those narrow black boots of his. He is said to wear them even when he sleeps." It is best you say very little to him, as he has a quick temper, and if you think

Tiberius dotes on your stepfather, his affection for Caligula knows no bounds."

"I hear screams at night, even from my quarters, and there are chambers under the palace down into the cliffs that are said to hold runaway slaves, particularly young women, that are treated most shamefully. There are rites, rumors have it, that involve young boys in particularly painful positions, and though I have seen almost everything in the games, even I keep my silence."

I am fearful for Rome when he becomes Emperor, but I must keep my mind focused on my immediate safety."

"When will court begin?" I queried.

"After Tiberius has brought all of the patrons before him to receive homage. Though he is not revered as his ancestors, his adopted son is completely consumed in requiring honors to be shown to the point of worship. He hears voices, it is said, and they make him to be a God. I don't hold much to that, but the forms must be followed, or Caligula has temper tantrums that spill over into court. Tiberius has become more and more timid, and dismissed his best general, Sejanus, to Rome. The Senate has remained in Rome, and they follow Sejanus, who seems to be playing all sides, favoring Tiberius one week, Caligula another."

"Tiberius was wise in his early years, and still manages to make good decisions, even if it has to be sorted through the mirror of his favorite. But you know how that is, your court is not without its own customs."

"So this hearing is just a mock trial?"

"Not at all," Antonia continued, "but forms must be observed. You have a Greek court, a Roman court, and a Jewish court side by side in your country, and one often doesn't speak to the other, does it?"

I had to concede her point on this one. I had seen for my own eyes that Persian law, Greek, Hebrew custom, and all other reviews were subsumed to the power of the iron boots of Rome, and here those boots were little and black.

I watched for Antipas and Agrippa to be called forth.

As Agrippa spent more of his time in Rome than in Galilee or Syria, he rose when called and spoke the proper phrases. Antipas followed suit, as he came to the court about once a year, but was not as familiar with daily changes in custom.

Agrippa was given leave to speak. "My uncle Antipas has ruled long and well in Galilee, o Emperor, and has kept back the depredations of the Persians for some time. However, I have reason to believe that some of the battles may have been mockery for the sake of Rome, and he is gathering his own armies. Daily the garrisons in the Decapolis grow larger, and they are not all Roman, but gathered from Persia, Dacia, and Syria. I fear he is growing a private army without your knowledge, hidden away in the fortresses of the Dead Sea."

"Antipas, what say you? Why is your army grown so great that you do not depend on Rome for protection?" spoke Claudius, "are not our armies good enough for you, or do you seek to be king?"

"Your excellency," spoke Antipas quietly, holding himself erect, "I protect what is my own from the armies to the South. King Aretus is still annoyed that I sent his daughter home, and I must defend myself."

"But why do you not call upon Rome, there are garrisons in Syria, and beyond the Jordan?"

"Yes, your excellency," he again spoke softly, "but Rome is far away, and we are close at hand, and the armies are aimed at me, not at Rome."

"An argument we have heard before. Agrippa keeps us well informed."

At this Tiberius interrupted. "I hear you use your designation as 'friend of the Emperor' for trade of your own. Is this true?"

"Emperor, my factors have kept you aware of my desire to move the Persian trade route to Galilee, and that will only keep them more under the eye of Syria, a faithful Roman province than Nabataea, which is independent of Rome. You, yourself, told me that the threads of the merchants, which you control, form a network throughout the Empire. I only thought to bring it into closer ties to your factors."

"In that you are wise," spoke the Emperor. "I find no fault in that. I expect to hear from you that your factors will weave for me, as well as for you. I am particularly fond of the gold threads from Babylon. I expect a bolt by the end of the year. See to it—as a surety—Herod."

"Claudius," he spoke to Caligula testily. "Is there something else? I had feared you had something greater to report than a few soldiers and some merchants who are squabbling. Herod Antipas seems to be the wisest person to rule his own province, even as a Tetrarch. He sees where we do not. Is there something else? Are there other issues that you wish to discuss?"

Claudius Caligula pondered. "Antipas counters well, but he still bears watching. He does not often come to court, so we do not know what he is doing. He has holdings in Gaul, in Cilicia, in Syracuse, and in Cyrene. Was this all your doing?"

"My friends prosper when they follow my lead," responded Antipas. One of your own uncles lost his villa on a bet with you over a bolt of cloth—silk cloth, I might add."

Antipas continued, this time much more stridently, and his temper was flaring. "Should I not prevent a useless gamble, and secure it more closely to myself? The house of Herod and the house of Claudius retain many of the same factors."

"Antipas, be calm, I am still your friend, spoke Tiberius unexpectedly. "I hear you bring a letter from Cyrene," spoke the Emperor, returning to the trial.

"Yes, Emperor. My factors are spread throughout the Great Sea and I hear unrest against my people. Where we Jews are few in number, we have often invested wisely, and that, for some reason, seems resented. Your family is small, but your holdings are large, should not our gens be welcomed?"

"Agrippa, what say you to this? Do you concur?"

"Yes, Emperor, and your excellency Claudius," he spoke. "I, too, have holdings in Tarsus, where we are welcomed, and in Cyrene, where there is growing resentment. I have sought marriage alliances for my children, would this help to seal a broken trust?"

"I am aware of your daughter Berenice, but she is quite young. Claudius, is there someone you would recommend to keep an eye on the situation?"

"I would suggest Felix, a commander in Rome, for Drusilla. This would seal a family tie, and ensure that we have eyes in Judaea."

"But she is only four, and she has already been promised to another!" Agrippa objected.

"And you would rather not have a centurion at your door, is that it?" spoke Claudius Caligula. "You know I favor you, but should things change in that regard, we must speak of this at a later time. She is still the best match."

"Well thought, Claudius, but I do agree with Antipas that prior arrangements must be honored. However, we do have Antipas. Antipas, what of your daughter, Salomé? Is she here among the women? Do they treat her well?"

"Your cousin Augusta Antonia has been most kind to take her under her wing. I trust that you, and she, can find a match suitable."

"The gens Claudius might consider it, but I have heard that you have a younger brother who has been without a wife for many years, and he travels often to Italy. Perhaps this will build trust between your family and ours. He is trained in Roman law and custom, and will seal our friendship more closely."

"Philip, is he well? He has kept himself away from the family."

"There is no illness, not that I can see," spoke Tiberius. "He attends the Senate with your older brother Herod Phillip—now why did your father name them both Philip?"

"The women name the children in my country, your majesty." In Hebrew, they have entirely different names, but one is named after Philip of Macedon, as my father was enamored of the Greeks, and when the second young boy was born, his half-brother was more than 12 years old. Philip the Elder has been advising Philip the Younger for years, and now the Elder is aged, and will need a matrona to run their combined household."

"I think we have found a match that will be suitable then," concluded the Emperor. "I trust you will be seeing him before you leave Italy?"

"Yes, it has been almost a dozen years since Salomé last saw her father, and it is time that she know him. Philip the Younger will then have an opportunity to meet his prospective bride in a court setting before the bans are issued."

"The house of Claudius will expect to preside over the Roman wedding then. A friend of the Empire must have the attention of the masses. Claudius, I leave this in your hands, and you know the Senate of Rome better than I do now."

I blanched. Claudius to arrange for my marriage? I looked at Antonia and she had a forced smile. "I think we can manage this, Salomé, "she spoke. "Caligula's mother can still persuade him in this. It is not as bad as you hear it."

The court continued, and Antipas was questioned closely on his factor's words about Cyrene, but the anxious moments when he seemed to be accused of treason had passed, for the moment. Herodias was nervous and watchful until the flamen pronounced the court done with a ritual hail to Claudius and an honoring of Tiberius as they swept from the room.

I shuddered. There was much more going on in this court between Agrippa and Antipas, as if an old wound had been festering. Agrippa seemed cordial, and smiling, but I could feel that he had the bite of the Herods in him, perhaps a ferret, not a fox, but not the innocent he had seemed.

"It seems you are bound to Rome, my daughter," spoke Antipas. "I have not seen my brothers in five years, and it is time you were reacquainted with your father, and your husband-to-be. You will be a matrona, and we must arrange for your householding. A Roman fosterage is not an easy life, and this is your first taste of the Roman court."

Agrippa spoke. "I have sent for my ship to take you to the Tiber. Herod Phillip will greet you at the port, so that you need never be afraid for your safety."

I thought to myself. Afraid for my safety? With the double-thinking of Antipas and Agrippa, what could I possibly expect? There was no safety in these men. I must hope for some signal that someone I knew would companion me.

Herodias spoke gently, "I have sent for Georgio to accompany us to Rome, he knows more languages and odd people that we need not be nervous. He was Herod Philip's servant before he became mine, and he will know what to do."

I breathed easier. Though Antipas had not made any untoward advances since the death of the Baptist, I was always careful never to be alone with him, though he kept me at his footstool whenever he held his own courts. Having Georgio as the household guard would keep all of us in good hands.

Augusta Antonia spoke. "Your grandmother Berenice will accompany you to Rome as she must meet with Sejanus, as she now runs Archelaus's old villa in Gaul. She was left to keep the peace. Having your grandmother with you should help you become accustomed to the markets, the theatre, and the sometimes long separations for a woman with a soldier or a diplomat as a husband. Your husband is well traveled, and he studies the customs of many lands."

At this I brightened. "He can tell me of Babylon? Bat Mara has told me so little."

"Yes," she spoke. "His holdings are near Damascus, held by King Aretus of Nabatea, so he trades with both Petra and Babylon. He will be able to educate you about customs in ways that Bat Mara has not seen in at least 10 years."

My mind was filled with visions of tapestries, with unusual plants and animals. I had seen camels and horses since my youth. I now had an elephant, but I had heard of river horses and strange spotted cats. Maybe the dragons of the Villa Jovis would come to life in thread.

I still remember that day, even more than 60 years later, a day of excitement as we gathered our belongings, and gossiped of the new sights we would see. Some truth was there, and many false expectations, but such are the threads of the Empire, leading one through the maze.

CHAPTER 19

Sukkot

We sailed into Pereia, the port of Rome, at first light. My father himself came to greet us in his chariot as the boat came into harbor. He bowed in greeting to Antipas, their red hair matching, though his had now grown thin with touches of grey. His smile was genuine as he took Herodias' hand and helped her to the landing.

"My brother has treated you well, I see," he spoke gently.

"I am content," she responded, though I knew she was far from rested.

"Your daughter, Salomé, Philip," Herodias indicated me.

"I am your servant, my father," I spoke as the ritual demanded.

"Nonsense, my daughter, you have the look of queens in you, the fairest princess of Galilee. You have the eyes of your mother, and the hair of the Herods. Do not be shy, I will need to hear all about your doings. I do not travel often anymore."

And I had feared this homecoming. This gentle man was my father, and though he and my mother were estranged, his eyes held a spark that seemed to light up the pier. What years I had lost. I hoped for a few years to learn his wisdom.

"You have been anticipated, my brother, my daughter, my nephew, my sister," spoke my father slowly, to ensure we understood his welcome. "There are horses for each of you, and a cart for your possessions. You have traveled more lightly than we had heard. Our villa is in Rome itself, as I have many duties. It is an hour's journey, so we will have an opportunity to speak as we ride."

"I have been studying for many years both the laws of Rome and the writings of our forebears. In many ways, they both have sought justice. In the days of the Republic, the Senate was made of volunteers, all the statesmen were fully engaged as farmers or in commerce, and met in a council of landholders. This state of affairs was very similar to the time of the Judges of Israel, when there was no king. Now, we have an Emperor, no longer elected on a yearly basis, but ruling for life. With a ruler you get taxes, and soldiers, and conflicting views of justice, very similar to Israel, even with Solomon the Wise." It was clear he was a philosopher.

"I am a client king of the Empire, my daughter" he spoke, ensuring my footing in the chariot. "though my holdings are very small, so I must learn the laws of the land to keep the peace. I have left factors and householders in place on my lands, held in trust, and I never travel anymore, so I am looking forward to hearing from you, Salomé, of your adventures. You must be trained in our ways, but I must also learn yours."

I stammered, "but I am not a ruler, what can I share with you?"

You," he spoke tenderly, "see a side of court I do not. Women in Israel have more rights than many, but even there they cannot be seen in court unless specifically called. You are unique in that you are appointed a witness. Not lightly do I hold my responsibility to train you and help your sharpen your skills of observation. Brother Antipas, you are losing a treasure."

"I agree with you, though not for another year, we must work on her patrimony together, as she has two fathers and neither of us will want her to come to harm."

We rode in silence for a space. This side of Antipas I had rarely seen, and I was most mistrustful. My father in contrast was kind, and could not have been more understanding. My change of fortune in only moments took my breath, and speech, away.

The sand of the harbor gave way to rocks and green hills. Pine trees gave way to oaks as the city of Rome came into view, the Capitoline dome shining in the distance. The road wound into an avenue overhung with trees. I was reminded of the road from Galilee to Caesarea, the lines of trees on the hilltops and very steep hills reminding me of home.

We had arrived in Rome in time for the first night of Sukkot. We were far from Galilee, yet the Jewish community was thriving in Rome. Several houses of prayer had booths outside, through which the stars could be seen.

The seven days of Sukkot, the harvest festival, were a respite from our many hurried days. The evenings would be deliberately spent rejoicing over a good harvest, and thoughts of trouble were kept in abeyance. I was here in Rome to spend time with my father, and apparently, my husband-to-be, so I was nervous, and needed time to think.

"Please," spoke Philip, "let me have the servants wash your feet. Change your clothes and we will eat under the sukkah—it is still your custom, is it not?"

Antipas nodded, "we do not often have time to rejoice in a land at war. Thank you for the reminder."

I remember stretching out my toes as I took off the sandals for the servants to wash my feet. The ache of miles was in my legs, and this simple act of gracious hospitality told me more than a thousand words of my welcome.

I threw off my outer garments and changed into a simple chiton, and veiled my hair. Mother did the same. Antipas took off his cloak, and changed into a Roman tunic, but he still looked very weary. Berenice transformed herself from an aging widow into a matron, touching her hair only here and there with henna as if the journey had but lightly touched her. She seemed younger than my mother though she was 20 years her senior.

As we entered the atrium, we found Philip, my father, now accompanied by a younger man, enough like him in his face to be his twin but with different hair. He bowed in my direction. "I have heard from your father than you were beautiful, but the favor is all mine to see. Your letters have preceded you so I know that we are to be betrothed this night, so I will not touch you, but accept your father's kiss as mine from afar."

I blushed. This gracious man, whom I expected to be almost tottering from the rumors, was a strong and vigorous man. He had the raven hair of his mother, Cleopatra of Jerusalem, and his beard was full. He wore the dreadlocks of a scholar. His strength would be needed in the days to come. I felt safer for the first time.

We gathered in the garden and I found, separate from the sukkah, a canopy had been prepared. My father smiled.

"Though the ketubah is to be written over the next year, we felt it best to be prepared. The times are dangerous and uncertain, and though you must leave us within the week, let this night be your welcome."

I felt nervous. From only a word from my mother, a rumor of a queen, and a letter from afar, I was to be engaged upon first arriving from a far province to a man I had never met, whom I could see could care for me. I bowed my head and grasped the necklace my mother had placed around my neck. Pulling myself erect, I swept back my hair and veil so that my father could see the scarcely felt silver chain.

The twinkle, or did I imagine it, was all the answer I needed to know that he knew of my mother's gift to him of her dearest possession, their only child.

"We are witnesses," spoke Herod Phillip, "to a joining of houses. Do the guardians of these to be joined assent by the laws of Rome?"

"By the laws of the tetrarchs and the laws of the land," spoke Antipas.

"By the will of the matronas, and the witness of the elders," spoke Herodias.

"By my will as the patron of this house of Herod, then the law is fulfilled. For this year and a day these two will write their ketubah together, that both the houses of Rome be secured and the honor of the Jews be satisfied."

Herod Phillip the Younger turned to me, grasped my hands in his, and kissed me on both cheeks, as between equals." He then let go, and said softly, "may the year be swift, beloved." We were now betrothed, and I was legally part of his household, though I would spend the next year apart.

The official announcement of bans would take place before the Senate, but the marriage would wait until we had finished writing our contracts.

My head was reeling, though I had only a sip of wine before the cup was crushed. My father saw my distress and gently sat me on a couch though he was careful not to be more than a support. Patience he wore like a cloak, something so unlike my stepfather.

As the evening meal ended, I was given a scroll from Galilee from Bat Mara. Apparently, Herodias had anticipated my need and inquired before she left Galilee for advice on a ketubah, the contract I should expect from my husband to protect me in case of sudden widowhood. The letter had been forwarded to Herod Philip and was now presented to me.

Her letter was startling, as it came with unusual news. I had always thought of Bat Mara as old, yet she was only 45, very close to my mother's, and now my husband's age. She had seemed aged from her continuous blood flow, and bent like an old woman in pain as long as it had continued. She walked with poise, but had seemed fragile. Her graying hair had always made me think of a grandmother, or an aging aunt.

Now her knowledge of a ketubah was colored by an unusual occurrence. She wrote to me in a bold hand, as she was an educated woman. "In the year 3792, at Rosh Hoshanah, I received a request that I thought never to have. A fisherman has asked me to marry him. Now, I who have been called Mara, the bitter sea, will take my birth name of Hannah, a woman who prayed for her son in such deep sighs that the priests thought she was drunk. But I am not drunk, and this life of mine has become a celebration."

"The man you know, as he was your guardian in Galilee whenever Antipas could not watch you. The fisherman Tobias, who was always the butt of so many jokes of the soldiers, knows what mockery I had to survive for the many years of my illness."

"He found the mageed's teaching so inspiring that he sought me out, feeling that the gift of healing had restored me to the virginity of my youth, and that guarding you has given us all the children we are likely ever to have. As I am working with him to write our ketubah I will give you all the advice you may need, from an old woman's point of view, very like the woman whose name you bear, the only ruling queen of Israel in her own right."

"The purpose of a ketubah is to spell out clearly your patrimony, whether or not your parents are living, a stipend and a surety to ensure your life without poverty in case your husband should die suddenly from any cause."

"Though you are marrying into your uncle's house, with the unrest in Rome, you cannot guarantee that he will live or die, so that it is best you are protected, both by the laws of Rome and the laws of the Jews. We are an unusual people, we Jews, and we are fortunate that our contracts are respected by the courts of Rome, and we usually judge our own unless it is a crime against a non-Jew."

"As a Jewish woman of station, I will be able to give you advice that you might not hear, even from your mother, as she chose to marry outside the custom.

"You are being careful and hope for a good guardian. Be careful, be watchful, and find someone you can trust in Rome as you trust me here in Galilee."

"You are marrying a man more than 20 years your senior, one who has many estates, and who will need a matrona of wisdom, who is trained in the laws of Rome, of Syria, and of Galilee."

"You must put off the childish ways, though never the watchful ways of your mother. Keep your hand in the marketplace, in the women's quarters, with the women's mysteries, as they will guard you when you least expect it."

"As part of your ketubah, expect a yearly sum to be set aside specifically in investment, if at all possible, in land to support you with produce, and with earnings from businesses with which you are familiar, such as the dyers of Tyre, and the olive groves of Jericho. You have opportunities that I have not had since I was a young woman in Babylon, so learn all you can, invest all you can of your own earnings. Represent your household well in the world, find factors of your own, ask Antonia about merchants you can trust, as though she cannot often leave Capri, she keeps her sources of news well paid. Seek out the Jewish women who have married Roman men, as your grandmother has done, and do not be afraid to learn from them."

"You are a woman, now, a girl who has seen much beyond her years, and you have a responsibility for the next generation of young girls around the palace. Keep your eye on your young cousin, Drusilla. She may be betrothed, but she has now become much more of a puppet than you."

"As you know your letters, teach your servants sufficient to keep accounts so that neither you nor they will be cheated by too shrewd a merchant—but you have a good bargaining instinct, I need not fear for that."

"But back to the ketubah. Your marriage is arranged, and you will learn to love the man who is chosen for you. The ketubah is surety for your safety, but is the beginning of a marriage of minds. Treat it so, learn how your husband thinks in the negotiations which are brought to bear for your welfare."

Much can be learned in what is not said, as much as in what is written. I look forward to your correspondence, and hope to see you by the turn of the Roman year, in January, as we hope you will be a witness at our wedding."

"The scribe Marcus will deliver this into your hands with all speed, my seal, Hannah, known as Bat Mara."

•   •   •

I pondered this news. More swiftly than scribes had the information sought me out. From Antonia to the doulas of Syria I had been given clues, as if being handed a new quest at each turn, a different turn at the loom, and now I was to weave my own tapestry.

My father smiled. "Bat Mara also addressed me, and explained her request. I give you leave to go once you have returned from Gaul."

My head was spinning. From a moment, and with a word, Antipas was no longer my patron, though I would continue to travel with him. My protection had suddenly changed from a tetrarch to a Senator, and there would be much to learn in all of my many households.

WHISPERS OF EMPIRE

Synopsis

Salomé is presented to the Senate at Rome and witnesses the death of Sejanus at a banquet. She journeys to Gaul to learn the craft of ruling from her grandmother, Berenice of Syria. She begins to find her own network of soldiers and merchants. In the space of a year she has grown to a young woman of station, and takes on the robes and veil of a Roman matrona, learning to spar with words as well as dance.

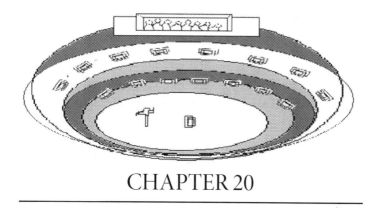

CHAPTER 20

The Senate

The week passed quickly. The fifth day of Sukkot coincided with the weekly meeting of the Senate, where Antipas, Agrippa, and both Herod Phillips were expected. My father Philip the Elder was a regular attendant at the Senate and had his own place in court. As a basilea (a client king) of a small province, he and Agrippa both attended the hearings regularly. As tetrarchs, my father and my husband-to-be could observe, but were not seated. Antipas felt slighted, Philip the Younger felt honored, such were the differences in their temperaments. The matronas of Rome had their place also, in a special gallery, though they could not succeed to an office. We women, neither Roman nor matronas, had no place at all, but this was a special occasion, and we were allowed, if veiled, to attend the hearings and listen with the matronas.

As Sejanus was in charge of the province of Gaul, we were expected in attendance at this meeting of the Senate at which Berenice would be questioned. Sejanus was the voice of the Emperor in Rome, as the most powerful general of the Empire, and so this was a signal honor.

Berenice, herself, would be called before the Senate, not an action lightly done. Once preliminary honors and the roll had been called, Sejanus spoke to the assembly. "Today we must hear from a queen in exile. The ethnarcy of Archelaus in Samaria has been disbanded some 20 years, and Pontius Pilate is now there as a ruler, but Archelaus' wife is still alive. She has petitioned for this hearing."

Agrippa, in his customary robes, held out his arm and escorted his mother to the plaza before the high seat. Berenice wore the blue of a Roman matron with a purple trim. Over this she had placed a white veil covering her head but leaving her face visible, part the Roman matrona, part Jewish modesty.

"I present to you my mother, the Queen Berenice, once of Samaria, known to this company. We hope that she will bring word of a bond of peace between our lands."

"Your words are strange, Agrippa, this intrigues me. Your majesty, I give you leave to speak."

Berenice came forward, with all the bearing of a matrona used to governing a household. "My son Agrippa is well known to you, as he is among the friends of the Emperor. I am an aging matrona, and not often given leave to speak. My husband Archelaus died some time ago, leaving me in charge of his holdings. It was my duty to be his eyes and ears, and speak, on rare occasion. I reared four children by his brother Aristobolus in his household. Because of this rare position, I can speak for both the women and the men of my household. Do I continue to have leave to speak?"

"Your words are clear, and spoken with rare and refreshing bluntness, your majesty," spoke Sejanus, "pray continue."

"Because this is a new alliance with a family known to you, it was felt best that I speak as a matrona, and one known to the gens of Claudius. Antipas has a foster daughter under his care, the Princess Salomé Alexandra, my granddaughter by his wife Herodias. We wish, this afternoon, to make petition for her engagement to Herod Philip the Younger, a member of the household of Philip of Rome, a Senator."

Sejanus paused. "This petition will need some discussion, but should be able to be part of the day's agenda. We invite you to return this afternoon at the ninth hour to conclude these matters."

The Senate took a few moments to whisper individual questions and the matronas left. From all the preparation, it was over. I was uncertain what to do until Berenice met me. "Come, we must go to the market, we may not have another opportunity."

"But we only just arrived, grandmother" I protested.

"The men must be about their deliberations, and your hearing is in but a few hours. We may as well enjoy the day while there is time."

"So quickly? I thought the petition was only preliminary. The Roman bans won't be issued for a year!"

"Apparently not. Word must have come ahead through Caligula's own guard. We wish to address the Senate while it is the mood to be generous. Herod Antipas is not well liked, but for the sake of your father Herod Philip, the Senate will listen to his petition. You are in an unusual place, son of a Senator estranged from his wife, but still caring for you as a gift from the marriage."

"You carry the kingdom of Israel, though dormant, in your heart, only you, I, Herodias, Berenice my granddaughter, and Drusilla, have that honor. Men are proud, but it is the women who bear the royal line."

"What do you mean?" I asked, puzzled.

"The line of the Herodians has grown thin. In his madness, your Grandfather Herod, called Great, systematically killed not only the male heirs of his household, fearing a rival, but the mothers of the line as well, leaving only the granddaughters in place. Those who marry these granddaughters are the heirs to the heritage of the Maccabees, and even the Romans are not ignorant of the depth of that heritage."

"If they choose to marry into the line (as will the Emperor's choice, Felix), they are accepting that responsibility of a kingship, even if they are called Tetrarch, or Governor, or King of Syria. Election in the Senate is one thing, bloodline, when it can be proved, is something else again."

•   •   •

It has now been years since this one word of revelation changed my life. At 70 years of age, I am beyond the thought of ancient Israel, and even the city of Jerusalem has been destroyed. but I still carry the blood in my veins. What shall my sons do when I am gone?

•   •   •

I was ignorant of these future times, however, as we traveled to the marketplace, and found it bustling with the many gods of wealth and commerce. Berenice noted each passerby as they stopped at one shrine or another, as Rome was a city of small spirits, household gods, the Lares and Penates of the Etruscans mingled with the palaces of Isis, Cybele, and Apollo, and even the bearded visage of Dushara, chief god of Petra.

We Jews were sometimes thought atheists, as we carried our own God within and would not burn a pinch to recognize the small spirits, but my mother had taught me to respect those small ones as angels of another people, their voices not heard by me, but certainly sacred to my Greek and Persian subjects.

I paused at the doors to the temple of Vesta, a place I had heard about from the aging Antonia, and pondered those women who lived within it. They worshipped, as I had come to believe, that same Divine Presence which protected Sarah, Leah, and Rachel, the mothers of Israel, the protector of the hearth and home. Perhaps I should inquire of them about the Empress.

I stopped Berenice and motioned her toward the doors, left open to widows, and children, and unmarried women. I was newly betrothed, and she was a matrona of station, but both of us were women in need of solace. This might be the last time I would be considered a maiden, I wished a moment of peace in the bustle.

An old woman in virginal white looked up as I entered. "You have the look of the Mother in you," she spoke to me. "Have you attended her before?"

"I come from Cyrene, and bring you greetings from the doulas there, I spoke, and from a dancer called Bat Mara."

"Those names are known in this place, not many men know that we keep close watch on all women of the empire, and particularly women of your station. Welcome to this refuge, Salomé Alexandra, you have been expected."

At this Berenice's eyes opened wide, "you know of the Vestals?"

"Almost nothing," I replied, "but Antonia herself told me not to neglect these walls, in case I were ever to need refuge from the troubles of the world, and Bat Mara long ago—had it only been two years—told me that my life would be filled with fire and flood. I would not be ignorant of the Shekinah in her face as the protector of women in this place."

The aging vestal smiled, "you listen well. Only one who had met the doulas would know that they keep in touch with all the healers of the Empire. The herbs of the Han and of the Houza are taught in their precincts, and the bay leaf of Apollo will open doors in the midst of war."

Berenice shook her head in amazement. "I thought I knew all of the byways, and certainly knew of the shrines of the people, but I never thought to ask the herbalists for guidance."

"I learned long ago," I spoke, "that servants see everything, and that those who market spices, herbs, and medicines have long ears. You have only to ask—with discretion—and your rule will be enhanced. Without them, your kingdom will fall—with them, you will always prosper."

"Holy vestal," I addressed the priestess, was this the precinct where Empress Julia fled?"

"Yes, she came to us when she first was pregnant with Procula. She was the favorite of the Emperor, but once she became pregnant, he renounced her and she had no place to turn. It was almost 15 years before she was again allowed in public sight, and Tiberius was willing to welcome her in her age, and legitimize their daughter. She grew old in these walls, but her daughter was destined for greatness. One never knows how the seed will grow when it is grown, but Procula exceeded our expectations."

"You know that I am destined to be back in Judaea within 5 years," spoke Berenice to the vestal. "Agrippa is petitioning for Archelaus old possessions. With all the many changes, I am likely to be in Jerusalem, oddly enough, sooner than Salomé."

"Our best voice is the woman named Bat Mara, who is now to be married." —It was now my turn to be amazed at the woman's knowledge— "Seek her out in Caesarea and ask her for her advice. She knows the herbalists of Jerusalem, and the old women who act as shroudmakers for the dead. There was a woman named Magdala, who sells nard and frankincense, who would be your best contact."

"We must take our leave from you, good vestal," spoke Berenice, bowing low. "I wish to purchase some items for Salomé before the afternoon's court. She should be dressed as a Roman maiden for this occasion."

"Your wisdom is well spent. Do not hesitate to wear blue and white, even in the Roman cut, Salomé. Your faith and that of your husband are the same, so you need not hide it here. Peace be upon thee."

"Shalom to you, good vestal. I will remember you to Bat Mara when I see her."

•   •   •

The merchants were particularly vexing this day of all days. The price would be high for a simple sash, but low for the sandals to go with it, followed by continual bickering for that last veil that I must have, in blue and white stripes, to mark me a Jewish woman being betrothed. This betrothal was a formality, as all that was necessary by my family had been done, but if one was to expect the Romans to honor Jewish family law, I had been taught early that the Romans deserved the same respect.

Marriage law had always been a fine line for every kingdom subjected to Rome, as each land had its own customs. Rome made no laws within a "gens," the Roman "clan" system, but the "paterfamilias", the head of household as the oldest male. was considered absolute ruler. With a word, a father could disown, or lavish praise, subtract all honors, or single out a child for a unique status. Only the Vestals held more power than a Roman father, and they used it but rarely.

Yet my position with two fathers, one a basileus, and one a tetrarch, put me under two distinct households, each with its own customs. In this rare instance, Antipas and Philip were in agreement, choosing to look beyond their disputes to the common interest of their heiress, who would give honor, and—it was to be hoped to Antipas—a respite from suspicion. I must dress the part.

The thin silver necklace was for Philip, and that would be set off by silver coins in my headdress. The blue and white was for my husband Philip, cut as a Roman maiden, to honor the court where I was to appear. The band about my waist was of blue silk, to honor my father Antipas, who was known for his trade.

We returned to the gallery of the matronas, above the Senate floor, and awaited the debates to signal our presence was acknowledged. There were many matters of dispute, some honors to be given, as Sejanus was the greatest of the legionnaires, and honored the soldiers much more than Caesar Tiberius.

Sejanus now called Senator Herod Philip to the floor. "As a client king of the Empire, you serve in the Senate by right. Your brothers have shown themselves capable of ruling tetrarchies, is it your wish to betroth your daughter to your brother Herod Philip of Syria, by the laws of Rome, as well as that of your own country?"

"I do, Commander, I wish her to pledge her Juno to his Genius."

"The lares and penates of your kindred. Will she take your brother's Gods as her own?" Sejanus probed.

"She brings her own God with her, and that one is his as well, I find no fault in that, Commander."

"You must teach me of your faith, as it is rare that we of Rome will witness the marriage of the Hebrews. I give you leave to speak," he turned, speaking to me.

"My speech will be brief," I replied, "as rarely a woman has graced this presence. The God of Ancient Ways is better represented by scholars, among which my father Herod Philip—of your number, and my betrothed—with your will, are to be counted. If your interest is genuine, they will speak with you privately. I ask only leave to worship as I will, and my betrothed to do the same."

"A woman with discretion, I see," spoke Sejanus. "I now know why you have consented to this marriage. May your daughter and her beloved's lives be fruitful, and may she bear heirs to your house." He turned to the hall. "Good senators, do I have your assent to this betrothal?"

The Senate rose as one voice, "Hail, voice of Caesar, we give our assent." I glanced at my mother and thought, had her betrothal been announced with such fervor?

Berenice motioned for us to keep silent. "My excellent Commander, I thank you for your wisdom. May I venture another question while I have your authority?"

"I have noticed a number of soldiers around the villa, and feel as if I am under siege. Is there any way you can be less visible, and yet ensure my safety?" Berenice trembled.

Sejanus chuckled. "You think like a householder. You know that visibility is only the surface. We can be invisible, but know that we will be there. The vineyards will always have extra workers. However, this brings up a question, what do you know of Archelaus' former holdings in Galilee?"

Berenice bowed low. "I married him after he came to exile, so I know very little, but Antipas and Agrippa alike have kept a clear accounting of the properties, most were turned back to the Roman overseers, but the city of Samaria seemed to have been in dispute."

"You do listen well, and this key will help us in our next question. You are given leave to return to the matronas."

Sejanus spoke carefully. "Antipas, your stepdaughter is quite lovely and she wears the Roman robes well, but the band of silk about her waist is something quite unusual. You know that Tiberius has been very clear about that trade."

Antipas spoke boldly. "I am a friend of Caesar, and follow his trading patterns. We have the same factors, and so I do have the ear of some merchants both from India and from the Han.

"The Nabateans have cornered the trade with India," he continued, "but Persia has always traded with Galilee for the Han, no matter who holds the caravan routes."

"Would you be interested in a private partnership with the generals? The Emperor does not have control everywhere, and we often are looking for eyes in far places."

Berenice froze. I noticed her discomfort. She motioned me to silence and we continued to listen carefully, more to the words not said than to explicit instructions. And to think my choice of fashion would arouse such suspicions.

Antipas pondered. "I must think on this, the silk trade has many twists and turns, just like a weaver at the loom. What do you have in mind?"

Sejanus turned and looked around the room. With the exception of the women and this small band of outliers who were not Roman, most of the ears present were from the army. "Agrippa has served in Gaul, so he knows how far the legions travel. We could add to your merchants those of Britain, and the northlands. Germania is rapidly growing in trade with Italy."

"Agrippa and I will confer and bring you an answer after the next holiday. We understand you just returned from Germania with some slaves and wish to show them off. Let us have time to look at your market goods before we commit ourselves."

Sejanus smiled, but there was a glint of wolf-like animosity in his eyes. "We will give you an opportunity to see our wares, and weigh carefully the addition of our legions to your trading partners. It is now Thursday, the 23rd of September, I give you until the Ides, Monday, October 3, 10 days, at the next meeting of the Senate, whether we should include you in the fair."

Antipas and Agrippa bowed low, and escorted we women from the hall. I did not breathe until we were well away from the Forum. I paused and whispered to my father, "My lord, I was afraid for you, Sejanus seems quite ambitious, and speaks for more than himself."

Antipas kept his voice low. "Wait until we are back at the Villa, I must prepare to go to Gaul at once."

To keep appearances calm, we stopped in the market, gathered some supplies for Herod Philip's household, and talked of inconsequentials until we were well away from the center of the city. As we passed a rather large estate full of cedars, Antipas reigned the chariots in and gathered us all close.

"I do not want anyone to hear it, particularly Herod Philip's servants, as I do not know where their loyalties lie. We are now in front of the estate of Antonia, so we have silent and watchful trusted servants."

"Sejanus has grown dangerous, and simply giving me the hint of trade with the Germans let me know that he is close to open revolt against Emperor Tiberius. Berenice, you are my brother's most trusted ally, and you have the ears of Antonia. Do you have a scribe you can trust to deliver a message? Couch it how you like, but Antonia must warn the Emperor. Talk about new trade, and the Emperor's favorite, mention Claudius' recent siege of Vienne, anything that will hint at larger armies than expected, but Tiberius must be warned."

Berenice chuckled bitterly, "and I thought my husband mad when he talked of so many Roman soldiers in Lugdunum and Vienne even ten years ago, and now they have infiltrated the vineyards. Even in his madness Archelaus was quite perceptive, and Sejanus did not turn a hair. Sejanus even hinted that his spies were everywhere."

Berenice paused and summed up her thoughts. "I will speak to my scribe in the women's quarters and send it with the evening scrolls."

Agrippa and Antipas looked at each other with intense scrutiny, unsure whether to trust each other or work at cross purposes. Agrippa wished for more land, and was hungry for power, but he also knew that the Emperor, and his heir

Claudius, held those reigns, not Sejanus of Rome. He sighed deeply. "The women of the Empire tend to settle things behind doors in ways that men cannot. In this you do well, Antipas, as Antonia with a word can topple a plot that clearly has been building for some time."

Berenice dictated a letter full of misdirection. "The fashions of Rome are changing and the women of Rome are now wearing hints of color in their garments, silk accents to show that they are women of wealth, but not ostentatious. There are new blond slaves out of the north, and a great market day is to be held shortly after the Ides to show off the goods of the legions. Sejanus must be quite proud of his new arrangements to protect the Empire's borders without being obtrusive. He needs someone to observe and congratulate him on his shrewdness."

"That should be enough threads to build a tapestry," spoke Berenice. "Salomé, could I have that sash you are wearing?" She tied up the scroll and gave it to Georgio who would be riding off to Pareia and then to Capri. This message required a personal courier who would not be questioned. "To the hands of Pallas and Antonia" she directed. "At your command," he spoke and was on his way.

The ride back to Herod Philip's estate continued without incident but we all spent the next several days in anxiety. Agrippa and Antipas were secretive, and abruptly fell silent whenever I would enter a room.

From my father, however, I soon learned that it was well that Georgio had been the chosen servant. He knew all the byways, and had been so much a part of Roman society that even the legionnaires did not see him arriving at Pereia alone to be unusual. He had departed for Capri within the hour on a nightly courier ship and would return within a week.

CHAPTER 21

Messages

Agrippa and Antipas called a family counsel two days after Georgio had departed. "From all that Sejanus has said," Agrippa spoke, "we feel that one of us, at least, must go to Gaul to confirm or deny what we have heard. Sejanus cannot be trusted to tell the truth."

"In addition," said Antipas, "we must check closer to Rome in case there is an immediate uprising in the offing. One of us, therefore, must ride north to the gladiatorial camp and attempt to ferret out news. Both of us are well-known faces in both Gaul and Asia, so no one will question our coming to observe this new batch of soldiers."

"I have chosen to go to Gaul, Mother" spoke Agrippa, "as I know the servants in your house, and can check on any newcomers. Therefore, Antipas will go to the training camp."

And so my uncles left, and we were left to wonder.

•   •   •

Berenice seemed to age visibly over the next few days. She stopped using henna in her hair, so the auburn gold turned to silver and her worry lines became prominent. She paced the rooms, looking at the hills, and praying silently. She was worried that she had said too much or that her veiled hints would be misunderstood. A woman's word was not often heard, and trying to convey such momentous news entirely by gossip was something that she had honed over years, but would it succeed where others had failed?

Georgio came directly to the women's quarters when he returned. He was about to ask for a private audience when Antipas was announced, arriving still steaming from the road.

Georgio whispered to him, "I am glad that there were many dispatches, and for once, that both you and Agrippa have friends in high places. I did not have to choose between multiple loyalties and could simply deliver each scroll to the proper authority." He glanced at Antipas, hesitant not to give offense.

Antipas nodded his head in acknowledgement and spoke, "you do not offend, you had your work to do, I have accomplished mine. Give your report first, and I shall fill in gaps you may not have."

Herod Philip let us into a central courtyard lit with torches and carefully extinguished all lights that would show from the street. This meeting was a private council, and he wanted no gossip in the market.

When all was prepared, Georgio took the stance of a messenger about to recite. The atmosphere was so tense that we felt that it should have been noticed beyond the walls. Georgio spoke, "You should know that Pallas, who is Antonia's most trusted slave, has been watching Sejanus for some time. When I brought Berenice's letter, he was the first to read it before Antonia was called."

"This last missive brought up a number of convergences, none of which alone could have been conclusive. First, Sejanus is an equestor, of the second rank, not from the praetors of Rome, and thus not usually allowed to become a Senator. He holds rank entirely because of Tiberius' patronage. By contrast, Antipas and Agrippa have both been trained in the legions, and the legions are where Sejanus holds most of his influence."

His hand has been slow in moving, removing one Senator or another over the past 10 years and replacing them with friends who promote the generals, not the nobility."

"His offer of increased influence to both Antipas and Agrippa is within his power, and would not be seen as treason concealed. As an equestor, he trades in horses, and keeps himself informed of all the movements of anyone who supplies the garrisons, and in that both your Antipas and Agrippa excel. His questions in court were not unusual, and perhaps not suspicious on the surface, but for someone like Berenice, who sees much more clearly from outside of Rome from its most important province, anything that influences trade is important."

"Second, and this, to you, is perhaps the more interesting, Sejanus convinced Tiberius not to trust his own mother, Livia. Though she was a spitfire, she was not completely untrustworthy.

She was accused of poisoning her various rivals, and even her other sons, so perhaps Tiberius is to be forgiven for not wanting to be around her, but from my observations she was ambitious, not murderous. Her death only three years ago still keeps him at bay and away from Rome. Claudius Caligula was her favorite, so in this, oddly enough, you have an ally from a peculiar direction.

"Pallas has been the go-between for Antonia to Caligula for many years, and for him to receive this letter confirming yet another query about a hero of the legions to aggrandize his own power is as much as an admission of guilt. Claudius Caligula has been informed and is most concerned, as Sejanus trained him in the arts of war and this is a direct affront to his own loyalty. Whispers of empire-building have become as loud as a herald's cry for Tiberius, and something must be done."

At this Antipas raised his hand. "This information confirms what I have spend three days investigating. I met many men in the gladiator camp north of here, but none other quite as influential as Plebius Vetonius. I have worked with him for years, you may remember him Herodias."

"He was with the guard in Syria, wasn't he, when I first married Philip?" she queried.

"Yes, a very influential man, he was in the entourage of Germanicus, Tiberius' first adopted son, who was head of the Eastern Roman Legion.

He and I have crossed paths any number of times from here to Gaul and back to Parthia. It has been about 15 years since we spent any significant time together, but he still holds a grudge."

"Why," I spoke. "You speak as if this troubles you."

"Being a friend of the Emperor is not all the honor that one expects. I brokered one peace treaty many years ago with the Parthians, working with Germanicus, but the king we took hostage was killed in Cappadocia, and so we were now having to start negotiations all over again with the new king Artabanus, who was not about to be made a vassal of Rome. Vetalius was sent to meet with the king in a pavilion erected in the middle of a bridge over the Euphrates, the only territory that could not be claimed by either Rome or Parthia.

At the conclusion of the ceremony, I prepared a feast of peace, and was careful to record all the proceedings, including identifying Darius, the son of King Artabanus, who was to be brought back to Rome as a hostage. I sent a swift messenger back to Rome with gifts from Parthia, including a giant named Eleazar, by swift ship.

Vetalius arrived shortly after, bringing what he thought would be welcome news, along with the prince. Instead, he found the Emperor fully informed and he was given less honor, he believed, than if he had brought the word himself.

"For that slip of protocol, he sees me but seldom now, and though we still must work together, he is hesitant to share information if he believes he will lose honor in doing so. The fact that he spoke to me at all shows how serious he takes his duties."

"I had arrived at nightfall," Antipas continued, "hoping to see any of the older legionnaires and ask them about both Gaul and Germany. I had served on both fronts, so if anyone would be in the training camp who was an old soldier I would recognize them. Vetalius was the last one I expected to see."

"Rather than put me off as he has often in the past," Antipas continued, "he brought me watered wine and had a footsoldier wash my feet. After the hospitaility, he seemed both reticent to talk, yet also compelled."

"Only when I was rested from the hasty journey did he say, over a shared cup, 'we are old soldiers you and I, and you have the ear of the Emperor.' "

"I nodded and murmured, 'is there news for the Emperor then?'"

"I do not like you Antipas," Vetalius spoke, "but I like dishonor less. Sejanus is not to be trusted."

"He is a Senator, and appointed by the Emperor as his voice, who am I to speak against him?"

"I am one of the few Senators who can speak against him," Vetalius continued, "and not be silenced, but now, the tale of the soldiers is that he will be Emperor soon."

"What is that?" I questioned, brought up short as he was anticipating my question.

"Sejanus is preparing this camp for funeral games, and the old soldiers can speak of nothing else. He will give them honor before they die, they say, and for that they will follow him anywhere."

"Why does that concern you?"

"Had Sejanus even nominally declared the funeral games as sponsored by Tiberius or even Gaius, I would suspect nothing, but this time, he speaks of Sejanus Triumph".

"He takes the prerogative of the Emperor?"

"Exactly," Vitellius concluded, "only the Emperor can call for funeral games and the gladiatorial contests that go with them. It is his right as the Divine Emperor to do so, as a High Priest for Rome, anyone else would be perceived to have blasphemed."

"Tiberius has refused to be called a God, and so has delegated his authority to Sejanus. But Gaius has certainly gone back to those honorifics. What are you saying?"

"That it is a choice between the Divine Sejanus now, and the Divine Caligula, and the legions are in Sejanus' call, not the Emperor's, nor his heir's."

"You have heard this?"

"In murmurs only, but the weapons are piled higher every day, and more and more legions have been called within a day's journey of Rome. This move has been being prepared since the day Tiberius retired to Capri."

"And Tiberius does not suspect?"

"Sejanus has had all the power for more than ten years, regardless of the protocol, and so Tiberius has few choices. He can make some preparations, and hope to have some influence, but he lives on Capri because he is terrified, only Caligula is our hope now."

"Hope, that popinjay?" I spoke bluntly. "He is the Emperor's heir, and is thought mad by everyone, but you believe he can actually bring honor back to the Empire."

"Yes."

"I will think on this, Vetalius, because you tell me with nothing to gain, something that I seldom have run across in a soldier."

"Come with me, then, and see the training, do you have a day?" "One day, only, I must return to Rome by tomorrow at the 3rd hour."

"Then stay with me this evening, and we can walk among the fires."

We walked together and he pointed out the cages of bears and lions brought from Gaul, and the great wild oxen of Germania.

"These beasts are to be used in the games, and so the men use them to encourage them to train all the more. The wild ox is prized in Germania as the most dangerous of beasts, and is only approached by laying a pit trap and working with at least six more men as a rite of passage. The German soldiers look at the games as their last passage with honor into the afterlife, better to die in battle with a beast then to die at home and sick of death and stench."

"I knew of the funeral rites, but there must be something else you brought me to see."

"Look at the cages, do you see the space below them?"

"I see what looks like spaces for rollers, is there something else?"

"Only four rollers are needed, as they connect to chariot wheels. The other holes are storage for spears, swords, and pikes."

"Then we have a Trojan Ox here?" I laughed.

"Indeed, weapons at ready, with soldiers trained for battle, and in the front of the Emperor's own heir."

"Then Sejanus expects Caligula soon?"

"Not only expects him, but looks forward to the deception. A triumph, before a soldier and Emperor's heir he trained himself, but done in such a way that even Caligula will not see."

"How did you find out?"

"Through keeping silent and saying what was expected. By acting loyal to the legions as if they were above the Emperor, not at his call. Come, take your rest, and I will show you the final piece tomorrow."

And so I slept, and woke at dawn to the mustering of soldiers doing exercises. I watched for the morning, and as a soldier I could tell that they were not training just for their last battle in an arena to the roar of crowds, but for much more. I shuddered. For this was betrayal."

"I rode hard to get here by tonight, and am glad that I have arrived in time to speak with you and Georgio. Is there news from Capri, then?" Antipas concluded.

Georgio smiled. "The final portion of the letter from Antonia is simple. Antonia sends greetings and asks for you to contact her household to prepare a banquet on the 18th of October. She is sending an invitation to Sejanus to come and hints that Caligula is to be expected."

"Caligula is coming here?" I stuttered.

"Will Sejanus suspect anything?"

"Not from Caligula, he presumes he is simply here to preen. But Caligula—though sometimes overbearing—is also perceptive, and this is not a good time to be on his bad side."

Philip stopped and smiled. "I would suggest that you dress conservatively, Salomé, and above all, don't wear silk."

"Never wear silk again?" I blurted.

"No, just this once, it will be signal to Caligula's guards that they are to leave you alone," he explained. "They are not known for their self-control, and you have had enough of their pawing. The women of Rome are used to it, and have many ways to deflect too much attention, but you are newly betrothed, and I do not wish you to be made an example of their high spirits."

"Sejanus will think this banquet is in his honor as a fitting crown to his triumph, I think," spoke Antipas. I must join Caligula, much as I dislike him, and at the triumph. He also does not like me, but with news from me to confirm his suspicions, even he cannot ignore the slight."

"What shall we do, they are not expecting us at the Triumph, are they?" inquired Herodias."

"No," Antipas smiled ruthlessly. "As much as you have the freedom of the hetera, and the judgment of the Vestals, you do not need to be present, as our faith is respected, even by Sejanus. He will consider you to be prudent not to come to the prequel to games dedicated to other Gods, but I..."

"Yes," observed Herodia. "You will not be suspect, you are simply an old soldier observing the new one at his height," observed Herodias, "you have chosen aright to try to mend quarrels with Caligula, as Agrippa is always at his side now. For once, you will have the news."

"Georgio," I exclaimed. "you have saved me from rape, murder, and theft before, I place my safety in your hands."

"Then all will be well your highness," he addressed me with my new station. "Her Wisdom sends you word to remain calm, as fire will come of this, and you should be warned."

"My trust in you has proved itself again, Georgio" breathed Berenice. "Herodias chose you well to keep her daughter safe."

"I am servant to all the Herods, Salomé has enjoyed a rare respite from a family quarrel, and I revel in these short moments." He sighed as he spoke, and then he shook himself and laughed. "And the men of Rome never suspect that their women are neither blind, nor deaf, nor unobservant."

Herodias laughed ruefully. "I took you away from Rome into a place even more filled with quarrels, I hope you have found some peace here."

"For a few days," Georgio chuckled. "After next week, much will be thrown into chaos, you must be prepared, and you will be watched. You can gather everything you need here in the women's quarters. Just be ready to go quickly, as the change in atmosphere may be sudden."

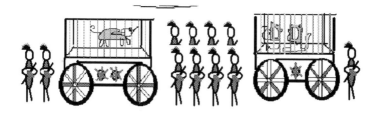

CHAPTER 22

Sejanus' Triumph

The triumph, as Antipas related, had stretched out the length of the Circus Maximus. Though the Coliseum would be the site of the games, the Circus had existed for more than 200 years, and was the only place to bring out all of the soldiers, prisoners, and beasts to be exhibited or paraded all at once.

Soldiers, both the blond Celtoi and Germanii of the northlands, and the Nubians and Phoenicians, darkened by the sun of Africa, came in rank after rank.

As this was Sejanus triumph, the chief cages were of beasts of the northlands, and the slaves from all over Hybernia, wherever the foot of Rome had been planted for the past 10 years, the length of time that Sejanus had ruled in all but name over the Senate.

Caligula had ridden into Rome to the announcement of trumpets the night before, and had set aside his own quarters for soldiers and took his place beside them in the barracks, the one act that often made him loved, no matter his eccentric behavior, because he had grown up in the legions. He was still young, scarcely 20, but it was clear he commanded with a word, and his black boots were distinctive.

Antipas was invited to sit with him in his own place in the Circus, a signal honor, and one he hoped would not catch the eye of Sejanus. As the cages of oxen and wolves came through the legions, Antipas whispered to Caligula. "Do you notice the size of the cages?"

"I see nothing unusual, the cages of the elephants when they are captured are not any larger," spoke Caligula.

"I would agree, your Wisdom, but notice the construction. You were raised in the legions of Gaul, what do you see?"

"Do you notice where they are located? And who is drawing them?" Antipas continued.

"It is the newest slaves, they think it a signal honor, they may be the next to die, and this would be a fitting way for a soldier, in battle with their beast of initiation," Caligula responded, "you know the followers of Mithra are throughout the Empire."

"Spoken like one who knows the mysteries," Herod assented. "But these are not from that school, these are the newest slaves from Germany, where they do not know Perses," Herod automatically made a sign of a spear, without thinking.

"Antipas, you forget yourself, this is a public place," chided Caligula.

"I speak as one initiate to another, by whatever Name is given, you must look to the wheels."

"I know that carving, I served in Hibernia" spoke Caligula.

"Yes, the Celtoi are great woodcarvers, but this one is unusual, do you see?"

""I know...wait," Caligula hesitated. "I know that design, I have built enough of them. Sejanus insisted that I not be treated differently."

Antipas hesitated, "Divinity, I have notice something curious. Do you know of elephants?"

Caligula laughed. "Are you complaining for my gift? I assure you it was not given to weigh you down."

Antipas laughed, but there was no humor in it. "Divinity, if you know elephants, then you know the size of their cages, the cages they are using for this triumph."

"I do, I had not noticed anything unusual," Caligula spoke.

Antipas ventured slowly, "These cages look right from our distance, until you look at the wheels."

"The wheels, they are well balanced for their load," observed Caligula.

"Yes, but they are both narrower and higher than the standard. Look at the edge of the bars, and the depth of the bottoms. The carvings are large, but if you compare them with the cages of the wolves, then you can see that they have false bottoms. If they were riding alone, just with horses and escorts, I would not be concerned, but they are surrounded by new soldiers, soldiers who would guard those sacred oxen with their lives."

"With their lives, what do they cover?" queried Caligula.

"Do I have leave to speak, your Majesty, I would accuse your friend" my stepfather spoke guardedly.

"Agrippa has vouched for your observations, what do you know?"

"Your enemies conspire. These cages were finished but a day's journey north of here. They conceal arsenals ready to be deployed as soon as Sejanus gives word. Only my suspicions could confirm this, through soldiers who have been loyal to you, though my personal foes."

"You have spoken with the camp trainers," Caligula observed. "Was Vetalius among them?"

"He was," spoke Antipas.

"Then I believe you. He has held a grudge against you for longer than I have been among the soldiers, and only he could know the inside of Sejanus' camps and not be suspected," Caligula concluded. "So Sejanus hopes to repeat the storming of Troy, this time with Celtic soldiers," he chuckled. "The Celtoi moved from Troas when Anaeas fled to Italy, now he wants them to start the battle again. Shrewd, effective, if only there were was not a Appolonius in his midst, Vetalius the wise, he would have succeeded."

"What shall we do, then your Majesty?" Antipas had asked.

"There is a certain banquet that Sejanus is holding in three days...after this 'triumph' of his. It is my personal request that you NOT attend."

Antipas was dumbfounded.

"If you are not there, then Sejanus will not suspect my sources of news. He thinks me mad and ignorant, and this saddens me, more than you can know. I had hoped..." he stopped. "But no matter."

Antipas broke off his recounting. "The rest of the triumph was more of the same, though some more unusual beasts came in with the Nubians, some striped horses, and even a river horse, held in a special tank drawn by several oxen. I hope to show you these someday."

"I believe the banquet should occupy your hours now, my wife, my daughter, my mother," spoke Antipas. "I cannot be seen on the street, and should stay in your villa, with your leave, my brother." He spoke the last line to Herod Philip, my father, something I never expected him to ask.

"My house is yours. Once my wife was the cost of my life, now I will not repay your current kindness with evil," spoke Philip.

"Then we are at peace, may we part friends." Antipas bowed deeply.

"Until that day, the private quarters are yours. The servants will be instructed that you are to be served in peace, and all inquirers will be told you are still away with the legions."

"No need to lie, just tell them to say that I have not been seen. That will be true enough and I will leave notes so that they are not caught in a lie," spoke Antipas.

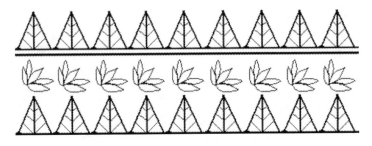

CHAPTER 23

Villa Antonia

Augusta Antonia kept a house away from the city. It was defended with several inner layers of porticos, so that though it looked open and airy, it was well fortified, and no one could enter without at least five guards noticing their arrival.

The many walls, even without doors, kept the noise from the street from the central pool, filled with water lilies from Egypt, and decorated with both Roman and Egyptian motifs. Antonia's father was Mark Antony, whose second wife Cleopatra had dominated the Roman world for more than 30 years. Her mother Octavia was Augustus' sister, so she was now the matriarch of the Augustines.

Octavian Augustus had come back to Rome in triumph, but losing his lifelong friend Mark Antony at the battle of the Nile had cost him in years of care appearing in a moment. At unguarded times, he mourned the loss even until he died, so Antonia had remembered her father and Egypt as a kind of silent eulogy to his memory.

Mark Anthony had been a kingmaker, putting Herod the Great on the throne, confirming the kingship of Aretus, Nabatean King of Petra without a fight, and showing sufficient strength to lay a clear border between Rome and the Persians.

When he died, he controlled half of the Empire by personal friendships, so his loss was deeply felt.

"Pontia of the Plebians," spoke the heralds. This was one of the women of the gens Pontius. Pilate had married a woman of far greater station than he, and so the women of his line were now slowly being seen at state banquets.

"General Sejanus and company", spoke the herald. Antonia turned from our alcove and swept across the room, welcoming Sejanus and a dozen soldiers. "Your Excellency, let me seat you here in this place of honor, I hear you have only recently returned?" motioning him to the largest of the divans.

"And here, a place for your soldiers." She clapped her hands and servant girls came with fruit and wine. Sejanus controlled himself, but the soldiers clearly were distracted. "Please, be rested, and refreshed. Your cloaks, if you please?"

Two soldiers removed their cloaks. Three did not, but moved back to corners of the room to keep watch. Antonia, recognizing the bodyguards, called her own servants in turn.

"Guards, please help these gentlemen find the best views. We wish to entertain, not cause them worry."

The menservants slowly circled the hall, offering to wash our feet, and offering towels for our hands. While all the food would be in nibbles, and small bites, it was still best to start fresh.

Sejanus visibly relaxed. He was always wary, but much was done to put him at ease. A servant boy and girl both attended to him, and he ruffled the boy's hair, and fondled the girl distractedly as he leaned back on the couch.

We ate a course of fresh greens, tossed in olive oil, with barley loaves to dip in the extra oil. My fingers were greasy but easily cleaned on the good bread. All seemed well.

A round of wine from Sicily was poured and then a bell sounded. Antonia clapped her hands and the hall fell silent. She smiled, and became the herald. "My friends, a rare honor. His Divinity, Gaius Caligula, heir to the Empire, and his sister Julia Drusilla."

"Antonia, your honor is beyond fathoming, you are a Goddess like your mother."

Augusta Antonia pretended to blush, nodded once and then spoke. "This banquet is in your honor, and the honor of the legions, I am your servant. How may I aid you?"

"By feasting, and drinking, and boasting of your own honors, as this is your house. Do not be afraid of me, I did not come to accuse, merely to observe." He smiled but there was a spark in his eye that was far from sane.

And so the feast began. It was lavish, and long, and filled with long pauses, at which servants with sistrums would stir through the hall like the whisper of leaves through the trees. Snow had been brought by runners from the Alps, and we ate it with honey, and fresh fruit to clear our palates between courses. Antonia spared no expense, and her banquets were much coveted.

Sejanus was expansive, and took to making outlandish jests, comparing one servant or another to the new slaves of Germania, or the lowlands of the Rhine.

Tacitus rose, and gifted us with a speech praising the virtues of a well-run household, talking long enough for everyone to settle their last palates and be rested.

But it was not to be.

As the hush fell over the room, as it usually did after a prolonged speech, Gaius Caligula rose and addressed the

General. Caligula was small, but he was standing, and he seemed to tower over Sejanus, who was lying relaxed on a couch.

Caligula spoke carefully, "Commander Sejanus, what of the legions?"

Sejanus nodded laconically. "We presented our new tributes in the Forum on the Ides, your Excellency, and will hold games in the Stadium tomorrow. Many blond slaves out of the north; word of a new garrison at Vienne. We trust this is pleasing to the Emperor."

"All honor to myself and to the Emperor, as you are our voice here. And the new soldiers, have they shown their training well?"

"Even the new soldiers out of Gaul are becoming toughened by their travels. The road keeps them strong. The gentleness of the Senate does not suit them."

"Ever the soldier, Sejanus," he observed. "But I trust the Friends of the Emperor," he stated flatly.

Sejanus buckled under the stare. His ears were not deceived, and the taste of the wine was bitter. "Old women, I should have known. What friends of the Emperor can they be to defy a soldier's choice?"

Caligula winced, "I arrived here watchful, hoping that I was misled. You expected me to preen, and bring my servants in and have myself addressed as a God, instead I speak of Antonia as the Goddess she is, and the mistress of her own household."

"I watched you a week ago as you led a triumph through the streets with your new pretty slaves, all those strong blond boys. Do they cry in pain and bleed like others, or are they some phantoms, ghost-white as they are."

"Your Excellency, I do not wish to offend, I wished only to show off to the Romans what the legions have brought."

"You are deceived, your Excellency."

"You would lie to a liar? You flatter me, Sejanus."

Caligula took a cup, crushed a leaf in it, and motioned a servant for wine. "You are given a choice, take this cup from my hand, and be buried in peace, or your family will lose all of its honors. The choice is yours."

I blanched. Here, before the hall, Caligula was offering Sejanus hemlock, the choice of martyrdom, or downfall.

Sejanus crumpled. He could see that his soldiers were outnumbered; each had very carefully been put in a place to watch the hall, but not their backs. He stared at Antonia, and his eyes gleamed insanely. "I shall not drink," he cried, tossing the wine in Caligula's face. He then leapt to his feet, and fell on his own sword.

Caligula looked at the bleeding soldier. "I gave you the choice to drink, and preserve your household. You will die as a Roman, but your family ceases to be. They will not die, but the household of Sejanus is no more. Guard!"

One of Sejanus soldiers came forward. "His head" spoke Caligula. The soldier nodded, lifted up his master's body, held up his head by the hair, and cut it off with a stroke."

I shuddered. Was I always to see John's face before my eyes, in faces of madness in my dreams? But no, this was not John, this was a true traitor, and justice had been served.

Augusta Antonia clapped, and servants came and took the body away, where it was thrown down the stairs to the public street, to be buried or burned as a common criminal. The head was wrapped in a cloth. "Deliver this to his wife, she will know what to do," she spoke to two servants. The two servants rushed away, trembling visibly.

With his head, his wife would know that she no longer had a household. Her slaves would be auctioned within two days, and she herself, and her children, if she did not seek refuge within the day with her parents, would be considered complicit and die as her husband. In a moment, it was done. The justice of Rome, when it did strike, was quick, and brooked no appeal.

Caligula, for once, did not laugh. He shook himself, and as if to someone invisible he spoke, "he had been strong and I worshiped him, and now he is gone."

I realized how much this night had cost him. Gaius Caligula was a trained soldier and had grown up in the garrisons. Sejanus was the head general of the legions, and so the one he had relied upon to always be honorable. The downfall was hard for him to bear. Even in his swift justice, he could be moved. I kept my silence, but I would remember this night for many years. A troubled young man, overlaid with the weight of an Empire, mingled with a seer who heard voices. What was I to believe? I am still finding my own answers.

Caligula, still quite vulnerable, looked in my direction. "And what is this? This is not an old woman, but a young woman, the jewel who has been placed under my care. Not the first time a man is beheaded in front of you, is it? You may look innocent my dear, but you are older than time."

He turned, as if to a voice. "Ah, she is a messenger, that is why she is here," he spoke to the air. "What message to me this night, then, Princess?"

I pulled myself together and spoke clearly, "the justice of Rome is swift, and you, too, are not now so innocent. Are we called upon to kill Gods?"

Caligula fell silent.

I paused and something emboldened me. "But the voices are always there?

"Yes," he spoke, and his eyes glistened with tears. "The Gods weep when they are mocked, and I am thought mad."

"I also hear voices on the wind. I have been taught to listen." I spoke gently to honor his mourning.

"Your message is heard, then, the voices on the wind confirm it. You will witness many things, fire and flood, and see kings die, and new kings rise where there is no kingdom now. I will not touch you, as the flames would burn me. You shine like a torch and I will never allow my soldiers to sully you." He spoke like a prophet, and seemed afraid of himself.

"I am your servant," I spoke the words as if prompted.

"Never, Princess, you will be crowned Queen long after I am dead. Remember me with kindness," he spoke at last, clicked his iron heels and whirled out of the hall.

After a palpable silence, the hall breathed all at once, with servants being hailed for more wine, everyone calling for anything to clear the brain and help them pretend that murders always accompanied a state dinner. Perhaps, in their Rome, it was not unusual, they did have the Circus after all, something I would not attend.

Berenice and Herodias spoke softly to each other, and then rose together and went to Augusta Antonia. Bowing low they asked to leave. Antonia called two soldiers. "Escort my friends all the way to the house of Herod Philip. I do not want them harmed."

And so we left as we had come, shrouded in cloaks and carried in sedan chairs so none could tell who we were unless they followed us all the way to the villa. I slept like a stone, and woke to a thunderstorm.

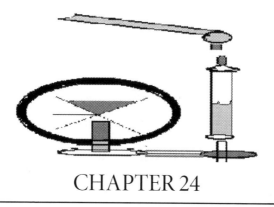

CHAPTER 24

Rain

Everything was dank. We were packing to go to Gaul, but nothing would stay dry. The winter rains had now come and they seemed endless. I decided I should write Bat Mara and let her know I would be returning to Galilee in the month of February, a perfect time for the cleansing rituals I would need after this murderous set of courts.

To think that it had been less than one year since my dance for the Baptist, and I could not escape its consequences. I was to be married, and my heart would need this year for cleansing. Bat Mara would need to give me more advice. How could I move on with my life and the responsibilities of a household, the wife of a basileus who was also a scholar, when I was barely through with the whirlwind of a year of constant moves and the hostility of strangers? I knew a queen, a poisoner, priests of a religion that I had been trained to fear, and—I mused—an elephant.

The drip of the rain from the roof into the pool was like a water clock, beating out the moments of time, and it gave me a respite from my packing. My mother had seen many things, but now it was my turn to stop and think, and wonder—and ponder. My betrothed husband Philip was very solicitous, and knew that I had witnessed very difficult things. Only time would heal, and he had promised to wait.

But enough of the water clock. I wrung out my cloak and began to sort out my veils. Each one was a memory of a bargain at the fair, or some special gift from my mother, or one of the soldiers. This sparrow now had many brightly colored feathers, and must pack them all away.

The veil of blue. I stopped and remembered the dance, so many months ago, and the song without words that announced it to the hall. I began to hum almost tunelessly as the moves came back to me. I was alone in this courtyard, and I rose to my feet, stretching as I had not in many months, in preparation for dancing. Perhaps the Eternal could hear my prayer and had sent her healing tears. We were told in our prayers that when we cried for healing, it was God the Mother who would answer.

I moaned, and let the tears come. I cried and cried, to myself, and then to the walls. The rain came down and covered my cries so that I could mourn alone. I had not known how bitter growing up all at once could be. I would no longer have a childhood, Caligula had robbed me of that last spark of innocence with a sword stroke. But my own voices came, clear and strong on the wind, and I, at last, understood what Shaqilath had been saying. I called to the wind, and knew that my thoughts and memories were felt by her, so many miles away in the Court of the Lions. Was she, even now, training her daughter in the ways of statecraft?

I felt the touch of a hand on my shoulder. My grandmother had come up behind me. "Yes, my sparrow, it is good to cry, once you are on the throne, there will be few times you can find solitude."

"Sparrow?" I queried.

"It was I who gave you that name," she laughed, "from the sparrows in the roofline of your father's villa just above us."

"They would come and go at sunrise and sunset, as if to mark the moods of the house. You were a winsome child, with a ready smile, so Sparrow became my name for you."

And now I have a grandmother, I thought. "Why did you not travel to Judaea?"

"I fled Herod the Great's wrath, and only escaped because Agrippa was two years old, and Herod, for some reason, would not murder a young widow with a child. Rome seemed safer than Jerusalem, and now Agrippa has found favor with the Emperor. My flight into exile was a near thing, and I almost drowned in shipwreck on the way from Tyre. My four children were raised in Rome, and that is how Herodias met Antipas, and now Philip has met you. I married Archelaus after he fled to Gaul and lost his property in Judaea, but I have always missed Samaria and Galilee. Is there still snow on Hebron every winter? I see the mountains, so much taller here, and think of home."

"Yes, the snows are bright on the mountaintops," I replied. "Can you now return?"

"I might, I was Archelaus' eyes and ears, but I have been on my own for many years. I invested his fortune wisely. I now own property in Gaul, in Greece, in Alexandria, and in Cyprus, and when his properties were taken over in Judaea, they left us one house alone in Samaria, but only on the condition that he would never return there. I am welcome, but my children are not, at least not yet."

"Why is that?"

"As you can see, I have the ear of the Emperor, so this is the privilege they give me. I am only one old woman, after all, what can I do?"

I smiled. One old woman, even Sejanus saw through that.

"I hear you have a granddaughter named after you?"

"Yes, Agrippa dotes on her, you heard her mentioned in Capri, she is only 4 years old, but already she is betrothed to the King of Lebanon."

"Why so young?"

"She makes peace between several households, and he has promised to convert to Judaism when they are married when she turns 13."

"Do you think it will happen?"

"The world may go where it will. I know I never expected to be married to Archelaus, but when you have four children to raise in a strange city, and there is a man of wealth who is recently widowed, you learn to take your best opportunity. All of my children have done well. Agrippa is now a centurion, my son Herod is king of Chalcis, Aristobolus has married the princess of Elesa, and my daughter Herodias has given me you. I know that you will not fail me."

"Fail you, how?"

"You will be a ruler someday, something I always have known. You marry into a kingly line, and you will be counted a witness to many things."

"A witness?"

"Women of station are few in the Empire, and those who can testify in court even fewer. They must be women of station, who rule in their own right when their husbands are abroad. Many women gossip, and live a pampered life in a harem. Not we few. We must be the matriarchs, the householders, the shrewd midwives. You have learned from your mother, but now pass out of her care for a while. For the next year, you will live with me, and learn the ways of Rome."

"Then I am not going to Gaul?"

"On the contrary. Yes, you are, you are going to see your stepfather's new home, but you will spend more time with me than with him. We have more than a dozen years to catch up, and with our villas together in the same province, less than a day's riding apart, you will be able to see how to run the affairs of a busy household with many responsibilities. The city of Rome is unsafe for the next year, while the legionnaires fight out the succession, but Gaul is well protected."

"But Sejanus said?"

"I know my own soldiers, and they are loyal to me. A few extra legionnaires in the vineyards will not disrupt my household. Better to know the spies, and keep watch on them, than to pretend that they are not there. One does not become an old woman in the Empire without knowing when to leave a situation alone."

My grandmother then braided my hair and put it up into a style I wore from then on, that of a Roman lady of station. The flowing mane of hair running in the breeze I would only savor on rare occasions. I felt I aged 10 years on that morning in the rain. My childhood was put aside, and I must listen to every word, learn the accounting of a household, keep clear watch over the cellars to keep away vermin, things that I had always left for servants to do. A braid, and a chiton, a change of bearing, and it was done. I had entered my father's villa as a child, now I was a woman, so aged in a single year as to be unrecognizable, even to myself.

Berenice advised me. "I have survived three marriages by being always ready to walk away from everything. If my home is under siege, I always know the safe rooms, and the unwatched corridors. I wear my wealth openly, but if I have to dress in drab to hide from invasion, I become the beggar on the street. Pandora herself could not do better, and she has me as a patron."

"Pandora! The witch?"

"Yes, she has at least nine households that keep her employed, each in a different city so she can flee in a moment. I see her but seldom, but she was raised in Gaul, and has taught me the herbs of the hillsides there. My kitchen is prized and my table is seldom without guests. But all those who visit me know to be polite. Old woman indeed! I may not have the title of Augusta, but she and I have played a game of friendly rivalry for years." She clapped her hands. "Now we must finish your packing."

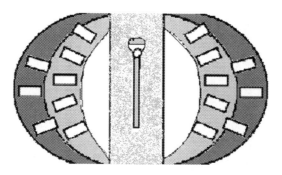

CHAPTER 25

Lugdunum

Lugdunum, the City of Light, was built at the confluence of the two rivers, the Rhone and Suone. Almost 75 years had passed since Julius Caesar had conquered Gaul and the city had grown rapidly to become the administrative center of the province. Roads stretched to Germania, northwest to the great Ocean, west to Aquitania, and south, the road we rode, from Italy. On an island in the middle of the waters was the monument to Emperor Augustus, and the priesthood that was established for the imperial shrine. The altar with tall end poles, marked the Sanctuary of the Three Gauls, and was inscribed with the names of all the Gallic tribes. I thought of the badges of the tribes of Israel on the gates of the temple in Jerusalem. The city drew from all the quarters of the Empire, so we were hardly noticed as we arrived on our Persian horses, drawing Egyptian style four-wheeled chariots. The roads of Rome were well established.

Lugdunum was named after Lugh, the Brigantian God of Light, and the city was filled with temples from around the Empire. The cult of Isis was well established, temples to Jupiter, and Apollo were on opposite sides of the forum. The most prominent temple, other than the Imperial one, was the shrine to the Matres, the three sacred mothers, who were honored throughout Europe. Always they would be invoked for every decision involving the prosperity of the city.

True to their word, the architects had been busy on the construction of the Villa Antipas on a hillside rich with vineyards. The vineyards had apparently been established for some years, as their lines were extensive, even in the winter. There were workers selectively pruning back the vines, leaving the stumps and the supporting structures, but taking most of the loose twigs. The shoots would grow rapidly, but for now most of the hillside was brown, except for the occasional cedar tree marking the edge of a field.

I remembered Berenice's words about being willing to be brown and drab, and I thought of these plants. Every year they would be pruned back to almost nothing, but the next year, they would leap as if making up in a single spring a century of deprivation. This past year had been my pruning time, stripping away all of my childhood fantasies, and leaving roots waiting for the springs of adulthood.

Berenice's hair shone, still red and golden, though she was more than 60 years of age. "One day soon, Salomé, my hair will turn white, and you will know that I am fading. Remember me in your age, for it can happen in a moment." She signaled for the chariots to start again, and we rode into the Villa Antipas where Agrippa and Antipas awaited our arrival.

Sunset was touching all the hills as Berenice took off her headdress and shook out her hair and combed it out as we paused within sight of the Villa Archelaus, on the hillside beyond on the road from Lugdunum to Vienne. "I am home, Salomé, and here Archelaus always wanted to see my hair shine. Now he is gone, almost 20 years, but he fancied me his Queen of Heaven, like Berenice of Egypt."

The sun faded as we left the horses to be watered and took ourselves immediately to the baths to get rid of the dust of travel. The builders had finished the calidarium, the heated baths filled by hypocausts from the river, a rare luxury in Galilee, but here a necessary part of life in Gaul. I could learn to enjoy this time, however brief it might be.

I sat with my grandmother in the gathering darkness, watching the stars. She mused, "Queen of Heaven, "she breathed. "O my child, look at the stars above you. Before you were born, Bat Mara used to sit with me, homesick for Babylon, but she was already old beyond her years. She told me one night, not long after we met, 'the stars do not change, but our stories are always growing. Each year, a new mageed, a storyteller, comes along, and paints new pictures on the heavens. A thousand years ago, it was the Babylonians, pointing out the wandering stars, the planets, after which we name the days of the week. We keep their stories alive every day without knowing.'

'Your name, your Majesty, speaks of the stars. In Egypt they tell a story about a Queen, with golden hair like yours, who made a vow to give it to the Gods if her husband Ptolemy came home from battle. She shaved her head, and Isis took it and placed it in the heavens, between the Lady and the Charioteer, an emblem of her protection. You are descended from her, and your hair will fade only when your work is done—but her stars will never fade. Live wisely, my lady.' "

"The night sky is full of wonders, Salomé," she sighed, "and we learn from it what we can. She is the only queen of history I know with her own stars. Will there ever be another?"

I wondered how Bat Mara's mageed was getting along, with his stories of lilies, and stormclouds, wind, and weather. I would see her in two months, so much to share.

•   •   •

Agrippa, though younger than my stepfather by more than 30 years, had taken charge of the household. He and Antipas were in constant consultation over which servants to trust, which soldiers would be the best in the field. Agrippa had served in Vienne in his many travels, and Lugdunum was the center of Gaul's administration, so he knew which of the councilors of the city to listen to, and which to shun.

The equites, the titled horse soldiers, were the height of freedman society and they sought favors from every landed royalty, praetor, or Senator that chose to build in Lugdunum. As the Herods were known horse traders they had noted the Arabian steeds pulling our chariots, though we had not seen them, and soon were sending messengers to obtain an audience. The Fair of the Three Gauls had been held since the founding of the city and was now held every year in the Amphitheatre. Surely Herod Antipas, known from Galilee to Cyrene for his trade with horses would want to establish a market here.

Would there be more "baggage" I wondered, some subtle undercurrent of weapons or silk, or subterfuge. I listened carefully to the messengers and then asked Berenice for advice.

"You are adept at listening, Salomé," she spoke, "as silk threads connect the Empire even here in Gaul. Roman soldiers rotate throughout the Empire, and a centurion who has served in Judaea is just as likely to be serving in Lugdunum the following year. Only Rome has a larger trading base. Caligula speculates in the market and is fast approaching his credit limit with my factors in Alexandria. Though the faces are different, the same greed courses through Caligula as did Archelaus. Caligula is likely to survive a few years longer, but he gambles far too freely, and I cannot be watching my son Agrippa all the time. However, this trade of Antipas may give me some leverage, if he will listen to a mother's advice."

I found myself having to make choices. I could understand Berenice's loyalty to her son, and my mother to her husband, but what was mine? I was a newly engaged woman of wealth, and needed to find a middle road. As I was no longer, technically, my stepfather's silent witness, I found myself at loose ends. Until he formally dismissed me from his court, therefore, I would attempt to keep apprised of developments. Court had become a second home to me, even if I was no longer the center of attention.

I joined my mother in the great audience hall, at the moment open-aired as the ceiling had not yet been finished. The workers, as Antipas was now in state, worked on the kitchens and began to fit out the stables and did their best to keep the noise level down when the equites came to call. Antipas had to rely on Agrippa for stablemasters and groomsmen beyond his basic entourage, as he had come with only one charioteer when he fled Rome in the middle of the night.

A contingent of his own soldiers and workers from Galilee would be joining the household within a few days as they had already been in transit when we were in Capri. The architect was his personal representative from the palace at Caesarea Philippi and he wanted this villa to be laid out in a similar fashion, though at a reduced scale. In Lugdunum, however, he intended to have a stablemaster familiar with Arabian and Persian horses, as he already maintained a good reputation for fine breeds.

Georgio had contacted several Persian tradesmen and now came to introduce them to Herod. "Your excellency," Georgio bowed, "the tradesman Lu Tsang of the Han" indicating a man in saffron robes. My eyes widened. Was this the monk from Gadarenes? "He brings greetings from the court of the Han, and from your factor in Petra."

Antipas leaned forward, "Is Aretas moving again? Do I need to watch my outposts?"

The monk bowed low. "Our embassy keeps its ears open, and we fear you may need to return to Galilee soon. We trade with both Persian and Mongol breeders, and the east is quite restless. But I bring you good word from Gadarenes."

"You dissemble well, what word?"

"A certain golden carpet has arrived at the border, and its sheen is quite rare. We realize that you keep watch for these goods, what should we do with it?"

"A man with black boots has requested it as surety, and I wish him to be able to pay his debts. See to it that it is not delayed." By this I knew that Caligula would get his carpet.

Apparently, Antipas had been prepared since before our leaving Caesarea for his court appearance in Capri. "Where shall it be sent, your excellency?" continued the monk.

"To the factors at Alexandria, they do business with both my household and his, and they are expecting more of the same." Herod spoke, "Georgio, ensure the receipt is written in Farsi as well as in Latin, we wish no misunderstandings."

I could feel the wheels turning in my mind. Hired swords came with this shipment, but they would be covered under trade goods. If caught, soldiers protecting cloth would be understood as caravansary escorts, not as mercenaries. Shrewd indeed.

"Wish the ambassador well, and tell him I hope to see him at the Gadarenes' fair next spring."

"As you wish," spoke Lu. "Are you in need of more horses, a stronger breed perhaps?" he queried.

"Yes, strong lines of black horses, and a select few for the marketplace. We wish to build a reputation here for the best of the breed, not castoffs."

The markets Antipas started here in Lugdunum would last throughout my lifetime. Even when he lost his position elsewhere, Herod would maintain his reputation to the last.

Georgio found me in the garden after the audience. "I know that you wish to send a letter to Queen Shaqilath. Tradesman Lu is perhaps your best method. He will be in Petra before the month is over, and can be discreet. Do not betray your house, but trust your instincts."

I wished to be discreet. I found my blue silk kirtle and cut a ribbon from it. I took a quill and a small piece of parchment and wrote:

"To Queen Shaqilath of Petra, the Sparrow sends greetings. My husband Philip of Galianthis is a kind and generous man. I am secure in my own place for the moment, and wish you safety. The winds blow where they will, and I will listen for your voice."

With the silk and the indication of marriage, that would carry quite a bit of news without betraying any confidence. I sought out Georgio and asked that he deliver it to Lu for his journey. I felt the breeze on my cheek and knew that this was my first words as a ruler of a household. So small, and yet carrying volumes.

How many soldiers, weavers, and cooks would I be sending word through over the years. It now seems countless, but each message, however brief, would start my network of informants on its way, and though weeks and months would sometimes pass before return, each message gave me one more taste of freedom, away from my stepfather at last.

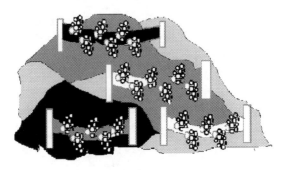

CHAPTER 26

Berenice

I woke at dawn to the sounds of neighing horses. The Market of the Three Gauls was to take place soon, near the first of November, and I was looking forward to learning my place in this new province. Far from being a backwater, the city of Vienne and Villa Archelaus was close to Lugdunum and supplied stabling for many of the wealthier householders, and the vineyards were sweet and were heavy with fruit.

I had been whisked away to Villa Archelaus less than three days prior, just as Herod Antipas' negotiations were getting interesting. Who knew which horse trader would show up at his door, begging favors, a word with a Friend of the Emperor, if you please? The fawning became amusing, even if it looked somewhat ludicrous on grizzled old soldiers seeking out what I had perceived as a man unfamiliar with their ways.

I learned, soon enough, that Antipas thrived on the attention as it took him back to his earlier days as a legionnaire, a part of his life I had never known. In his early 20s he had traveled Gaul, and Belgia, and even parts of Germania before he came to Rome and met my mother at a banquet.

This portion of his life was 20 years past, when he had been only scarcely older than I now was, so this was an old soldier having new wine with the newest recruits. The language was coarse, and in some flight of impulse, I was ordered to Villa Archelaus to spend time with my grandmother.

My grandmother sat like an old spider at her weaving. She was amused, and her eyes sparkled. Her hair was still red, though as she had warned, it was rapidly turning gray. Not a day went by when I did not see a change of a wrinkle, or another turn of hair from the shining auburn to ancient silver.

As had happened in Rome, she now used henna only occasionally, when she needed to appear before outsiders, but in her own household she no longer tried to keep up appearances.

"You are young, and know only Judea and its markets. Now I must teach you the ways of a Roman matrona, you must learn books, dockets, accounts, and have a swift memory for faces, genealogies, and family connections. I know you observe well, or you would not have survived so far, but now comes the work of the scholar."

"I have learned Greek, grandmother, and some Latin, is there more?"

"The Eastern Empire is largely Greek so learning your letters and commentaries in that language has served you well, but now you are in the West, and the language of the West is Latin. You must learn the great orators, read the words of Julius Caesar, and learn why Gaul was so precious to him. Though he was deposed as a tyrant who conquered quickly, wishing to match Alexander in his strength, still his memoirs are the best record we have of the conquest, still working itself out five generations hence."

My grandfather Antipater was given Roman citizenship by him. Herod the Great, my uncle and your grandfather, was put on the throne by Marc Anthony and Octavian Augustus. Our family has been caught up in the affairs of Rome from that day forward. The city of Lugdunum has become the shining city of lights, honoring Augustus and Julius as Divine.

"Gaul is in three parts, and the Three Gauls were the first province Julius Caesar conquered. It was the heritage he passed to Octavian, and now Lugdunum rivals Rome in the number of trade routes and fairs that take place in its precincts. You must be at market, and observe."

"Do they bargain as much here as in Damascus?"

"Not as much, they are more shrewd, and devious. They offer a high price, and you must visit early in the day, or be the last customer as evening falls to get any true bargains. The more you know of the goods that are being sold and the families who sell them, the more you will know which merchants to avoid, and which to pursue, and which to pay even a high price."

And so I began listening to my grandmother's merchants, starting with silk—that rarity that had caused me such grief—woven into tapestries from Persia. I moved to linens from Egypt, then began inquiring of herbal dyers from Gaul as well as Tyre. Agents of distant households were included, and the occasional purveyor of perfumes and sleeping draughts.

With this latter, I inquired, "Grandmother, this latest merchant seemed to have a rare knowledge of sleeping draughts, is he also a strega, a poisoner?"

"No, but he knows where to find them. You remember Pandora? She was born in a village near here, so we always lay aside some time near the harvest to hear her rumors of wars, households who should be watched for, and learn what new medicinals she may have researched, their properties, and most especially, their antidotes. For every sickness caused by plants, there is also a cure, and sometimes they are confused."

"Confused, how?" I queried.

"If I give you a plant and you are healthy, these potions will you make you look sick, dyspepsic, uncomfortable, though you are only slightly injured," she murmured.

"Sometimes you can play ill for a month to keep from being bothered by particularly insistent merchants, and if they do manage to get through you can be quite convincing, pale and wan, and looking feverish, without actually causing yourself harm. Guile can be more valuable than gold if played right."

I was to learn how useful that small subterfuge was when I bore my first child. The sickness could be cured with judicious teas, but if someone not pregnant took them, they would be queasy for four days.

I was able to keep everyone away by rumors long enough to actually know my first-born son without having courtiers hanging on his every move.

•   •   •

Brittania also traded in tin and copper, as not all the swords and weapons were made of Damascus steel or the tempered iron of Greece. The bronze and brass was made into cookware, the copper salts were used as mordants for brilliant dyes found only in Hibernia.

I began to watch for these colors, as the oranges and brilliant greens could not be made with plants in the Galilee. Berenice's weavers were famous, so many merchants came through her home. Because Berenice was still a woman of wealth, and expected to entertain dignitaries, she required dinner robes of all guests, and provided servants to wash both their feet and their hands upon entering her home. This required an anteroom, and a certain dignity, which established an order that kept the house from becoming rough and tumultuous.

She was a firm believer in prevention, so we kept a very clean kitchen, and—as she was a scrupulous observant Jew—two complete preparation areas to ensure that we kept kosher. To simplify matters, we ate mostly fish rather than meat or fowl, using meat only on ceremonial occasions so that it could be carefully slaughtered and ensuring purity.

Nothing escaped my grandmother's notice, however, not a broken horseshoe, or a fevered cook. If a servant took ill, he or she was immediately removed to a separate area of the house and kept observed until a full recovery.

Berenice had not been lying to Sejanus when she mentioned the soldiers invading the vineyards. She kept a watch force, and knew ever soldier by name, so any rotation or new face was immediately noted.

What a difference from Antipas' household. Though he also kept a strict kitchen, he was a soldier, and his language and that of the court, was not censored. Like, but so unlike, I would form my own path between the worlds. All these factors came into play as we left her household for the Fair of Three Gauls.

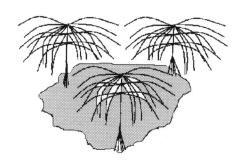

CHAPTER 27

Three Gauls

What Rome lacked in its opulence was the splendor of autumn. As the leaves faded around Lugdunum, the woods were golden and the willows wore yellow ribbons in the breeze. Though many of the households took every branch of the willow for baskets, we kept a few for their beauty, and almost a sign of ostentatious wealth as we could afford not to trim them but leave them to bend as weeping maidens over the edges of the ponds.

The bells of a horse jangled under me as I rode with Antipas, Agrippa, Herodias, and Herod into the great Market of the Three Gauls, and the performances, contests, and displays to come. We were the new faces come to fair, and we wished to be seen.

The Fair had been founded by Julius Caesar and now after 100 years was an event not to be missed. Each tribe in Gaul had its favorites, its colors, its household dress, its customs, its dances, and all were on display. The tribes of Judah rarely showed their colors except in the fall, and here were people of many tribes drawn together, not only from Gaul, but from Cyrene, Germania, Greece, and Nubia.

Our cousins the Ptolemy's had fled to Nubia after the fall of Cleopatra, but now were people of distinction throughout the Empire, and they brought the wealth of Ethiopia even to Gaul. One could see rare striped furs, and river horse hide shields on display along with spears made from the iron of the hills beyond the cataracts of the Nile.

The merchants were dark-faced men, dressed in bright white, and the contrast was dazzling. The spice merchants were represented, and the fabled odors of Edom, and saffrons of India wafted through the marketplace making our mouths water even at the third hour of the day. The spices were from our own ships, the merchant fleet that Antipas had managed to secure during our stay in Syracuse, bargaining under the Cretan ambassador's nose, and from his own servants when he was indisposed. I looked forward to rich stews as the nights were beginning to turn crisp.

Lugdunum was the capital of the ancient province of Celtica, renamed Lugdunensis by Augustus, but the people still called themselves Celts. The sole Roman garrison guarded the Roman mint, the largest building of the province, but all the armies of the Rhine converged during the Fair as this was a time of trade between all the peoples.

Georgio was in his element as an old soldier, as there were legionnaires everywhere. Two weeks of hard riding from Rome, the legionnaires owned Lugdunum as the Senate owned Rome, and the difference was clear. Soldiers were given way as princes would be in the Forum. Now I understood Berenice's consternation, for no place was without soldiers.

However, the priestesses of the Mother were given the same deference as Vestals, so I was not as anxious as I would have been. Jerusalem had many soldiers, so it was familiar.

The ancient priests of the Celtoi, the Druids, were still in evidence at the fair, and were called upon to bless the games. After the opening, in which Berenice and Agrippa were both called out, we found ourselves in a sea of merchants.

The word had gone out from Caligula rather quickly and I seemed to always have a cordon around me, soldiers gently steering away any who would get close to the niece of the heir to the Emperor's friend. Whereas in Judaea or in Galilee I was taunted by the Roman soldiers, here I was their pet, the exotic. I was not the ordinary, and the change was refreshing—to a point. I wanted to learn to bargain at these fairs, and with a soldier at my elbow, I couldn't gossip as freely. How would the sparrow find her seeds in this dry ground? Well, there were ways to test this. "Good merchant, have you any cotton cloth today? I need something with a sheen to it." My Latin was broken, but I needed to practice.

"Smoothe by weave, or by thread?" spoke the merchant.

"By thread," I spoke. This merchant knew his cloth.

"Syria or Egypt?" he spoke again.

"Syria, from the north coast," I spoke.

The merchant smiled. "I have something of what you desire, though precious little, the winds have not been favorable this season. Will this do? I have but a cubit."

The fabric he brought was unusual, it was utilitarian Syrian cotton, but it was shot through carefully with what looked like silk threads, so carefully woven that it had the sheen that was soft, not coarse.

"Where did you come by this cloth?"

"Merchants from Persia weave it themselves, from their own stores. Tapestries take many threads, but these judicious weaves carry the strength of cotton without losing the beauty of the silk."

"Not from further East then?"

"No, for many years we had to wait for the long road across the Himalayas, but now we grow the mulberry trees ourselves. The silkworm does not thrive as well in Persia as in Cathay, but our cloth is still beautiful in its own way."

"It is indeed, you have made a sale this day, and I will buy all you have. Know that I will look for more from this source? How will I know your mark?"

"Look for the winged man on our tents, we are keepers of the flame."

"So far from home?"

"You forget the legions, Mithras is well known here. His sign protects us."

The soldier next to me made an odd gesture. The merchant returned a countersign. "We are brothers then, ooldier."

By this I knew that the legions would also be a source of news. What would I now learn that had been closed to me in Galilee?

I turned to the soldier. "Since you have become my keeper, can you share your secret?"

"Only that we have our own passwords among brothers, and you seem to have a way with keeping silence. Our Mysteries are for the men, as the Mothers are for the women, so we respect you as long as you keep your distance."

"I have eyes, but I also have a heart. Know that you have a friend in Galilee, soldier, what is your name?"

"Xerxes is my name in Farsi, Ahasuerus in your tongue, but they call me Longinus from the size of my spear. The Romans do not speak other languages well, and they think us all Barbarians. Why do you ask?"

"As you seem to be assigned to me and I will be returning to the Galilee within a few months, we may as well learn to converse. I am not used to an escort in the market," I ventured.

"My sisters also love to gossip and only in Persia can they be free to do so, you are a rarity in Rome, a woman with both a tongue and discretion. It will be an honor."

"Then riddle me this, how do Persians and Jews keep such close quarters and yet not share their faiths?" I queried.

"I believe that your books tell you of this tale, Salomé, your own story of Ahasuerus and the beautiful Queen Esther. For us, it is the greatest of our kings before Alexander, Cyrus the Wise, who chose her above all others to be his Queen. Her influence was great, commanding an empire to honor all the faiths within it, not simply the king's belief."

"As this was the teaching of Zoroaster, that a man's conscience is a gift from Ahura Mazda, the Wise Lord who makes all good, Cyrus chose to protect those whom his own edicts had declared outlaw, and opened up the borders to your old holdings in what is now Judaea, but was then Canaan and lower Assyria." This soldier was proud of his faith.

"I remember her story well, Xerxes," I continued, "but thought that it was Xerxes the conqueror who was Ahasuerus, Cyrus' son. For many of us, because the names were Persian, even we considered it a fable as to how Marduk, your greatest god, brought Ishtar, the queen of love from the heavens to be the wife of the king."

"It is strange that we have kept the story true in our tales, recognizing that though you Jews took Persian names of Mordecai and Esther, you kept your own faith, even through a telling that paralleled our own stories of Divine intervention. Perhaps over time, the Wise Lord will bring us both to truth." He smiled, giving a sign I knew to be that of Perseus, the Warrior, whom he emulated.

"I have learned discretion early, as without having open ears, I could not have kept my head in Herod's court." I replied, making a countersign without thought.

Xerxes was amazed. "Who taught you that sign?"

"An old dancer was my teacher, who had lived in Babylon for many years. She taught me many signs as she gave me instruction. I thought they were common knowledge in Persia?" I observed.

"No, the signs are kept to families, so unless she was trained by Persian women, she would never have seen the signs, and certainly not in public," he spoke, "but you use your gestures as if they are simply a part of you" he clarified.

"When you learn them as gestures of dance, and they are woven into your moves, you don't think of them, and they are automatic, as if speaking to a friend across a crowded room."

"Your teacher was wise," spoke Xerxes. "Did she assign meanings to them?" he continued

"No, she simply taught them as calls and responses between adept and apprentice," I replied, suddenly shy. "The passcodes are ancient, and as gestures they are simply countersigns.

"You know no secrets that the young would not pick up, but that is all I can confirm. Likewise, I observe your customs, often without clear meaning. You reenact your story of Esther and Ahasuerus every year, even in Persia, as we retell the story of our greatest Warrior hidden away throughout the Empire. Who knows whose story will last the longest without corruption?" Xerxes commented.

"In truth, I will need to write to my teacher and let her know that she was taught well. She is now quite old."

"I will ensure your safety from this moment onward, young sparrow."

"Sparrow?" I queried, startled.

"You fly in your mind above the battlements, is that not your name from your Grandmother?" he smiled.

"Does Berenice leave me no secrets then?"

"From her guards, nothing, but we keep our voices unheard unless spoken to," he replied with a chuckle.

A sailor, an heir to the Empire, and the unexpected gift of trust from a Persian soldier. My family brought me many gifts as well as curses. I would need each one to keep alive in just a few years.

I had thought I had but one month to be prepared for my journey back to Galilee. Bat Mara, however, heard of my plans, and by the end of November had sent me a letter, moving the wedding to mid-March, between Purim and Passover, a befitting time for purification. My head was spinning with names, faces, and ploys.

I was questioned every afternoon, and tutored, and I had thought Bat Mara's training was rough. This tested my mind, and every skill in subterfuge I knew would not turn the tutors aside. And so for November, well into December, coming up to the Feast of Lights, I remained in Berenice's home.

Berenice introduced me to factors from Egypt and from Crete, ones not known to Antipas. "Your stepfather and betrothed are busy in their own matters, this way you will always have your own source of income."

Like the tossing of the dice she was very careful when the odds were long against her, but her early investments in winter wheat and Egyptian cotton had borne fruit. In Egypt, her holdings were mostly monetary. Judea had gone through drought in the past 20 years, but her household were always well fed from fields near the Nile, and when silks became precious, her early investments in cotton made her merchants quite wealthy.

She took only a portion from each merchant, at judicious intervals, and only if her portion would not put them in jeopardy. She ran a bank in Alexandria, financed by her holdings, and Caligula himself had taken loans from it. This woman was my grandmother, and yet she held the Empire in her small hands.

Today was Crete. By a loan gone bad, she now owned three ships and was working on turning it into a fleet. Wine and apples from Gaul were to go to Crete in exchange for olive oil and quinces, a fair exchange, and one which would be seasonal, and thus steady, money. The original owner of the ships was now her hireling, but she had a soft spot for him. A shipwreck was what had turned his loan into a liability, and that was a chance for every merchant every time he went to sea.

"Gathos, I realize that you have had a very bad blow from this most recent mishap, but realize my position, I cannot extend you more funds. My merchants have never been happier than when you return, but with this shipwreck, I cannot loan you reserve. You have little to bargain with."

"Your Majesty," pleaded the merchant, "all my family knows is the sea and not the land. Do not leave me destitute."

"I have only one choice before me, I can take you as a servant, and you forfeit the ships, but you stay at sea. You are a captain, and have a family, but the deeds to the ships are mine."

"Leave me one to my name."

"You will appear before the merchants of Crete with no change, but the deeds are mine. With work for the next three years, you may be able to buy your way back to one ship, but the other two will remain mine, and I expect you will inspect and bring in at least two more to the fleet by the end of next year. We currently sail from Gaul to Crete and back again, but I wish to add Alexandria and Tyre to the bargain, so we may bring cloth to this end of the Empire. I can make a bargain with you, but only if you step down."

"You will not shame me before my peers?"

"No, not even the galley master will know, but between us you will keep your word. You know you started there, on a trireme, more than 20 years ago. Archelaus saw promise in you, and I don't want the investment wasted. I introduce you, today, to my granddaughter, Salomé. I mean to leave those ships to her, for investment in the silks of Tyre, so she also will know your secret, but we guard our own."

"Tyre. it has been many years since I was home." Berenice the golden-haired matrona seemed to fade for a moment, and I saw an old woman in her place. Then, in an instant, it was my grandmother again.

"Grandmother, do I have leave to speak?" I ventured.

"Yes, do you have something to add?" she replied, curious.

"I recognized the name Gathos from an old legend of ours. Goliath of Gath was a giant, and this captain of yours seems to have his strength. Are you perhaps Phoenician?"

"My family is known in Tyre, and have plied the waters of the Great Sea since Hannibal. What do you know of the children of the sea?"

"I met a priest of Tyre in Cyrene and respect your customs. Did you have an older brother who died in the flames?"

"That was the cost of the God to our family, your Highness," he bowed low.

"The first-born is often the most precious, and the weakest of your line, so I know that the flames are in your eyes. I will confirm my grandmother's vow to you. Treat us well, and the flame of your household will never go out. Betray us, and the priest of Tyre will hear from me."

"Your Excellency, do not betray my trust."

"No Gathos, my pledge on it, I will have my ships by the end of next year, and I plan to wear silk to a wedding in Galilee in the Spring. Bring me that silk, and our bargain is sealed." Berenice smiled with pride, and I knew I had won my place in her heart. The sparrow was now a hawk, worthy of her inheritance.

CHAPTER 28

Small Moments

Small moments come back to me as I think of my grandmother. Though the horse fair would take up every waking minute of my stepfather, I was caught up instead in the small doings of running a large estate. Waking up in the morning to a houseful of servants was not unusual, but being the one giving those servants orders, watching over accounts, berating one while praising another in the same moment was a gift I learned at Berenice's feet.

"Leona," she spoke, "make sure to bleach these linens more brightly, they need to contrast against the wood grain, not fade against it. Andros, your carving is exquisite, can you bring out the claws of the lions in the next couch, I am looking for a certain effect when I next give a banquet." In this way, she would gently reprove, but also give direction so that she would get what she wanted without coercion.

"Sparrow, I am giving you charge over the weavers, that seems to be your gift. See if you can choose something that will set off these Egyptian alabasters." She spoke these words in front of the spinners, so that they knew they should listen to me.

I thought of a tapestry I had seen in Gadarenes, and I laughed. I thought a moment. "Ducks hidden in the reeds, I want you to be subtle. I would like to hang this behind the tables in such a way as the ducks look alive, and about to peck at the grain in these bowls."

"Always give a person at feast something to capture the eye," spoke my grandmother, "if you need to distract them from what you are saying, do it with beauty, not with ugliness."

I thought of the ravens of my dance, so long ago, always watching for some bright thing to take away to their nests. "Here," I said to the weavers, opening my purse. "Take these copper coins and hide them in the tree limbs as you weave. They will capture the setting sun which comes just across the portico there. . . and over here, we need something dark, the whitewash is blinding. Cover it with lacework, something with an open weave in greens and browns."

"You change the seasons at will, your Excellency. It is now the wine harvest, and you bring summer to the hall," spoke the chief spinster.

"Yes, make it bright as midsummer so that we toast the sun as it fades away."

Berenice chuckled, "You would make this the garden of your dances, but without death."

"I will honor my mother and my grandmother, her hair of red gold, and yours becoming silver. Cinnamon and alabaster, a good combination."

"You will always charm with your words, my sparrow," she spoke, "I am blessed that we have met again. Now walk with me."

She took me to the vineyards. "See those workmen? The ones with the braided hair?" She pointed out three or four whose hair seemed to be woven with leaves and branches."

"Sejanus' spies? I thought he was dead, I saw him die!"

"Do you think that cutting the head would kill that serpent? His soldiers have sprung up like the Hydra with many heads instead of his one. Rome will be restless for another generation. The peace of Augustus is fast fading, and I fear for Rome, even though I am financing the new Emperor."

"Then you know of Caligula's plans?"

"He and my son Agrippa have been friends since youth, I know that they gamble, and are spendthrifts, but something tells me that I have my small part to play, and even though Caligula may become a demon to some, there is destiny which must be played out."

"What do you mean, grandmother?"

"Sometimes the gentle can only be seen by contrast to the cruel. The whip of an old master is felt to be better than freedom to one born a slave. A new day will come, but like slaves being freed without learning, it will not be an easy change."

"Then what do you do?"

"I plant small seeds here in my garden," she indicated the herb garden, now beginning to go to seed. "My servants are all freedmen, not one will give birth to slaves in the next generation, but I fear that this entire age will pass away before something new arrives. I hear about a prophet who heals with a word, but I think that even he will have to fade before the might of Rome before something better arises."

"You have heard of Yoshua, the storyteller?"

"Bat Mara mentions him often in her letters to me, and he always speaks of the small things, the sparrows, and the flowers in a garden. For that reason, like roses at the end of winter, I have hope."

Three emperors have come and gone in my lifetime, and yet, I have survived. Perhaps it was for just for this moment, and this winter, to see you, my fragile rose, come to womanhood. Learn to cherish those small stories, as you will be a woman of station, and far outlive me."

"Do you have a foreboding?"

"Like Bat Mara, I occasionally glimpse things that might be, and things that will be, and they are sometimes confused. I see you with a crown of gold, surrounded by flowering trees, and yet at the same time, there is fire around you, like a burning city. Which will be the truth, I wonder?"

"But come, let us continue our walk."

And so we took the slow path around the fields, the last apple trees being plucked, the press of the vineyards, the winter plowing begun—each thing in its order. She knew someone in every field, and no one frowned when they saw her coming. At each place she stopped and pointed out a broken fence, a worker trimming a hedge, each place that sought pruning.

"This is my pruning time, Salomé. Everything I have built is being cut back, and I lay away for the winter, as it will come soon enough. My prayer is to see you married, but I am not sure that I will. Come and drink wine with me, and let us toast the sunset."

And so we sat, for almost two months, while the world went as it will, and I learned the small things before the great ones overshadowed this wintry bower.

•   •   •

One evening, as the Roman month of January was about to begin, Berenice took me to her wardrobe. She unpinned her hair, and its golden cloud swirled out from the Roman headdress she wore in public. Now the gold was lined deeply with silver, and her face had become aged.

"My dear sparrow, I have many things to teach you, yet I fear that we may not have as much time together as I would like. I have, perhaps, five years more before I will fall silent, and so I want to show you some heirlooms of my house."

"The first, though, is significant, as it is my ketubah, from when Archelaus and I were married. As one of the very first contracts to be written, as I was marrying a descendant of Salomé Alexandra, it was very special. I was no longer young. I was not a blushing bride to be, but one already with grown children when my mother came to the throne, and Archelaus was not a man whom many liked. But through the years, I have realized that sometimes law and custom are interwoven, and because this one document has enabled me to hold onto these lands and the power in the Senate that they have given me, you should know of its existence."

"Jewish law and custom are highly unusual in the Roman Empire, as we are a scattered people. Though we have an official place of origin, our peoples carry their customs with them, and their ways of doing things far from Jerusalem. We have synagogues in almost every province, one dedicated to Ptolemy and Berenice of Egypt, several in Carthage, even one named after Emperor Augustus.

"We seem to be entwined with the powers of every country we dwell in. This ketubah is honored in all of them, spelling out my rights to my husband's property, his dowry, and his lands. As a will, it is parallel to any Roman document of law, and as respected." She carefully unrolled the document further. "It is written in Aramaic, older than the Greeks or the Romans in its use in our courts, and readable even in Babylon. Never forget your ketubah, Salomé, as it will protect you in Rome, in Syria, and wherever else you may travel."

"The second is this single bronze coin. It is the smallest denomination of Jewish coinage, with two pomegranates and a cornucopia on it, and is poorly made. But it was given to me at our wedding by Archelaus as a symbol of my acceptance. Everything else in the wedding was trappings, accepting his coin was to accept his life. It is the small things that make a life, not the big ones, and something as insignificant as this coin, now given in the temple as widow's pensions, may affect all of your life to come."

"The third is my bridal veil, made of silk and covered with gold coins. This veil was put on my head by Archelaus himself the morning of our wedding as I came to him from my mikvah, before anyone else could see me. Though we were grown aged, and had married before, this simple act ensured that Archelaus knew whom he was to marry and that there would be no surprises at the public ceremony."

"This custom goes back to Jacob and Leah, when she was presented to him as his beloved bride Rachel. When he lifted the veil at his bridal bed, she was not the bride he had chosen, though she remained faithful to him for more than 50 years. From that point on, the husband himself will veil the bride the morning of a wedding to ensure that his beloved is his chosen, and no other."

"You learned a dance of seven veils, in which you stripped away all purity. Over this next year, as your flows come, you should dedicate them to purification, and restoration. You are wounded, and this will help to make you whole. Your mother sent you to me for healing, as only a woman as aged as I, beyond the flows of womanhood, is given that responsibility."

"I also give you this bottle of rose water as a gift to Bat Mara. You will be leaving within the week for Galilee, as she has selected you as her bridal attendant. You will watch over her in her mikvah, as she has many years to wash clean."

"Her beloved rabbi may have pronounced her healed, but even he, when he cleanses lepers, sends them to be cleansed before they return to their homes and families. You will act for her as if she were a bride of 14, and lead her through the prayers of remembering and moon times, and this act will help to heal you as well."

"Grandmother," I breathed, "why would she choose me?"

"You were a weapon in her hand, and so she feels that it is best that you also become the physician and the healer. Although the death of the Baptist on a whim was not unusual, particularly among Persian satrapies, in which Herod sometimes places himself, you did not prepare for that dance as a simple murderer, but through prayer as if you were an avenging angel, and that makes this next year all the more necessary."

"You have seen death at your right hand with the Baptist, and at your left with Sejanus, now you must learn to give life, and blessing Bat Mara at her mikvah will leave you with clean hands and a pure heart. We are given the privilege of repairing the world. Go to Galilee with my blessings, as I do not know if you will see me in wealth much longer."

I rose, bowed formally, and went to my rooms and began to choose what I should take on my journey. The bottle of rosewater I put with the silver chain of my father. Small things indeed, able to fit into a very small pouch, yet I value them still, above any cloth of gold.

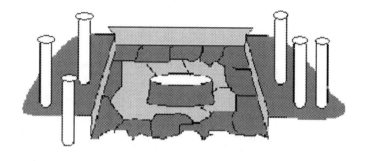

CHAPTER 29

Masillia

Berenice woke me in the morning to begin to travel to Galilee. My journey would be in easy stages, as we had two months before I was expected, and Berenice, this time, would be going back to Samaria, for the first time in 20 years. Georgio would be accompanying us, as the most trusted body servant of the household.

As we traveled southward, we followed the aqueducts along the high ridges. They crossed valleys and were one of the major wonders of the Empire, bringing water during times of drought, and enduring even through earthquakes. The ones that had fallen in Gadarenes were brand new, but with the repairs, they would now last a lifetime.

We would be traveling first to Masillia, one of the last remaining Greek trading ports in the middle of the Roman Empire. Though it had been conquered 50 years ago, it still retained the customs of forum and philosophy, even with a ruling body of senators, and a respect for learning that endured even in the rough soldier's life that the Empire had become. Georgio was at home here, as he seemed to be everywhere, as Greek was his second language beyond his homeland.

"As we are going to Crete, I wished to check with the merchants who have been storing our apples. It is now past the frost, and Berenice has been fortunate to have trees that bear fruit up to the winter snows," he observed.

"As the Great Sea retains its warmth," he continued, "the trees survive to bear this last crop which we will be shipping to Crete in exchange for cotton. The weavers of Crete make beautiful striped cloth of purples, blues, and very pale greens, like the ocean around them. There are rumors that they can take the ink of the octopus, and blend it with certain sea salts to make dies that will never fade."

"I would like to see that cloth, as my favorite fabrics seem to be fading under the Gallic sun, and I am missing the Spring," spoke Berenice.

"Then we will seek out the weavers when we arrive, your Majesty," Georgio addressed Berenice. "Your fleet has been thriving, one storm will not sweep away years of prosperity. The Jewish colonies have been thriving as well, and I believe you will be welcome."

"Why so, Georgio?" queried Berenice.

"Well, Pandora's reputation has preceded you, so you are known by certain herbalists as one who will buy sleeping draughts, but largely it is because you are the daughter of Salomé Alexandra."

"Why would that make a difference?" she spoke. "Salomé is more than 70 years dead."

"You have spent so much time at Rome that you do not hear all the rumors. After Archelaus's death, there were several rival factions, and one of the largest was in Crete. You have a distant cousin who was reputed to be one of Herod the Great's by-blows, by the name of Jonathan."

"As the grandson of the High Priest, or so it is said, he was looked upon as a revival of the Maccabeans, so many followed him as not only an heir to Herod the Great but one who carried the line of the last high priest. He and you are of an age, so you may be able to find common ground."

Georgio addressed me, then, clearly, "Though he died before you were born, Salomé, any descendent of Herod the Great is welcome in Crete, as it has one of the oldest Jewish colonies in the Roman Empire."

As of this moment, I, and my young cousin Berenice, barely two, and her sister, Drusilla, now only four, bore the hopes of many I had never met. And now I was marrying a Senator.

Again I learned the power that women of station have that they never realize until they seek to marry. If they grow up ignorant of their peers, it is only upon signing a marriage contract that they often learn the weight of years that depend upon their lives. What choices this? I must now learn the full circle of my husband's responsibilities, and his acquaintances. My mother had taught me much about the court of Herod, but I had not paid attention to the courts of women, who often survived their husbands and became sought after widows of influence.

As a first step, I asked Georgio to take me to the forum here in Masillia to see how it compared to Caesarea Phillipi. Now that I was a betrothed woman, my robes were much more conservative and I was expected to walk with a bodyguard, but I was not restricted here in Gaul as I would have been in Syria.

I could listen, and possibly reply to a point of discussion though today I simply wanted to listen to the topics of the day. The marketplace of ideas called the Greek forum is unique in the Roman Empire. It is a place where anyone can talk and hold discussion, and choose as a starting point practically any point of philosophy. Both men and women have risen to lifetime fame as debaters, poets, and dreamers. Diotima, Aristotle, Sappho, Appolonius, these names of legend were known even in Galilee.

The topic today was the subject of memory. Is there anything new under the sun? This subject intrigued me as I seem to have found myself wandering into myths and legends. Perhaps a debate would hone my thoughts for when I would later have to rule on precedents and legal matters.

"Freeman and soldiers, listen to my words," spoke the orator, a man in the robes of a younger son of one of the local merchant houses. "I would propose that we cannot dream the future, only remember the past. When we sleep, we review our past lives, we remember when the ancients built great cities, and think these thoughts are our own. But when we awake, we forget the source, and act as if we are instructed to see something new? Is there a counter?"

"My noble sir," spoke a soldier, "the fact that you wear a younger son's robes must be taken into account. A dream of greatness can be explained by always striving to be something you are not, the heir to the house. Can this, perhaps, be the source of your dreams, and your thoughts?"

"I am not certain that either of you have the truth," spoke a beggar. "I was born to my station, and can educate myself through your debate, something that could not have happened had I been born in another time and another place. Is this, for me, not something new?"

The merchant spoke again, "As a scribe, I trade in scrolls, and seek out scholars when something is unusual. Babylon is a thousand years old, and yet we still read their ancient writings. In this memory is sustained."

A slave scratched at his sleeve, and rubbed his shaved head. "As a slave, my master entrusts me with his sons, to educate them in oratory, grammar, and even the rudiments of law. I would be manumitted, but I would lose in freedom of body, what I now gain in freedom of thought."

The orator spoke again, "Are these stations changed, or are they new? I do not know. "My friends, you leave with both question and counter. The memories of ancients are as my dreams describe, and yet here is a man born to a lowly station who with his efforts grows beyond his means. Is there an equality of spirit when our differences are so stark?"

My thoughts coalesced. I had been told by Bat Mara that I would see fire and flood, sword and strife, before I found peace. She spoke of the clouds clearing, and these speakers gave voice to my often repeated inner debates. I was an only child, and so neither younger nor older. I was born to wealth, but knew many beggars. All my life I was surrounded by soldiers. As a woman, I was born with a path that threaded between them all. Had I been born in Cappadocia, I might have entered the army and no one would have been surprised. The Amazons left their traces everywhere. But here I stood, listening to the voices around me.

"Georgio," I turned, "would you teach me to protect myself?"

Georgio eyed me carefully, "you have more wit than many others your age, you already have many defenses, is there something more?"

"I realize my life is on a knife edge, and I would rather not have it pointed at me. Is there anything in your training that could help me to do something knew, something not expected by bodyguards?"

"I will think on this. Why would this debate conjure such thoughts?"

"It was the beggar, he spoke right through the soldier and the philosopher to me. He is not limited to station, nor training, but to his own desire for learning. Where I have grown, and I have learned, has been through listening to others and then choosing for myself, neither a nobleman nor a soldier's life. I need you, as a soldier, to advise me, I will need a philosopher to keep me honest. But most of all, I may need a beggar at my court to ensure that my body is as sharp as my wits."

"I will think on this, mistress" spoke Georgio at length. "You need to be trained in law and counsel, but you can use the services of a gymnast. Bat Mara trained you well in the dance, but your body, of late, has been neglected. When we arrive in Crete, I will inquire."

He whispered to me, "You must know that Berenice has become anxious for her health, and growing much more certain that she will not live for much longer than your wedding. We must put many things in place, be patient."

I touched the thread of silver at my neck, and thought of its links. Each new experience bound me to my destiny as certainly as this chain. What would be the next circle to be added to its length?

CHAPTER 30

Sparring Partners

Georgio had traveled with the legions, and had learned combat techniques from every manner of soldier. True to his word, he sought out a system of combat which would protect an unarmed person of slight weight. From Persia he had made contacts with the saffron-robed monks who often acted as bodyguards. From Sparta, he had learned unarmed combat and the spirit of the battle companions, learning to trust that person with your life.

I thought sea legs only referred to keeping one's balance and keeping from sickness over the waves as a ship tossed and turned. From Georgio I soon learned a whole new meaning, one which would enable me to defend myself in dangerous situations, when other women would have become victims. Gaining these sea legs was even more grueling than stability on land and sea. Georgio taught me balance even when wheeling through the air so that I could crumple with a blow and so sustain no damage, and yet, when necessary, hold like steel to a stance.

I had heard from my father that the women of the Celts fought beside the men, as naked as they, stripped bare to frighten their enemies and just as vicious. I had heard of Amazons from Scythia, legends, I thought, but in my life the legends were real, and the facts were so few. If I were caught alone, away from bodyguards, I must be prepared.

And so began a course of study that has kept me limber my many years. Each day a gymnast continues to work with me, so that though I am old, and my bones ache, my body remains supple as the day I began my dance. I know now what Bat Mara knew, that a body kept fit will ward off disease, even when it seems crippling.

The week in Masilia passed quickly, and we found ourselves on board the family quadreme bound for Sardinia. We would be touching on many ports, often for only an hour, while loading the annual shipment of quinces, or fabric, or wine, or oil. Each had its place in the hold, and each had an eager market awaiting it in Crete, or Cyprus, or Tarsus. My grandmother's holdings in each place were small, often but a single office, but their influence reached many ears, so she often knew when a credit would not be honored long before the factor. With a word here, and a carefully placed messenger there, she often allayed domestic unrest without a single blow. In this, she surpassed both Antipas and Agrippa. In later years, Agrippa would follow her example and be known throughout the Empire for his good judgment, but he learned it from his mother.

The trip to Sardinia was over a smooth sea, so I had the opportunity to sit on the deck with my grandmother. Her hair was now radiant again, the troubles of the past weeks had all but faded, but the lines in her face had remained.

I could recognize that her words of age had been prophetic, age would come quickly, so I listened to her every word.

"Sparrow," she spoke. "You may notice that I often spar with Georgio, even when he is right."

"Yes, Grandmother," I replied, "it seems a pattern with you."

"Like a well-placed foot will trip even the heaviest soldier, I keep my wits sharp by my words. Though soft-spoken, when one has been listening, one can bypass hours of dissent by a gentle reproof."

"I notice," she continued, "that you have continued your dancing, though with a different purpose now."

"Yes, I thought it wise to be prepared."

"This misdirection is good. Keeping your reputation as a dancer while learning unarmed combat by what looks for all the world to be simple movements will keep you safe."

"It is my form of sparring — I do not do as well as you on that account, Grandmother."

"Nonsense, you have already proved yourself in my gardens and in my feast hall, praise and instruction will gain more than reproof and sullenness. You spread a reputation as a mind-reader when you are simply observant," she spoke smiling.

Her smiles reduced her age lines to barely visible, but I knew that it was only a matter of months. "I will be passing soon, I will probably not survive past Galilee, but you must be trained. We do not have more than a few months, but you must know my factors, my ships, those merchants I trust, as Antipas will not stay in power more than another few years. You have become a worthy sparring partner, and many will rely on you to be a calm voice in the midst of troubles."

"But I am just betrothed, I have no power." I spoke, numbed.

"You are now betrothed to a powerful man, though he seems soft-spoken. He owns a small property in Syria, but it is a key to everything that is happening in the Galilee. Though he seems to own nothing, and be content to be your father's guardian, it keeps him close to Rome and able to intervene with a word so that a situation which could become explosive can be defused. I have supplied Caligula with many funds over the years, through moneys invested in Carthage, in Alexandria, in Athens, in many small holdings and large.

My grandmother looked deeply in my eyes. "There are many weapons you possess, and your dancing is but one. Appearances deceive, as you well know, and so today we will do the one thing no one will expect, to show that you are the heir to all I hold. Today the dance changes, and as before Bat Mara painted your face, and veiled you in crimson, today you wear gold, adorn yourself in costume, and take a new role. You will put off the clothes of the child and today, before all my servants, they will see you as a matrona, a woman to be reckoned with. The coin of my dowry you will wear in your hair, this littlest of things, to remember your long dance."

"You are the heir to my properties, and my accounts. Agrippa does not know them all, Antipas has been kept unaware. He follows Caligula's and Tiberius' fortunes, but my factors have been there before him. Be watchful, you are being taken to Bat Mara to give her a worthy marriage, and to heal your soul, but know that you will carry many other prayers with you."

And so the change began. My grandmother's hair, once hidden, became her cloak of ermine. My hair, once my glory, now became wrapped in a bun, and covered in a veil. No more the coquette, the temptress, I was now a queen of the Romans, the Syrians, and the Jews, no matter how small my holdings, and I must be an example.

And prayers, I thought. Who would have thought that one such as I would carry prayers to heaven. I now knew what the Phoenician first-born must feel, the burning of the dross of my soul through all that I had watched. This was the gift I would give to my teacher, who had been forced to make me a weapon against my stepfather.